The
REALLY
DEAD WIVES
of
NEW JERSEY

a novel

ASTRID DAHL

SIMON & SCHUSTER PAPERBACKS

New York | Amsterdam/Antwerp | London
Toronto | Sydney | New Delhi

An Imprint of Simon & Schuster, LLC
1230 Avenue of the Americas
New York, NY 10020

Copyright © 2025 by Anna Dorn

First Simon & Schuster trade paperback edition January 2025

SIMON & SCHUSTER PAPERBACKS and colophon are registered trademarks of Simon & Schuster, LLC

For information about special discounts for bulk purchases, please contact Simon & Schuster Special Sales at 1-866-506-1949 or business@simonandschuster.com.

The Simon & Schuster Speakers Bureau can bring authors to your live event. For more information or to book an event, contact the Simon & Schuster Speakers Bureau at 1-866-248-3049 or visit our website at www.simonspeakers.com.

Interior design by Joy O'Meara

Manufactured in the United States of America

10 9 8 7 6 5 4 3 2 1

Library of Congress Cataloging-in-Publication Data is available.

ISBN 978-1-6680-6488-7
ISBN 978-1-6680-6489-4 (ebook)

CAST

Renee (43): Single mom, fan favorite, bisexual. Tagline: *I may play for both teams, but when it comes to being real, I always bring my A game.*

Carmela (47): Tempestuous bitch, sexy (but scary) Italian supremacist. Tagline: *I don't bite but I do scratch, and these talons are 100 percent Italian.*

Valerie (46): Carmela's sister-in-law and puppet, airhead, has prosthetic foot. Tagline: *They say to put your best foot forward, so I make sure mine is custom-made . . . and covered in diamonds!*

Birdie (Age unknown): Grande dame, wealthy widow, delusional. Tagline: *When life gives me lemons, I make citron pressé on my yacht in Saint-Tropez.*

Hope (33): Outsider, singer-songwriter, Californian. Tagline: *I checked out of the Hotel California with only my guitar—in Jersey, I hope to be a star.*

Leo (44): Hope's husband, Valerie's brother, Carmela's brother-in-law. Handsome diva. Carmela calls him "Leona" due to an abundance of feminine features.

Ruby (13): Renee's daughter. Aspiring pop star. Adorable, sassy, hormonal.

Pierre (29): Birdie's adult son and assistant. Equestrian. Likely gay. Breastfed until he was two years old.

Bianca (18): Carmela's daughter and polar opposite. Timid, soft-spoken, nearly invisible.

CREW

Eden (37): Showrunner, hustler, tough as nails. Hope's cousin.

Johnny (45): Director of photography. Low-profile, low-drama. Neither seen nor heard.

Caleb (36): Audio supervisor. Tall and lanky. In love with Eden.

Aria (48): Network exec. Blond bob. 5' 1". Objectively terrifying.

PROLOGUE

Eden's star is missing.

Breathless from climbing a third staircase, Eden fantasizes about working in scripted television. Actors aren't perfect, but they're easier to wrangle. They're used to being vessels for other people's ideas, have given up any notion of agency a long time ago. These reality stars think they run the show. But Eden runs the show. She's the literal showrunner of *Garden State Goddesses*, the third-most-popular show on Huzzah, America's premier network for reality television.

Eden Bennett has earned the right to be cocky.

Growing up, Eden wanted to make documentaries. She worshipped Werner Herzog and Adam Curtis and the Maysles, watched and rewatched *Grizzly Man* and *HyperNormalisation* and *Grey Gardens*. But she soon learned that documentarian is not an actual job for someone without a rather sizable trust fund. Despite this, Eden continued to be driven by the adage that truth is stranger than fiction. She wanted to capture the uncanniness of real people. So she's been working her way up the ladder at Huzzah for the past fifteen years. At thirty-seven, she's finally become a showrunner. But when she imagined achieving this milestone, she did not envision climbing countless staircases in a remote equestrian suburb to find her star, who keeps disappearing from the fucking party.

Eden was promoted to showrunner for many reasons: her undying work ethic, her tenacity, and her ability to push and prod her stars toward the most dramatic conclusions on camera. This season, she thought her job would be easier because her star is also her cousin, her flesh and blood, someone she's known her whole life, someone who would be easy to tame.

But that assumption has turned out to be dead wrong.

Making her way to the third floor, Eden takes a second to catch her breath. A bead of sweat develops on her forehead despite the chill in the air. If there's one thing she's learned from nearly three seasons of *Garden State Goddesses*, it's that rich people's homes are drafty as hell. High ceilings, creaky floors. Eden tiptoes down the hallway, the hardwood floors whining with each step, and peers into yet another guest bedroom, which is empty like the others. Still no sign of Hope.

Hope Fontana, née Hope Bennett, grew up with Eden in Weed, California. In New Jersey, when you say you're from California, people imagine Santa Monica, somewhere sunny and glamorous. Weed gets fifty-five inches of snow a year. And when you say you're from Northern California, people say, "Oh, I love San Francisco!" Eden wishes she were from San Francisco, which is right smack in the middle of the state, instead of Weed, a three-thousand-person city six hours north of the Bay Area. People assume the city is named for the psychotropic plant, but it's actually named after Abner Weed, who founded a lumber mill there. Now the city's gas stations sell shirts and key chains that say I LOVE WEED and then CALIFORNIA in very small script underneath. Eden's parents would protest the sale of such merchandise, calling it "diabolical blasphemy."

Eden's parents aren't just religious; they're zealots. Together, Eden's dad and Hope's dad founded a rather demented church called Brother God that Eden doesn't like to think about. When she and Hope were kids, their mobile homes shared a blow-up swimming pool in the backyard. That little pool was about the only bright spot in a very dark childhood. That and running around the woods, playing make-believe, watching Mount Shasta shine in the distance, imagining escape. Eventually, Eden did escape. And she helped Hope escape too. Of course, the act wasn't entirely selfless. Selflessness is a luxury Eden has never been able to afford. Growing up, it might have killed her—if not literally, then at least figuratively. So, fine, yes, Eden needed Hope, needs Hope.

But she isn't in the next bedroom or the one after that. Nor is she in the third-floor closets or the bathrooms. Behind one door, Eden finds a back staircase she didn't notice before, peers down, and sees—to her dismay—just empty space. She shuts the door and returns to the main staircase, walking briskly to stay warm amid the draft. Hopefully by the time she descends, her cousin will have miraculously returned and something dramatic will be happening in front of the cameras. Maybe someone will be yelling at Hope for her disappearance, acting out Eden's emotions for her. The Goddesses often act out Eden's emotions. But Hope rarely does. She rarely does anything Eden asks.

But casting Hope filled a void on the show that Eden needed to fill. Eden had her fan favorite—Renee, the single mom, modest, real. She had her villain—Carmela, the explosive bully, clever enough that viewers love to watch her from afar and are glad they don't know anyone like her IRL. She had her ditz—Valerie, Carmela's sister-in-law and also her puppet, dumb but pretty, with a Mafia-tied family. And she had her sloppy grande dame—Birdie St. Clair, who has multiple massive properties to film in, like the one Eden is scaling now, and is on the type of strong pharmaceutical cocktail that turns nearly every sentence she speaks into a meme.

For example, when Eden came to set up this afternoon, Birdie told Eden, in a vaguely French accent, that she'd just returned from Europe, where she'd "been on a yacht with Puff Daddy," which she'd pronounced *Pouff Dada*. Eden knew Birdie hadn't been to Europe, as her crew had filmed Birdie in New Jersey several times in the past week, and Sean Combs hasn't gone by Puff Daddy in nearly twenty years. When Birdie went to get glam, her son, Pierre, told Eden that Birdie had been prescribed a new medication for her arthritis and was therefore loopy. Eden nodded in understanding, as if Birdie wasn't always loopy, as if she weren't always drugged. Eden senses that a reality television reckoning is upon them, that they won't be able to get away with this type of flagrant exploitation much longer. Eden still has a conscience, she thinks, but she's been hardened by time and trauma and also ambition. This is her first season as showrunner, which means her career is on the line, her paycheck is on the line. Which means she isn't going to worry about whether she or Huzzah are exploiting Birdie St. Clair, who has multiple homes with over fifteen rooms each. Birdie is fine. Eden has a one-bedroom rental in Hoboken. Eden needs to find Hope.

Soon Eden is back on the first floor, out of breath again and avoiding the cameras so she won't have to be edited out later. She peeks into the great room and sees a bunch of people she doesn't recognize, paid extras, none of her stars. Eden wants to scream. She snakes her way down the hallway and toward the kitchen. Maybe the women are congregating in there. Maybe Hope left the party. Maybe she drove all the way back to Weed, California. Maybe they could follow her, catch it on camera. Audiences go crazy for cults, and while Eden didn't identify it as such growing up, subsequent therapists have suggested to Eden that her upbringing was, at the very least, "cultish."

Casting Hope killed three birds with one stone. The third bird was extricating Hope from said "cultish" living situation. This was the least important bird for Eden, but it was probably big for Hope. This bird helps Eden feel better about the other two birds, the ones that mattered to her, the ones that are far from selfless.

Bird two: Leo Fontana. Eden would be lying if she didn't admit that she'd brought Leo to her cousin's wedding in San Francisco with at least a small desire that he'd meet a future Goddess, someone he could bring into the Fontana family and intensify their chokehold on the *Garden State* franchise. As Valerie's brother and Carmela's brother-in-law, Leo was already on the show some, but he was a ham and a diva and viewers wanted more. So that was the stone in casting Hope—Leo's entry point to more airtime, which Eden saw as dollar signs.

Bird one, the largest and most important bird, was needing an outsider. Someone to upset the status quo. These bitches are so insular, so obsessed with family and loyalty and the right kind of cookies at Christmas (Neapolitans, amaretti, pignoli). Their Sicilian American heritage is everything to them. Eden almost considered changing her last name to Benetta so they'd respect her more. Eden knew that someone as Anglo and doe-eyed as Hope marrying into the Fontana family would cause everyone to fucking lose it. And she was fucking right. They fucking lost it. Eden is almost always fucking right when it comes to her job.

But she's wrong about the women being in the kitchen, which is larger than Eden's apartment, and also empty except for the catering staff. No Hope. Hopeless. Eden chuckles to herself at the wordplay, then stops. It's not funny. She needs to find Hope so she can deliver a compelling season and move into an apartment that's bigger than this kitchen. Eden notices a door she didn't see before. Maybe there are more rooms behind it. This house is so fucking big.

"Can I help you, miss?" asks Birdie's head of staff. Luz? Birdie's staff is bigger than Eden's cast. Luz, if that's her name, looks stressed. Birdie probably works her to the ground. Or Pierre, rather, who seems to be sailing the ship. If Luz had a larger role on her show, Eden would try to find out what's beneath those anguished eyes. But Luz is not a main character, so Eden keeps moving.

"Just looking for the ladies," Eden says, then turns toward the door.

Eden exits the kitchen and—without warning—a scream pierces the air. Not the fun scream of a party, but a haunting, terrified scream. She pauses, heart thudding in her chest, trying to locate the placement of the scream, from where in this massive house it originated. Before she can react, a body comes hurling at her. Eden can't register who it is, just senses a flash of movement and limbs and hair. And the words, landing like a brick in Eden's chest:

"She isn't breathing!"

Part One

Mirror, mirror, on the wall,
who's the shadiest of them all?

—KENYA MOORE, *THE REAL HOUSEWIVES OF ATLANTA*

ONE

Six months earlier

Hope was leaning up against a cherry red Ferrari F40 in a wedding dress. She supposed the average bride would have been worried about the dress, but Hope was worried about the car. This 1987 model was arguably the best Italian car ever made. Hope only knew this from dating Leo, whose family owned a vintage Italian car business. And that business, Medusa Motors, was where Hope was getting married today. A car dealership wedding had at first sounded a little peculiar to Hope, but Leo had convinced her it would be glamorous. His brother and sister had both gotten married here, and he explained that they'd completely transformed the place.

It was transformed today, too, with lush red velvet carpets that trailed across the polished concrete, string lights that would shine bright once the sun went down, and only the most expensive cars on display, including the red F40 on which she was still leaning. After six months with Leo, Hope had developed a genuine love for cars. She enjoyed learning about their specifications and even test-drove them after hours when Leo allowed. Her two favorite cars were the red F40 and the Pagani Zonda C12, which debuted in 1999 at the Geneva Motor Show, could accelerate to 60 mph in four seconds, and resembled something from a sci-fi film of the variety Hope was not allowed to watch as a kid.

Six months with Leo had introduced Hope to so much. It was the longest time she'd been outside of Northern California, a place Hope had convinced herself she loved likely because alternatives felt elusive. She lacked the ambition and courage of her cousin Eden, who'd left at seventeen on a Greyhound Bus for New York City, and her sister, Faith, who'd hitchhiked to San Francisco at nineteen and never returned. Hope had left fifteen years later, at which point staying hadn't felt like an option.

Hope had met Leo at Faith's wedding. Before that, Hope hadn't left Weed in years. Brother God considered Faith fallen for leaving. Growing up, Hope always felt caught between her parents, whom she loved despite their flaws, and her sister, whom she also loved but who hated her parents and Brother God and rebelled at every opportunity. Eden was like that too, always angry and provocative. Hope was dutiful—until fairly recently.

She knew Brother God had issues, but the church had positive elements as well. Hope enjoyed reading the Bible and found many passages uplifting. Recently, she'd been thinking a lot about Isaiah 43:2: *When you walk through fire you shall not be burned, and the flames shall not consume you.* But mostly, she loved singing. In Weed, Hope had always been active in the choir, and eventually her father had let her lead it, until he'd taken that away—a fact Hope preferred not to dwell on. Hope missed the choir most. She missed her parents too, or the version of them that had liked her, before everything went up in smoke.

Once she had freed herself from Brother God's controlling shackles, going to Faith's wedding was a no-brainer. And it was there that Eden introduced Hope to her platonic date, Leo. Hope was enchanted. Leo was warm and charming and instantly made her feel safe. He was also easy on the eyes, with sharp cheekbones softened by waves of dark hair. He reminded Hope of someone she already knew well. She'd been comfortable enough to go back with him that night to his hotel room, something she'd never done before. Weed didn't even really have hotels. Leo's hotel was spectacular, on top of a hill with panoramic views of the glittering bay. Hope felt exhilarated in a way she never had. When Leo offered to fly her out to New Jersey the next week, she felt she had no choice but to say yes. There was nothing left for her in Weed after what had happened. In fact, she hadn't gone back since.

Hope had never been to the East Coast, and she was instantly blown away by how green it was. Weed had trees, but it was much drier, the forests often in flames. Hope had mostly known dry land and open space, mountains very far in the distance. New Jersey had no mountains, just green, rolling hills. It felt safe somehow, like she was enveloped by leafy trees and soft clouds. And oh my gosh, the clouds! Due to a lack of moisture in the air, Weed never had clouds of the soft, pillowy type that New Jersey did. Hope spent one entire afternoon lying on the grass in Leo's yard, finding baby animals in the sky.

A bead of sweat dripped down Hope's arm. She'd originally liked the idea of an August wedding—she and Leo had both been eager to get married quickly—but she hadn't realized how hot it would be. In Weed, it rarely got above 80 degrees. Currently, Hope felt like she was in a steam room. She'd had no idea the planet could get this humid. The temperature on her phone said 87, but it felt hotter. Leo reassured Hope that it would cool down once the sun set. And everyone loved partying on a warm summer night, he'd said. Weed never had warm nights; in the summer, the temperature would drop up to 40 degrees between afternoon and evening. Hope had been astounded at the Fontanas' Fourth of July pool party, when it was still balmy and warm after dark, and these little bugs started lighting up the air like magic. *Fireflies*, Leo had called them.

During that first week on the East Coast, Leo took Hope to New York City, which was unlike anything Hope had seen before. While her parents didn't believe in television or the internet, Hope had been able to secure both modern luxuries as an adult, as well as a small apartment on the edge of town that she rented with her waitressing money. So she'd seen New York City on a screen, in movies like *You've Got Mail*, but they hadn't captured the *feeling*. The city had its own pulse, a vibrant energy coursing through her and awakening her senses, as if she were seeing the world in a whole new spectrum of colors. They'd stayed at a five-star hotel on the edge of Central Park, which had exploded with pink due to spring. Hope couldn't believe she'd spent thirty-two years of her life without experiencing a proper spring, let alone spring in Central Park. Leo lived only an hour away from the city by car. So when Leo asked Hope to stay with him in New Jersey, to move in, to never go back to California, Hope knew the only answer was yes. Again, there was nothing left for her in Weed. She didn't even go back to collect her belongings. Leo bought her all new things.

The cars in front of Hope lit up gold as the sun lowered in the sky. This was the plan: Hope would walk down the aisle at golden hour. The light flickering on the cars made her think of the Neil Young song "After the Gold Rush." Hope didn't miss the Golden State, not really, but she missed her guitar. Since she'd started renting her own place a few years ago, she'd been making music in the privacy of her apartment and uploading songs to SoundCloud. People seemed to like them. She knew she wasn't exactly Neil Young, but she'd amassed a following larger than Weed's population. Thousands of people still seemed like a lot to Hope. New York City had over eight million people, which was almost three thousand times the size of Weed. Shady Pond, the suburb where Leo lived, where Hope was getting married, was roughly five times larger than Weed. But it seemed bigger than that. There was infinitely more to do here. Weed didn't even have a proper grocery store. Hope's parents grew their own food and Hope mostly ate at the diner where she'd worked, one of only a handful of restaurants in Weed. Shady Pond had movie theaters and restaurants and shopping centers. Leo's sister-in-law, Carmela, owned an upscale nail salon in the main shopping center. Carmela kind of scared Hope, but Hope liked the salon, where everything was sparkly and they served champagne.

Carmela would be Hope's castmate. This was where things got weird. Hope had agreed to something kind of crazy: to appear on *Garden State Goddesses*, an evidently popular reality television show she'd never seen before. Eden worked for the show and would be showrunner for the upcoming season. Eden had convinced Hope that she'd "shine" on the show, that it would be an optimal opportunity to make friends. Hope liked the idea of a community of girlfriends in Shady Pond, where she knew no one except for Leo. (Eden lived thirty minutes away in Hoboken.) And when Hope had admitted to Eden after a glass of champagne at the nail salon that she'd been making music, Eden told Hope that the show would be an ideal place to promote it, that she could develop a real audience. This possibility really appealed to Hope. Ever since she first heard Joni Mitchell, Hope had wanted to make music like hers—poetic and evocative. Joni Mitchell had moved to New York City in the '60s. Hope was giddy at the idea of following in her footsteps.

But Hope was still scared to be on the show. She'd never aspired to appear on camera before; in Weed, such a dream would have been as far-fetched as finding a mermaid in the local creek. Hope still hadn't watched the show; Eden told her it would be better if she didn't, that it would be easier to be herself. Hope felt pretty boring, but Eden convinced her she had an "easy charisma" that would translate well on camera. Eden could be very convincing. She had nearly convinced Hope to let her film the wedding for the season. In fact, she *had* convinced Hope and Leo, but Leo's parents had nixed it. They were old-school and skeptical of the show. They'd appeared on camera a few times, but filming their youngest son's wedding was a line they were unwilling to cross. Eden didn't push them. Leo's parents were polite to Hope but somewhat intimidating. Eden had said there were Mafia rumors, but that there were a lot of rumors in Shady Pond. And either way, Hope was protected. She liked the sound of that. Hope needed a little protection for once. Protecting herself had become exhausting, unsustainable, dangerous.

Hope jumped as the wedding planner called her name. The string quartet started. A knot took shape in her stomach.

She was eager to ditch her father's name and become Hope Fontana.

Hope Fontana, a new woman.

TWO

Renee had quit smoking thirteen years ago, when she got pregnant. But she was smoking a cigarette right now. Carmela had a way of bringing out Renee's vices. Everyone seemed to feel more courageous around her. Carmela Fontana was like a drug that way. Addictive, but probably bad for your health.

In the first two seasons of *Garden State Goddesses*, several castmates had quit, citing Carmela. Renee understood why these women feared Carmela—she had a sharp tongue, eyes that rivaled Sophia Loren's, and acrylic nails so sharp they should have been registered as lethal weapons. But Renee prided herself on seeing the best in everyone. Carmela was very funny and extremely loyal, and had impeccable style. Tonight, she wore a shimmery, body-conscious black dress with strappy navy blue heels. Oh, that was another of Carmela's attributes: at forty-seven, she had an incredible body. Her body was enviable for any age, really. Renee figured the chain-smoking curbed her appetite, and she had a Peloton in her garage. Once Renee went over there to film and Carmela was smoking a cigarette *on* the Peloton.

"My Spidey sense is going off," Carmela said, taking a drag. They were standing just outside the reception tent because Carmela didn't want her in-laws to see her smoking. But she was peeking through a slit in the awning, looking at Hope.

"Mine too," said Valerie, Carmela's sister-in-law and sister of the groom. Viewers described Valerie as "Carmela's puppet," an epithet with which Renee didn't entirely disagree.

"Something in the milk ain't clean," Carmela continued, staring right at Hope inside the tent, as if begging her to stare back.

"I can't believe she's going to be our sister-in-law," Valerie added, seemingly to please Carmela. Carmela was married to Valerie's older brother, and as of tonight, Hope was married to Valerie's younger brother. The Fontanas were a massive Sicilian family with alleged Mafia ties. People talked in Shady Pond, and Carmela's nail salon was just across the shopping center from Renee's store. Renee heard things. She also read things, on RadarOnline and on Shady Di, an anonymous Instagram account that circulated rumors about all of them, but it was harshest on the Fontanas, going so far as to speculate that Leo was responsible for Valerie's missing foot. RadarOnline and word on the street said it was Carmela. While Renee didn't believe Carmela was capable of that kind of violence, she had been burned enough times to know to keep Carmela at a distance. Renee and Carmela could be cordial and share a laugh, but they'd never be close. Boundaries were important in this town, crucial on reality television.

"I think she seems sweet," Renee cut in. Unlike Valerie, Renee wasn't afraid of Carmela. Viewers said Renee "played both sides," which Renee didn't necessarily see as a bad thing. Renee valued diplomacy more than her castmates did. Also, she was bisexual, so, metaphorically speaking, she did play for both teams. Shady Di had called her "bi for clout." They all hated Shady Di.

"Too sweet," said Carmela. "Untrustworthy, sweet. Bitch is hiding something, *Giuro su Dio*." Carmela crossed herself. The Fontanas were very Catholic. Renee's parents had been raised Catholic but had only imparted a lax version to her—Renee couldn't remember the last time she'd been in a church. And while Renee was Italian American, and her grandfather had been born in Italy, Renee did not feel as connected to "the motherland" as the Fontanas. Renee only knew a handful of Italian words and phrases—she knew that Carmela had just said, "I swear to God," because she said it a lot—and she'd never been to Italy. The Fontanas spoke Italish, peppering most of their conversations with Italian phrases.

"*Straniero,*" Carmella nearly spat.

Renee didn't know this word but assumed it was not flattering. It sounded like *stranger*.

"Do you think she's a natural blonde?" Valerie asked. Valerie was blond, but it definitely wasn't natural. She got her roots touched up once a month at the salon next to Renee's jewelry store. And when Renee had met Valerie years before the show started, when their kids had been in preschool together, Valerie's hair had been nearly jet-black.

"Probably." Carmela tapped her cigarette on the edge of a vintage Fiat's rearview mirror. "Sick freak of nature."

Renee never said it out loud, but she preferred Valerie's natural hair color. But Valerie was a bit of a bimbo, and Renee supposed it made sense she had the hair to match. As if on cue, she began to flap a baby pink fan in front of her face. It had been a hot day, and now it was a hot night. An outdoor wedding in August was an aggressive move. Renee didn't get why they didn't just wait until the fall to get married. The whole thing felt rushed.

Renee turned to watch Hope dance with Leo. They were an exceptionally attractive couple. Hope, with her wavy blond hair and innocent blue eyes, and Leo, with his long eyelashes and warm smile. Renee enjoyed watching them dance, which they did with grace and only made her feel slightly envious. Renee had been single for so long, she hardly remembered what it was like to dance with someone. Either way, she was excited to have Hope on the show. She was ready for another castmate who was *nice*. Well, Renee supposed Valerie was relatively pleasant when she wasn't with Carmela, but her friendliness often seemed fake, like artificial sweetener. Birdie wasn't mean, but she was so out to lunch she was basically an alien. Hope seemed genuine and normal. Renee was excited to get to know her better.

Birdie sashayed into Renee's line of sight. She was dancing with a younger man, as she often was. She fancied herself a cougar and frequently boasted about her active sex life, but Renee didn't totally buy it. Birdie was often slurring her words by 3 p.m., so Renee wasn't sure how she could be having these late-night sexcapades. The *Garden State Goddesses* were often lying to each other and themselves. The fans liked Renee because she was "real." She didn't say everything that came to mind, because that would be rude and immature, but Renee was a bad liar with a moral compass. She valued authenticity. The only time she found it acceptable to lie was to spare someone's feelings, like when Birdie said, "Don't you just *adore* my new mink?" Renee would respond, "Of course, darling," even though Renee found the fact that the animal's head was still attached a bit macabre. She supposed this was why viewers said she played both sides. But Eden said even the most likable reality TV stars had haters. She also said Renee was among the most likable of all time, but Renee figured Eden said that to everyone. Renee liked Eden, but her mother had taught her never to fully trust the person profiting off your labor.

"Don't you think?" Carmela stared right at Renee, who hadn't heard the first part of the question.

"Think what?" Renee asked.

Valerie laughed. "I knew she wasn't listening."

Carmela's scary side flared a bit. Her eyes widened, lips twitched. Renee thought Carmela was more bark than bite, that her bravado cloaked a deeply insecure person.

"Don't you think the new girl has secrets?" Carmela asked, eyes narrowing.

Before Renee could respond, a loud crash sounded from inside the reception tent. The women turned their gazes. Birdie was on the floor beside a number of broken glasses. The young man was no longer by her side, but a different young man rushed in: Birdie's son, Pierre, who had been given a decent amount of airtime on the first two seasons of the show. Aside from Ruby, he was the only other *Goddess* child who had his own confessional. Except Pierre wasn't a child. He was in his late twenties, likely gay, and astoundingly arrogant. Viewers seemed to get a kick out of him, probably because they were laughing *at* him—he had a nasal voice that always made it sound like he was whining, as well as mommy issues of Freudian proportions. But Pierre mistook their mockery for genuine adoration and had told Renee at last season's wrap party that the network should increase his pay as he was "carrying the show." Until that point, Renee hadn't realized he was getting paid at all. Ruby didn't get paid for appearing on the show, although Renee had used Ruby's popularity in her most recent negotiations to get a raise. Pierre certainly wasn't carrying the show, but right now he was swooping in to carry Birdie. He lifted her from the floor as wedding guests circled around, gawking. Sadly, it was a familiar sight. Birdie had a habit of becoming unbalanced after noon, horizontal once the sun went down.

Renee turned back to Carmela to answer her question. "Everyone," Renee said, taking the final drag of her cigarette, "has secrets."

THREE

Hope was getting antsy in Shady Pond.

Filming wouldn't start for another week, and Leo had insisted that Hope relax rather than get a short-term job. But Hope was lonely. In Weed, Hope knew everyone and was rarely alone. She went to work at the diner and had choir practice most nights—that is, until her dad took that away from her. Back in California, Hope cherished working on her music in her free time, but now all she had was free time: from the time she woke up to when Leo came home, always after 7 p.m. but sometimes as late as midnight. Business was thriving, which was how Leo could afford his three-bedroom home with a backyard and a pool, the biggest house Hope had ever been inside. But that meant hours were long, and Leo often had to wine and dine clients after work. Sometimes Hope attended these dinners, but that was lonely too, as they often talked about people she didn't know and sometimes spoke entirely in Italian. Leo's parents threw family dinners on Sunday evenings, but Hope felt similarly isolated there.

Hope had imagined becoming friends with Leo's sister, Valerie, but she was always in the corner whispering with Carmela, who seemed to hate Hope—constantly glaring at her and making pointed digs about Hope being from California. Hope had tried asking Valerie to get coffee a few times, just the two of them, but Valerie typically came up with some excuse involving her sons—she had three boys—or flaked last minute. Hope felt similarly rejected by her own cousin, Eden, who lived just thirty minutes away but always seemed to be busy with work whenever Hope asked her to get dinner or go to a movie. Hope's only real company in Shady Pond was herself.

Leo had gifted Hope a 1972 Fiat 500 in baby blue, Hope's favorite color. And she adored the car, so much so she was afraid to drive it. It seemed frail, and Hope wasn't familiar with these roads. She couldn't bear to think of getting in an accident and damaging the car. So Hope spent most of her days at home, the quiet house seeming to taunt her. Outside, manicured lawns rolled out like green carpets, the neighborhood's stillness punctuated only by the occasional distant bark of a dog. She made music in part because it made her feel less alone.

As soon as Hope had told Leo about her SoundCloud, he'd created a music room for her in one of his spare bedrooms. The result was nothing short of extravagant—a soundproofed home studio with recessed lighting, stocked with a guitar, a keyboard, drums, several microphones, a recording booth, leather couches, and a computer with a fancy program for mixing that Hope was still figuring out how to use. The setup was a far cry from the corner of her dingy apartment where she'd make music in Weed, a wooden chair by a window overlooking a parking lot.

Her new studio overwhelmed her a bit. Hope mostly stayed away from the electronics, preferring the acoustic guitar, a vintage cherry Gibson Dove, a model popular in the '60s and favored by the likes of Tom Petty, Cat Stevens, and Bob Dylan, musicians Hope had been drawn to when she'd first discovered music that wasn't about God. Hope had been homeschooled, so she hadn't even known non-hymnal music existed until she was a teenager and her sister, Faith, snuck her to McDonald's, where they were playing a band called the Black Eyed Peas. Faith loved the song, but Hope found it a bit raucous. It wasn't until she was in her twenties and started working at the diner, where her manager consistently played folk music from the '60s—Bob Dylan, Neil Young, and, most importantly, Joni Mitchell—that Hope really started to fall in love with secular music.

The Gibson Dove sounded like a bell, rich and bright, a vibrant contrast to the rustic twang of the scratched-up guitar she'd had in Weed. When Hope wasn't playing the guitar, she was writing lyrics or listening to music to inspire her. She'd started branching out of '60s folk during her last few years in Weed, enjoying music by Mazzy Star and Sharon Van Etten, who was from New Jersey. Van Etten had started playing electric guitar in her later work, as had Dylan and Joni Michell, which made Hope want to try electric too. But Leo had already given her so much, she couldn't possibly ask for another guitar. And besides, technology intimidated her. When she wasn't playing music, Hope was learning Italian on Duolingo, or lying out by the pool, looking at the clouds. She was so lonely she'd started talking to the clouds, as well as the trees in the yard. The oak tree over the pool, she'd named Cheyenne. She was that bored.

So this afternoon, when Hope's cell phone rang for the first time in days, she was thrilled to answer it, even though she didn't recognize the number and it was probably spam. But as it turned out, it wasn't spam. It was Renee Ricci, her future castmate. Hope had met Renee a few times and always liked her energy. She seemed genuine. And Eden had told Hope that Renee would be her favorite, that she was everyone's favorite.

"So," Renee said after a brief greeting. "Eden showed me your SoundCloud."

Hope's cheeks became hot. She'd never spoken to anyone but Eden, Leo, and one other person about her SoundCloud. All her fans were strangers. A wave of vulnerability washed over her. She felt exposed.

"I *love* your music," said Renee. "You have a really interesting voice."

Warmth blossomed in Hope's chest. "Thanks, that means the world to me." Hope was so lonely she would have been happy to hear from someone just calling to say *screw you*, but the fact that Renee was calling to compliment Hope's music felt like a dream. She was about to ask Renee if she wanted to get a drink when Renee kept talking.

"So my daughter, Ruby, she's thirteen," Renee said. "And she's *determined* to be a pop star. Like, literally, being the next Ariana Grande is all she ever talks about."

"That's so sweet," Hope said.

"Is it?" Renee laughed. "I'm kidding, she's adorable. But I was wondering, since you're so talented—could you give her voice lessons?"

Hope was silent, taken aback.

"I'd pay, obviously!"

"Oh, you don't need to pay me," Hope said. "I'd be thrilled to give your daughter voice lessons." But Hope was actually a little disappointed. She'd been hoping Renee was going to ask her to hang out. Hope wanted to be friends with Renee, to be friends with any adult in Shady Pond really, but everyone seemed so flashy and intimidating, in leopard-printed silks and fur coats with fake eyelashes and nails long enough to hurt someone. Renee wore jeans and her eyelashes seemed to be her own. She had a melodious laugh and reminded Hope of someone back home, someone she knew, just like when she'd first met Leo. Renee's daughter was probably cool too, and Hope had had enough practice with the choir to teach singing to anyone. Plus, Hope missed the choir like crazy. Helping Ruby might fill that void.

"Eden thinks it will be a great way to introduce you," Renee said, and it took a second for Hope to realize that Renee was talking about the show. This voice lesson would be filmed, on camera, for Hope's introduction to television audiences. Hope still couldn't believe she was doing this. Was she insane? Probably.

Hope cleared her throat. "That makes sense," she said. "I look forward to it."

"I love you!" Renee shouted, and Hope knew it was just an expression, but her heart leaped nonetheless.

The phone call was over too quickly.

And the house returned to being very, very quiet.

Sunlight glinted off the chrome toaster and cast an orange glow that flickered across the wall. It was nothing, just a trick of the light, but for a second, the air seemed charged with something dangerous. Hope shivered and made her way back to her music studio.

She needed to kill the silence.

FOUR

Renee's doorbell rang. Eden jogged to answer it. It was probably Hope, who still needed to be miked. Then Hope would have to ring the doorbell again and Renee would answer it on camera.

Eden was rarely nervous, but right now she was on edge. Hope was her first cousin, the closest thing Eden had to a sister, and Hope had never been on camera before. Eden was taking a significant risk in hiring her, both personally and professionally. She exhaled and opened the door.

Hope stood in a jean jacket over a paisley dress and not a smidge of makeup. Not a dab of mascara, an ounce of foundation, or a tinge of lip color. Barefaced. Normally, this would have pissed Eden off, but she didn't have time to be pissed. The camera crew was only booked for a few hours. She used to have a makeup artist for touch-ups, but eventually so many women had their own glam squads on retainer, it seemed like a waste of Huzzah's money to pay someone. So she had no makeup artist today.

Eden survived in this industry because she'd seen true darkness in her childhood and everything since felt like child's play. So Hope wasn't wearing makeup. No big deal. The viewers might love it, might find her "very real." The viewers loved real. Eden always knew this would be Hope's archetype: the innocent, naive one. The one who wouldn't think to put on makeup to appear on one of the most popular networks on television. Hope had never seen the show. She'd been raised in a cultish community in California without a television. She was a vintage photograph in a stream of Facetunes, her presence an echo of a forgotten time. This was just fine.

"Is everything okay?" Hope asked, and Eden realized she'd been silently staring at her cousin for far longer than appropriate. Being a reality TV producer often meant disregarding social niceties. Eden had never been particularly tactful to begin with, given she'd been homeschooled in said cultish environment. Eden was skilled at her job, but interpersonal relationships were trickier. Mostly, they felt like a distraction. For these reasons, she was still single at thirty-seven, and not entirely pressed about it.

"You aren't wearing makeup," Eden said.

"I didn't realize I needed to?" Hope said. "You told me to be myself."

Eden sighed. She was annoyed, but Hope was also exhibiting the very naïveté that would make her an excellent character.

"You're fine," Eden said, and then ushered her inside.

While Hope was being miked, Eden went to fetch Renee from the kitchen. "Do you mind putting a touch of mascara on Hope?" Eden asked. "Maybe a little foundation?"

"Of course," Renee said, then disappeared. The fans liked Renee because she was funny and kind and didn't put on airs. Eden liked Renee because she was cooperative and rarely complained.

Back in the foyer, Hope appeared utterly stunned while the cameramen miked her. She resembled a night creature caught in a car's headlights—startled and exposed. Beneath all the hardened defenses, a tiny inkling of guilt pinged in Eden's belly. She ignored it. She was skilled at ignoring her feelings. Some days, she hardly noticed them at all.

Renee came down the stairs holding a small makeup bag. Renee wore makeup but she didn't have a glam squad like the others. She was the modest one, a single mom in the smallest house on the franchise. She was still well-off, of course; she surely had more money than

Eden. Renee had married a financial analyst and gotten a healthy divorce settlement that included this house and enough money to start her own jewelry business. But she didn't front with the Lamborghinis and the hair extensions like the other women. Renee was Eden's street-smart girl next door. And Hope was the wide-eyed ingénue, a newly hatched chick stepping out of its shell for the very first time.

"Hi doll." Renee kissed Hope's cheek, and Eden could have sworn she saw Hope blush. That very tiny feeling of guilt panged again, and again, Eden ignored it. Hope would be fine. She would wise up. She had survived their cultish upbringing; she could survive this. Eden was giving her an enviable life, an opportunity to restart.

"I'm just going to touch you up real quick," Renee said, setting her makeup bag on a table and removing a tube of mascara.

Hope blinked and nodded, skittish. Eden needed to loosen her up. She went into the kitchen and smiled when she opened the fridge. She'd known she could count on Renee to have an open bottle of white wine. Eden took it out and poured it into a coffee mug, returned to the foyer.

"Here you are," Eden said, handing Hope the mug.

"Oh my God," said Renee. "I'm so rude. I should have offered you a drink, Hope, before attacking your face." Renee laughed.

"You're fine," Hope said. "My face is in more dire need than my thirst, apparently."

Renee laughed again. Eden smiled. They were bantering. They had chemistry. Everything was just perfect.

Hope took a big sip and nearly choked, causing Renee to drag mascara onto Hope's cheek.

"This isn't coffee," Hope said.

Renee disappeared again, hopefully to get makeup remover.

"It's wine," Eden said. "You need to unwind."

Hope consulted her watch. "It's not even three p.m."

Eden smiled. "That is a completely appropriate time to start drinking in suburban New Jersey."

Renee returned and wiped the mascara from Hope's cheek.

FIVE

Hope rang the doorbell for a second time this afternoon.

An hour earlier, she'd rung it the first time and wondered why on earth she had agreed to this. Opening the door, Eden had stared at Hope for what felt like five minutes, as if seeing her own cousin for the very first time. Eden wasn't looking at Hope like she was a person, but rather like she was a piece of clay to be sculpted. Hope supposed that was Eden's job—to see humans as clay, to mold them into more entertaining shapes. Hope loved Eden, but there always seemed to be something missing with her when it came to human interaction. She supposed it helped Eden in her job.

But Hope didn't want to be clay.

Things had gotten even weirder when Eden let Hope inside. Hope wasn't sure what she'd been expecting, but it wasn't what she saw in front of her. Hope counted five cameras in total, but there were maybe more. Two on tripods stationed strategically in the open-plan living room. Three smaller ones free-floating in the arms of men wearing all black. There were boom mics and lights set up throughout the space. It was as if the walls had sprouted eyes, all focused on her.

The men in black had surrounded Hope like satellites orbiting a celestial body. One man threaded a wire through Hope's bra and secured a tiny microphone just below her throat. The cold metal chilled her skin. Soon Renee was applying makeup to Hope's face, which actually felt kind of soothing. Eden had been right that Hope would like Renee. Her energy was inviting, as was her space, which was decorated in warm earth tones and smelled of cinnamon. Her daughter, Ruby, was adorable in a jean skirt, pink crop top, and high-top sneakers. She had Renee's curly brown hair and ice green eyes.

And now, ringing the doorbell the second time, Hope was ready to film the scene. She was excited even. When she heard footsteps approaching the door, a ripple of anticipation darted through Hope's veins.

"Hi!" Renee answered the door as if she was seeing Hope for the first time that afternoon.

The pretending would take some getting used to, but the wine had relaxed Hope a bit. And this time, as she entered, the cameras seemed less daunting, and the mic attached to her shirt felt somehow more natural, as though people walked around with microphones attached to them all the time. Renee ushered Hope into the living room and offered her coffee, which Hope accepted, thinking some caffeine might perk her up after the wine. But inside the mug was light yellow liquid. More wine. Hope shrugged and took a sip. She was feeling very free-spirited.

"Ruby! Get off TikTok and come down," Renee called upstairs.

Leo had recently explained TikTok to Hope, but she didn't really get it. He'd also told her about an Instagram account called Shady Di—"like Shady Pond plus Lady Diana," he had explained to Hope, as though Hope were a toddler—that circulated rumors on all the Goddesses. Leo was way more into Instagram than Hope, who'd only made an account because Eden told her it was important for the show. Hope had uploaded just one picture—her profile photo of her and Leo in Central Park on a perfect afternoon in late summer. The Shady Di profile photo featured a beautiful woman who Hope thought was Princess Diana, but who Leo had told her was actually a cast member on another reality TV show called Dorinda. Leo seemed amused by Shady Di, even when it insinuated awful things about him, but it made Hope uneasy.

"Okay, have fun you two!" Renee said, yanking Hope from her

thoughts and jetting off toward the front door. Hope hadn't realized Renee would be leaving. Maybe she wasn't really leaving. Perhaps this was another fiction for the show. Hope jumped when the front door slammed shut.

She took another sip of wine and sat at the freshly polished grand piano. It was positively pristine compared to the scarred instrument at the church. Positioned right beside the window, a corner of the lid lit up gold. She put her mug on the windowsill and her purse below the bench. Ruby stood tall beside her, seeming so much more confident than Hope felt.

Over a week ago, they'd discussed that Hope would help Ruby learn her favorite song, "Imagine" by Ariana Grande. Ruby already knew the song well, Renee had assured her, so Hope wouldn't have to do much—just play the basic chords on the piano and give Ruby light direction, but mostly encouragement. Hope had been practicing the chords every afternoon since in her music room. They were fairly simple, but the stakes were high—this would be her first time playing music on camera. It had to be perfect.

Hope started Ruby with basic scales and was immediately blown away. From her phone conversation with Renee, Hope had assumed Ruby's pop star aspirations were those of a typical thirteen-year-old girl, but Ruby could really sing. She also had a starlike confidence, was natural in front of the cameras like her mom, but with a flashier presentation. Hope was shocked by how high Ruby could go, almost as high as Ariana Grande herself, approaching that whistle register for which the pop star was famous. Ruby was so confident and soulful. Hope felt like Ruby should be teaching *her*. By the second chorus, Hope had completely forgotten the cameras were there. Her eyes started to well up.

"Are you okay?" Ruby asked afterward.

"Yes, you were amazing, why?"

"You're crying." Ruby popped her hip.

Hope's cheeks heated. "I was moved," she said, and reached for another sip of wine to steady herself.

"I slay, right?" Ruby said.

Hope almost spit out her wine. "Slay?"

Ruby cackled. "It's slang, mama," she said. "It means I'm on fire, like I'm crushing it, I'm a boss, I'm a beast, I'm lit, I'm the GOAT, I'm *queen*."

It sounded like Ruby was speaking a foreign language. She was so cute though. For the past decade or so, Hope had fantasized about having a little girl, but it had never seemed like an option. But now she had Leo, and sometimes, late at night, they'd name their future children. Hope wanted a girl and Leo wanted a boy, so they'd hopefully have both. Leo said the names would have to be Italian, which suited Hope because she liked Italian names. They were thinking Luca for a boy and Isabella for a girl. Hope figured they could call the girl Izzy, and Hope could teach her to sing like she was teaching Ruby now. Or maybe Izzy would be insanely talented like Ruby, and Izzy could teach Hope a thing or two. They could sing together. They could harmonize. They could have a family band. Hope's stomach fluttered with fantasies.

"Where did you go?" Ruby asked Hope, tapping her shoulder.

"I'm here!" Hope said, straightening up. "You ready to take it from the top?"

"Sure, but just one more because I don't want to strain my voice," Ruby said, like she was the teacher and Hope was the student, which was frankly how it should have been. Just as Hope started playing the first chord, her phone rang. She'd meant to silence it, but the wine had made her less vigilant. She reached for her purse to silence the call, but the name on the screen caused her heart to skip a beat.

Cheyenne.

Hope turned the phone off in a hurry.

"All good?" Ruby asked, tapping her sneaker on the floor.

"All good," Hope said.

Hope played the opening chords.

CONFESSIONAL TRANSCRIPT – *GARDEN STATE GODDESSES*

(SEASON 3)

RUBY RICCI

EDEN: Remember to speak in present tense, like instead of "I
    was excited to work with Hope—"

RUBY: "I *am* excited to work with Hope." I know, I know. This
    ain't my first rodeo, Eden.

EDEN: [*Laughs.*]

RUBY: Except it's a lie. I wasn't—sorry, *I'm not* excited to
    work with her. I have a voice coach already. She's so
    cool. Her name is Kayla and she went to high school with
    Lady Gaga. In New York City.

EDEN: Okay, let's forget about Kayla for now—

RUBY: Because Kayla isn't on the show. I know these things,
    Eden. And before you tell me, I know I have to answer
    my questions so that my answer makes sense on its own.
    Also, you should get Kayla on the show. Think about it!
    She's really cool and has an amazing voice. Not as good
    as mine though.

EDEN: I'll look into it. So, without mentioning Kayla, can
    you tell me how you're feeling when your mom tells you
    Hope is going to help you with your singing?

RUBY: When my mom tells me Hope is going to help me with
    my singing, it just feels a little . . . random? My mom is
    always so busy with the sh—um, sorry, with her business.
    She doesn't have time for me most of the time. I don't
    know, it just feels fake.

EDEN: Like your mom doesn't really care about your singing?

RUBY: Exactly! Sorry. My mom doesn't really seem to care
    about my life or my singing. So I'm confused about why
    this rando is coming over to help me. Also, I don't know
    her background. My last voice teacher trained with Lady
    Gaga. In New York City.

EDEN: Do you wish your mom lived in New York City?

RUBY: Duh! My dad lives there, but I only see him a few
    times a year. He lives on the twenty-fifth floor. You can

see everything from up there. And you don't hear any
street noise. Last time I was there, he took me to see
Wicked. It was . . . so slay.

EDEN: That sounds awesome. So what's your first impression
of Hope? What do you think when she walks in?

RUBY: When Hope walks in, the first thing I think is that
she's pretty. She has blond hair and it looks natural.
Everything about her seems natural. Almost like a
hippie? Her clothes are all flowy. My mom says she's
from California, I don't know, maybe that's how people
dress there. I've never been.

EDEN: And what do you think of her during the voice lesson?

RUBY: The voice lesson is fine. I love singing, so it's
impossible for me to not have fun. So I'm enjoying
myself. But Hope makes me a little nervous. And I never
get nervous. Seriously, ask anyone.

EDEN: What makes you nervous about her?

RUBY: Hope makes me nervous because she is so quiet, I can't
tell what she's thinking. There's this strange look in
her eyes. And then when I'm singing, she starts crying?
Like, I know I have a sick voice, but that is totally
weird. And then she gets this call on her phone, which
she didn't silence for some reason. And her face, like,
goes white. I'm not kidding.

EDEN: Who do you think calls her?

RUBY: I have no idea who called her. But I swear to God, she
looks like she's seen a freaking ghost.

SIX

Ariana Grande turned on automatically as Renee started the ignition. Ariana Grande was always playing in Renee's car, and truth be told, Renee was getting a little sick of her. Without Ruby here, Renee could play whatever she wanted. She switched the music to Madonna's *Ray of Light*, which transported her to freshman year at NYU, when this album was blasting from every dorm room and Renee had nary a wrinkle and the world felt full of promise.

Renee lived just a ten-minute drive from the jewelry store, where she needed to check on her new saleswoman. She liked to drop in unexpectedly to ensure her staff weren't on their phones or worse. Once she'd walked in on a new girl's boyfriend fingering her at the register, no joke. After promptly firing the girl, Renee had become more discerning with her hiring. It was a bigger deal now because the store got more visitors from the show. After eavesdropping on the new girl, Renee would meet Valerie and Carmela at the nail salon for a filmed pedicure scene. Eden wanted Renee to tell the girls about Hope helping Ruby last week, because it would likely anger Carmela, creating the type of explosion viewers loved. And Renee would do as told.

Renee had thick skin, and the *Garden State Goddesses* money was substantial enough that she was A-OK with following the showrunner's orders. Not only did she get a fat paycheck every season, but the advertising for her jewelry business was stellar. She hadn't been able to open a brick-and-mortar store until the show, and the space was almost always busy given the fans.

Renee pulled into her parking spot outside the Ruby, which she'd named for her daughter when Ruby was just three years old and Renee's store was only on Etsy. Now a thirteen-year-old diva, Ruby loved seeing her name outside the store. Renee locked the car, walked up to the storefront, and peeked her head inside. The new shopgirl was, to Renee's delight, not on her phone, nor was she being penetrated. Rather, she was talking to a customer with a warm expression on her face. There were four people in the store right now, not bad for a Tuesday afternoon. Renee waved discreetly and mouthed that she'd be back later, mostly to keep the new girl on her toes.

Carmela's nail salon was called Italians Do It Better, in case anyone wasn't clear that Carmela was an Italian supremacist, and it was a short walk across the parking lot. Renee could already see Valerie getting miked, chatting up the crew, probably about her sons, who were all named for Roman gods—Apollo, Jupiter, and Vulcan. Valerie could never shut up about her boys, which irked Carmela, who only had a girl, Bianca, a nerdy teenager a few years older than Ruby and literally nothing like Carmela in any way. Whereas Carmela was rail thin, bitchy, and assertive, Bianca was sweet, chubby, and shy. Renee supposed Bianca took after her dad, but she didn't really seem like him, either. Dino was a Fontana, the strong, silent type. He was less overtly intimidating than Carmela, but Renee wouldn't exactly call him approachable. In fact, there were rumors that he was in the Mafia, and Shady Di had claimed he didn't go anywhere without a loaded gun. Maybe Bianca was gentle as an act of rebellion against her aggressive parents. Either way, Carmela's inability to provide a son had apparently been an area of contention.

Once they were both miked, Valerie braided her arm through Renee's—she loved to perform an unearned closeness between them on camera—and they headed into the salon. Italians Do It Better wasn't totally Renee's style—too sparkly—but she could understand how the space was very appealing to a certain type of flashy new-money customer. Carmela had opened the salon nearly a decade ago, well before Renee had a brick-and-mortar for the Ruby, and each year it seemed to get glitzier. Gold veins ran through marble floors, reflecting the glow of gold-trimmed mirrors and ornate sconces on the walls. Crystal chandeliers hung from the ceiling and cast prisms across surfaces. She and Valerie were ushered to plush velvet chairs. Carmela appeared with an ice bucket and a bottle of Veuve. She popped the cork and squealed.

Carmela sat between Valerie and Renee, as had been pre-discussed. Carmela always sat in the middle, which no one ever questioned. Renee sort of liked being on the side, where she could pretend not to hear whatever Valerie was saying on the other side of Carmela if she got bored. While the nail technicians got started, weaving around the cameramen, the women chatted idly about various topics—the romantic autumn weather, the Roman gods, as Valerie often referred to her boys. Renee tried not to stare at Valerie's prosthetic foot, even as a camera visibly zoomed in on it. Valerie was the only person Renee knew with a prosthetic body part, and even after three seasons of filmed pedicures, the reveal was always a little shocking.

Valerie was cagey about the accident. All she'd say was that it happened when she was a kid at the Medusa Motors lot and she didn't like to talk about it. Shady Di speculated that her foot had been run over by a car driven by Leo. Several people had whispered to Renee late at night in hushed tones that Carmela had been there—she'd grown up next door to Medusa—and had something to do with it. This explained, her late-night whisperer would say, why Valerie seemed so afraid of Carmela, why she adopted every opinion Carmela had and followed her around like a little lapdog. She was afraid of Carmela getting to her other foot. But Renee didn't really buy this. She just thought Valerie was kind of dumb and had trouble thinking for herself. But Renee did feel bad about the accident, however it had happened.

The technicians began applying their colors—baby pink for Valerie, always pink (Carmela had famously called her "Italian Barbie" last season during a tiff); earthy red for Renee; and navy blue, nearly black for Carmela. When Renee raised her eyes from her toes, Eden's gaze met hers, conveying a nudging intensity. Renee knew what this meant. She took a deep breath and a deeper sip of champagne.

"So Hope came over the other day," Renee said as casually as possible as soon as there was a break in conversation. Carmela immediately stiffened. Renee imagined a cat arching its spine, hair erect. "She was helping Ruby," Renee continued.

"Why? Help with what?" Carmela's tone conjured that of a detective during a homicide interrogation.

"Singing," Renee said. "Hope has a nice voice."

Carmela scoffed. "Ruby sings better than half the chicks on *American Idol*," she said. "How could she possibly need help from Hope?"

"Yeah," Valerie added. "Ruby sings better than Mariah Carey."

Renee smiled. She was so proud of her daughter.

"Hope has a good voice too," Renee said. This was true. She didn't have Ruby's range or power, but she had an ethereal voice and a knack for melody based on her SoundCloud. "And she's an incredibly talented songwriter. She might be able to help Ruby make some original music." This idea was just now occurring to Renee. Ruby spent a lot of time practicing and perfecting her favorite songs but didn't seem to write any of her own music—at least not to Renee's knowledge. Ever since she'd become a teenager, her daughter had grown increasingly mysterious to Renee.

"What the fuck does Hope know about songwriting?" Carmela asked.

They weren't supposed to curse on camera, but Eden seemed to have grown tired of scolding Carmela, and the viewers seemed to like all the bleeps. Gifs of Carmela cursing were always going viral on Instagram.

"She makes folk music, like Joni Mitchell."

"Who is Joni Mitchell?" Valerie asked.

"Some California chick, right?" Carmela said.

Sometimes Renee felt like she was hanging out with Tweedledum and Tweedledee, and whenever she did, she just imagined that paycheck, moving closer to the city, her future store near NYU, and she'd pop some gum in her mouth and keep going.

"Ya," Renee said, chomping a piece of Trident. "A California chick. Who happens to be one of the most famous singer-songwriters of all time. And also she's from Canada."

"Why would Ruby want to sing like some rando Canadian?" Carmela asked. "I heard her sing Ariana Grande last time I was over. She sounded freaking phenomenal. Ariana Grande's Italian."

"So is Demi Lovato," Valerie added. "I love her. Ruby should sing her songs. Isn't Lady Gaga Italian? And Gwen Stefani—"

"Liza Minelli, Frank Sinatra, Bon Jovi," Carmela jumped in, pleased. "All the greats."

"Italians do it better!" Valerie chirped like a little dog.

Eden gave Renee another look that Renee understood.

"Well, Hope was great with her," Renee said. "Ruby really liked her." This last part wasn't entirely true. Ruby had said Hope was nice, but also a little weird, and that she'd started crying randomly, and then got this phone call in the middle of her song and acted strange about it. Renee had said Hope was probably just nervous around the cameras, and Ruby had just shrugged, then disappeared to her room to do whatever she did in there.

"She was probably just being polite," Carmela said. "Great girl."

"The sweetest," Valerie echoed. "I still want to set her up with my Apollo when they're old enough to date."

Valerie talked about setting up Ruby and Apollo *all the time*. Apollo was a grade younger than Ruby at school and Ruby thought he was obnoxious. She had zero interest. And either way, Renee thought Ruby was too young to date. Ruby was her baby girl. So whenever Valerie brought it up, Renee would just smile and change the subject.

"I think Hope and Ruby are going to keep working together," Renee said. "Probably once a week." Renee wasn't sure this was true. They hadn't planned any more voice lessons. But they might, it was possible, and Renee knew that Eden wanted a reaction from Carmela, so Renee was going to keep egging her on until she got one. "You know, Ruby's dad is pretty absent, so it's good for her to have parental figures around."

Carmella shot up in her seat.

Renee had known this would work.

"Are you fucking crazy?" Carmela barked. "Seriously, Renee, did you hit your head this morning? Ruby needs a father figure. She needs a *man* around. She does not need some nitwit from California teaching her God knows what. I wouldn't leave that freak alone with my daughter if someone paid me. Hope is probably going to teach Ruby to smoke pot. I bet she smokes it all the time."

"I think Hope is pretty straight-edge," Renee said, which felt true. She'd seemed alarmed by the idea of wine before dinnertime.

"It's always the innocent-seeming ones," Carmela hissed, "who are the most dangerous."

"Also, Leo told me they wanted to start trying soon." Her gum slid into her throat. Renee coughed to dislodge it, then accidentally swallowed it. "For a boy," she continued. This was completely true—Leo had confided in her when he'd called Renee about ordering a bracelet for Hope—and completely sure to get Carmela going. "Working with Ruby can help get Hope acquainted with being around children, with being a mom."

Renee watched the muscles around Carmela's eyes tense. She'd made the layup this time.

"If she wants practice, she can take my boys whenever!" Valerie chirped. "I need a break. My *nanny* needs a break."

Like a cat in the wild, Carmela shot up from her seat in a motion both elegant and violent. The nail technician jerked back, narrowly avoiding a collision.

"I'm over this conversation," Carmela declared, her voice as sharp as her acrylics. "*Basta! Finito!* Done!"

Carmela stormed toward the exit, nearly toppling a cameraman in her wake. She ripped her mic off as she charged through the door. Valerie got up and followed, an obedient little dog.

Renee sat back in her seat, confident that she was earning her paycheck.

She looked at Eden, who gave her a thumbs-up.

A knot formed in Renee's stomach. She took a deep breath, inhaling the scent of lavender and also acrid chemicals.

CONFESSIONAL TRANSCRIPT - *GARDEN STATE GODDESSES*

(SEASON 3)

VALERIE DULCE

VALERIE: Did you miss me, Eden?

EDEN: You have no idea. You remember the drill?

VALERIE: Like the back of my hand.

EDEN: Present tense, restate the question.

VALERIE: Remind me, which tense is present again?

EDEN: You know, I didn't have to explain this to Ruby. She's thirteen.

VALERIE: She's in school, when you learn all that crap. It's top of mind for her!

EDEN: Not "I went," but "I'm going." Not "I felt," but "I'm feeling." You're taking the viewer along for the ride as it's happening.

VALERIE: Right, right, gotcha.

EDEN: Can you spit out your gum?

VALERIE: I'm spitting out my gum. See, I get it!

EDEN: Really though, can you toss it? It messes with the sound.

VALERIE: [*Footsteps.*] Done!

EDEN: Why do you think Carmela is so triggered by Hope?

VALERIE: Triggered? I don't think Carmela is triggered by Hope. I think she just doesn't like her.

EDEN: Why do you think she doesn't like her?

VALERIE: How much time do you have?

EDEN: I have all the time in the world.

VALERIE: Okay. She doesn't trust her. Thinks she's sketchy. I mean, how did this chick from California end up in New Jersey? Married to my brother? Her own parents weren't at the wedding. No friends either. She just appeared from thin air. I mean, she's sweet and everything, but who is she?

EDEN: It seems like you don't trust her either.

VALERIE: I don't really trust Hope, no. But I was raised to be polite.

EDEN: Why is Carmela so upset that Hope is helping Ruby?

VALERIE: Carmela sees Renee like a sister. Sure, they've had their ups and downs, but once Carmela sees you as family, she becomes *very, very* protective.

EDEN: She doesn't see Hope as family? She and Hope are married to brothers. They're sisters-in-law.

VALERIE: Carmela doesn't see Hope as family.

EDEN: You really don't know who Joni Mitchell is?

VALERIE: Never heard of her.

EDEN: Have you been to California?

VALERIE: No, I've never been to California, but I've been to Florida! That's like the same, right? Sunshine, oranges, palm trees . . .

EDEN: What is your perception of people from California?

VALERIE: I imagine people from California to be like Hope, sort of. Spacy. Head in the clouds. Dreamers. Never saying what they think. No real values. They all just want to be famous.

EDEN: Don't you want to be famous?

VALERIE: I don't care whether I'm famous or not. I just want to give my boys a good life. Californians only care about themselves.

EDEN: Gotcha. Okay, back to the pedicure. How does it feel getting a pedicure with a prosthetic foot?

VALERIE: Seriously?

EDEN: New viewers will wonder.

VALERIE: I've had my prosthesis for, like, decades. I really don't think twice about it.

EDEN: You lost your foot at the Medusa Motors lot? As a child?

VALERIE: Eden, you really have no tact, do you?

EDEN: I ended up in reality television for a reason.

VALERIE: I lost my foot when I was eleven. I don't like to think about it. It was obviously very traumatic. And I'd prefer not to relive it. Over. And over.

EDEN: Carmela was with you that day, right? When you were kids?

VALERIE: I have to go pick up the boys. [*Footsteps.*]

SEVEN

Eden clicked her fob and got in her beat-up Honda Civic. With her salary bump this year, she could afford a sleeker car. She fantasized about a Range Rover. But she just didn't have time to make it to the dealership. When she wasn't working, she was thinking about work, looking at footage, making calls, talking to the Goddesses. Tonight, she was driving to Shady Pond for dinner with Hope. They were ostensibly getting dinner as cousins, to catch up, to see how Hope was settling in in Shady Pond. And that had initially been Eden's intention. But her producer brain tended to eclipse her relationship brain.

Eden kept thinking about the mysterious call that had visibly rattled Hope when they were filming Ruby's voice lesson the other week. After over a decade in reality television, Eden knew when someone was hiding something. It took work, but Eden always got the truth out—on camera. That's why she was paid the big bucks. And this time, she had a leg up. Hope was her family. Eden had taken care of Hope. Eden had gotten Hope out of Weed. She'd introduced her to a kind, handsome man with a huge house. Hope had gone from living in Nowheresville, California, with her abusive, cultish parents to a recently renovated three-bedroom home with a pool in a bustling New York City suburb. And Hope had done almost nothing to earn it, other than having big blue eyes of the variety men go crazy for. Hope owed Eden. She owed her everything.

As the sky turned purple over the Jersey Turnpike, her speaker exploded with the sound of an incoming call. Aria. The Huzzah exec and Eden's boss. The Huzzah exec on whom Eden had based most of her work personality. The Huzzah exec whom Eden wanted to become one day.

"Hi, Aria," Eden said. Eden always had to resist the urge to sing Aria's name. But Aria wasn't fun; she would hate it.

"Eden," Aria said. Always just Eden's name, no hello. Eden imagined Aria multitasking; she was always multitasking. Eden pictured her getting her nails done, always beige, or her hair colored, always icy blond, or ordering dinner on Postmates, always a steak salad. "Just checking in to see how filming is going. Any explosions? Reveals? Murders?" Aria laughed, but it wasn't a joyful laugh; it was an ominous one. Eden thought it was terrifying and iconic.

"It's going well," Eden said, trying to keep her voice measured, to not be overly enthusiastic in a way that would cause Aria to lecture her about resting on her laurels. "Carmela detests Hope, as expected."

"Doesn't Carmela hate everyone?" Aria said.

"Yeah but it's a little different this time," Eden said. "Hope is Carmela's sister-in-law."

"Right," Aria said. "Relevance?"

"They're stuck with each other," Eden said. "Show or not. So Carmela's, like, less of a snarky bitch, and more like a violent tiger protecting her young."

"Primal," Aria said. "Wonderful," she added flatly. "What else?"

"Hope got this phone call," Eden said. "And she seemed really shaken—it was like she had seen a ghost."

"Who was on the call?" Aria asked.

"I don't know," Eden said. Why had she brought it up? Aria was just going to berate her.

"You don't know?" Aria said. "Well, find out, honey." She paused, and Eden swore she could hear Aria thinking. "Anything on Shady Di?"

"I don't think they know about Hope yet," Eden said. Aria and Eden had been perusing the anonymous Instagram account for potential storylines since they found out it existed. But mostly, the account just posted rumors Eden had already heard a billion times— about Dino's Mafia ties, the Fontanas' mistreatment of Carmela, Birdie making her second husband disappear. . . .

"I have to run," Aria said, "but I promise you the bitch is hiding something. I could tell at the wedding. You know I have a sixth sense about these things. I know she's your cousin, so excuse me for saying this, but there is something really dark there. Please find out. Bye."

Aria hung up. Eden felt like an idiot for bringing up the call before knowing the answer. As the light left the sky, Eden tried in vain to quiet her producer brain, but she never really could. Various colleagues had recommended therapy to her after she'd passed out from sleep deprivation and dehydration while they were filming last year. Her DP, Johnny, had completely overreacted and called an ambulance, which had been embarrassing and unnecessary. The hospital had kept her overnight, which had been doubly humiliating. Eden couldn't afford to miss an entire night away from her laptop. As if she had time for therapy. Besides, her life was fine—great, even. Aria had just called her to chat! She was well on track to get staffed on *Manhattan Muses*, a far more popular franchise than *Garden State Goddesses*. Eden was sick of New Jersey, which she hated with a passion of the Christ her parents loved so much. New York was where she'd landed after escaping Weed, New York was her first *real* home, New York was where Aria lived, and New York was where Eden needed to end up. Getting a job on *Manhattan Muses* required delivering a *fantastic* season. So it didn't matter what Eden's conscience said. She was going to get the truth out of Hope.

The problem was, Eden really didn't know Hope that well. They'd been close as kids, but Eden had left Weed when Hope was just twelve years old, even younger than Ruby was now. They hadn't spoken from then on until Eden saw Hope at Faith's wedding two decades later. Eden had no idea what Hope had been up to in the meantime. She'd made references to the church choir, her eyes brightening as if she was singing backup for Beyoncé. She had talked about making her own music. But Eden had no idea about her personal life. Maybe the cousins had something in common in the sense that neither of them had much in the way of a personal life. But it seemed to make more sense for Eden, who had a prickly attitude and fierce self-assuredness that scared men away. But men had always been drawn to Hope. She had the type of wide-eyed naïveté that made men instinctively want to protect her. Surely Hope could have had her pick of the litter in Weed. Although Eden supposed the pickings were slim. Certainly no one in a thirty-mile radius had Leo's means.

At the wedding, Hope had had the same dreamy, ethereal quality she'd had as a kid. The same sandy blond hair and innocent blue eyes. But there was something different about her that Eden couldn't quite put her finger on. She seemed more confident, more defiant somehow. Growing up, she'd always been the obedient one. Whereas Eden and Faith were always getting in trouble, smoking cigarettes and drinking whiskey and having sex, counting the days until they could escape, Hope went to church and even seemed to like following Brother God's inane rules. But at Faith's wedding, something had been different. There was a restlessness to her, a hint of rebellion in her step. She had a spark, flickering and fierce. Aria was wrong; it wasn't a dark energy. It was a bright one. Beaming and destructive.

It was as if she were about to catch fire.

CONFESSIONAL TRANSCRIPT – *GARDEN STATE GODDESSES*

(SEASON 3)

HOPE FONTANA

EDEN: Are you comfortable?

HOPE: Yep. Just so I have it straight—I look at you when I
respond? And include the question in the answer?

EDEN: You got it. Ready?

HOPE: *[Inaudible.]*

EDEN: So I'll be asking you about your singing lesson with
Ruby. What do you think of Renee's house?

HOPE: Renee's house is warm and inviting. It smells like
cinnamon.

EDEN: What do you think of Ruby?

HOPE: Ruby is absolutely adorable. And those pipes! The girl
can sing. Honestly, I feel like she should be teaching
me.

EDEN: You get a call during the lesson.

HOPE: Yeah.

EDEN: Who is it?

HOPE: Someone from home.

EDEN: Can you include the question in the answer?

HOPE: Is this really relevant?

EDEN: Everything is relevant.

EIGHT

Eden was looking at Hope like she was clay again.

Hope was uneasy. They were seated at an Italian restaurant called Amore. Truth be told, Hope was sick of Italian food. But the decor was cute, with exposed-brick walls and trendy red lighting and vintage photos of beautiful women on the walls. Hope's gaze zoned in on a photo of a woman's profile. She had fair skin and thick, winged eyeliner like Carmela. Her features sort of resembled Carmela's too. They had the same olive skin and nearly black hair, long nose, and full, red lips. She was even holding a cigarette between her long nails.

"Who is that?" Hope asked, pointing to the photo.

Eden craned her head to see it. She squinted at the photo. "Oh," she said, as if locating information buried deep inside her brain. "I think that's Jenny Karezi. A Greek actress from the sixties. I don't know why she's in this Italian restaurant, or why I even know her name." Eden sipped her martini. "I wish I'd been obsessed with something more useful than film growing up, like the stock market or something." She sighed, then squinted at the photo again. "The owners must think she's Italian."

Hope was so sick of hearing about Italy. *The motherland*, Leo called it. Leo wanted to eat pasta and drink red wine every night. He wanted to watch *The Godfather* or *My Cousin Vinny* or *The Sopranos* for the billionth time. When Hope tried to put on Joni Mitchell, he'd tell her to switch it to Bon Jovi.

In a small act of defiance, tonight Hope had ordered the Greek salad, which now made her feel connected to the beautiful Greek actress in the frame in front of her. She'd also ordered a cosmopolitan, which Eden had actually introduced her to last time they'd had dinner, saying the cocktails were having "a comeback," probably thanks to the *Sex and the City* reboot. Hope had nodded as if she'd seen this show, which her parents had told her was "the work of the devil," which probably meant Eden's parents had told her the same thing, as their dads had started Brother God together.

Even though things had been weird when she left, Hope missed a few things about Weed. She missed the choir, where everyone treated her with respect, unlike Shady Pond, where everyone treated her like a child or an employee. She missed the snowcapped Cascade Mountains in the distance, which she used as a compass and to tell time. Here, Hope felt disoriented and lost. She frequently took the wrong exit on the freeway, ending up in a different suburb that looked almost identical to Shady Pond. It was unsettling, this sameness—rows of houses like echoes, lawns repeating, each turn a loop back to the start. Most of all, Hope missed Cheyenne. But she wasn't going to let herself dwell on that. Cheyenne was best left in past tense.

"She looks like Carmela," Hope said. "That actress, what's her name again?"

"Jenny Karezi and oh my God you should tell her," Eden said, looking at Hope like she was clay again. Hope knew Eden wanted Hope to tell Carmela this on camera. "She would die."

"Well, I don't want to kill her," Hope said, and Eden laughed again—not with her, but at her. Hope felt so lonely. She sipped her drink, which was pleasantly sweet. She'd never drunk much in Weed. Alcohol was strictly forbidden by Brother God, but as an adult, she'd occasionally have a glass of wine with friends or Cheyenne. But in Shady Pond, people drank wine like water. And Hope was starting to enjoy a nice buzz.

"So," Eden said when the waitress brought their entrees. "Are you ready for the New Beginnings party?"

Hope sighed and took a bite of her salad. Eden only wanted to talk about work. As soon as Hope had agreed to the show, Eden had been one-note—filming, filming, filming. Hope was so curious about the Eden behind this job. Did she have friends? Hobbies? A boyfriend? A girlfriend? Hope couldn't get a read on her sexuality. Her style was kind of androgynous, always a black leather jacket over a white T-shirt and black jeans, typically black boots or sometimes sneakers. She had a bunch of small tattoos on her forearms, and her hair was long and thick but frequently appeared in desperate need of a vigorous wash.

"I'm excited," Hope said to Eden, wanting to keep her cards close to her chest. As with most things in Shady Pond, Hope had mixed feelings about the party. She was excited to see Birdie St. Clair's house, which she called Chateau Blanche and which Hope supposed was technically an estate. Leo had told her Birdie had one of the largest houses in the tristate area. Hope asked what she did to afford such a big house, and Leo laughed at her, as everyone in Shady Pond loved to do. Leo said people with that kind of money didn't work.

Hope had only met Birdie a few times, and she seemed pretty spaced-out. Hope couldn't imagine her holding down any kind of job, and Leo said she'd never had to. She'd married a New Jersey real estate mogul when she was nineteen, divorced him for a lump sum, then married an even richer and much older hedge fund manager, who'd died over a decade ago. *Some suspected foul play*, Leo had said before pulling up a Shady Di post that creeped Hope out. She didn't want to see her future friend as a potential killer.

"Birdie's house is incredible," Eden said. "You're going to love it. It's like a palace." Eden bit into a piece of steak.

"Cool," Hope said. "Hey, I still haven't been to your place—I'd love to see it." Hope wanted to know about Eden the person as opposed to Eden the showrunner.

"For sure," Eden said, chewing. "You'll have to come over soon."

The invite felt hollow.

"How do you feel about your first filmed party?" Eden asked.

Hope sighed again. Always the show. "I feel good," Hope half lied. The New Beginnings party was meant to celebrate Birdie's newly established sobriety. Apparently she'd been sober since Hope's wedding, at which Birdie had fallen down while dancing and knocked over a tray of glasses. Everyone seemed to act like that was a typical occurrence, Birdie falling like that. Hope had known a few drunks in Weed, but only peripherally, people who would come into the diner. The drunks Hope knew tended to be shoddily dressed and unwashed; they didn't own massive estates and wear pink fur coats. Everything on the East Coast was backward.

The meal went on like this, with Eden peppering Hope with questions about the show, Hope trying to change the subject to Eden's personal life, and Eden steering it back to the show. After their waiter took their empty plates, Eden said she'd been speaking to the writers about Hope's tagline for the next season.

"Tagline?" Hope said.

"Oh, right," said Eden. "You haven't seen the show. So every Goddess has a tagline. They're fun. Let me think. Last season Carmela's was 'I don't bite, but I do scratch—and these talons are one hundred percent Italian.'" Eden laughed.

Hope didn't. "That's kind of scary."

"Bad example. Renee! Hers was 'I may play for both teams, but when it comes to being real: I always bring my A game.'"

Hope didn't get it. "Oh," she said.

"Get it?" Eden prodded, knowing Hope didn't. "She's bisexual, like she plays for both teams. Also, the viewers think she's wishy-washy, but also real. It's wordplay."

Hope swallowed. She hadn't realized Renee was bisexual.

"Okay," Hope said, unable to find other words.

"Do you want to hear what they came up with for you?"

Hope nodded, wary. She wasn't sure she wanted to know.

Eden grinned. "'I checked out of the Hotel California with only my guitar—in Jersey, I hope to be a star.'"

Hope blinked. The sentence was so silly. She didn't know what to say.

"Do you love it?" Eden asked.

"It's kind of, like . . ." Hope didn't want to offend Eden or the writers.

"It's corny, I know," Eden jumped in. "They all are! Are you familiar with camp?"

"Like, summer camp?" Hope hadn't learned about summer camp until she was an adult. As kids, she and Eden and all the other church kids had to work the community garden and help with church building repairs. Looking back, she was glad she hadn't known other kids were water-skiing and playing capture the flag all day.

Eden was laughing. "No," she said. "Not summer camp."

Hope didn't appreciate being condescended to. Eden was Hope's cousin, but right now they felt like strangers. Eden thought she was so smart and sophisticated. It was like Eden forgot Hope had seen her swim in her underwear as kids because their parents refused to buy them bathing suits.

"I mean sort of ironic and over-the-top," Eden continued. "Like, kitschy and theatrical."

"Okay," Hope said. She had no idea what Eden was talking about. "But I'm not sure I want to be a star." Hope did like the idea of having an audience for her music, but she didn't like how the tagline sounded. It was so arrogant.

"Well, you're going to be one," Eden said, and grinned. "A star, I mean. The show is popular, Hope. I told you this."

"Right," Hope said, again swirling with conflicting feelings.

A silence fell between them. Hope snatched the opportunity to ask a personal question. "You're so focused on the show, Eden," Hope said. "Do you ever have time to date?"

Eden laughed again. "I don't," she said. "Sounds nice though."

"What's your normal type?" Hope was fishing, but also desperate to talk about anything but work.

"Uh, it's been a while," Eden said. "Let me think. I had pretty terrible taste, come to think of it. Maybe that's why I stopped." Eden put her fork on her plate. "I like a project."

Hope took another sip of her cosmopolitan.

"What about you?" Eden asked.

Dammit. Hope wanted to keep the attention on Eden. "Don't you get enough of my life from the show? I want to know about you," Hope said.

"Well," Eden said, "in my many years in this business, I've found there's often a discrepancy between people's show lives and their real lives. The best Goddesses can merge the two. Like Renee. She's honest, doesn't hide things, and the viewers adore her." There was a tinge of aggression to Eden's voice. Was Hope being accused of something? She couldn't tell.

"Renee is great," Hope said.

"She is," Eden said. "I'm happy about the bisexual representation."

Was Eden coming out to Hope? She couldn't tell. Her cousin was so mysterious.

"So what about your type, Miss Hope? Do you typically go for pretty boys like Leo?"

Hope wished her cousin was remotely trustworthy so she could tell the truth. But since Hope didn't trust Eden, who refused to open up to her, she'd tell her another half-truth, as vague as Eden had been to her.

"Yes," Hope said. "I do typically go for pretty."

Then she put a fifty-dollar bill on the table and left the restaurant.

NINE

Renee rode in a black car with Carmela and Valerie to Birdie's New Beginnings party. The show typically arranged for black cars to take them to Chateau Blanche, which was about thirty minutes from Shady Pond. The catch was they typically rode with a cameraman and were fueled with champagne to create "content."

As usual, Carmela sat between Valerie and Renee, with the DP—Johnny, who'd been with them since season one—facing them. Eden had wanted the car to pick up Hope as well, but Carmela had threatened to not go if she had to ride with Hope. Carmela was coming down hard on Hope, even harder than she had on the new girl last season, but Renee was having trouble seeing Hope as a threat.

Without Eden in the car to prod them, the ride was fairly uneventful. Eventually, Johnny put down his camera and drank a glass of champagne with them. And before they knew it, they were on Rio Vista Drive, home to some of the most expensive mansions in New Jersey. Apparently Stevie Wonder lived in one of them. When Renee had first moved to Shady Pond, she'd thought those houses were big, but they had nothing on the homes here in Alpine, *and* Alpine was closer to the city. Last Renee had checked on Redfin, Birdie's house was valued at nearly $22 million.

Soon they were passing through Chateau Blanche's ornate gates, winding up that $22 million driveway. It was too dark to see it right now, but Renee knew that on the left was a big green expanse with horses, jumps, and stables. Birdie's son, Pierre, was an equestrian; he competed and everything—something called dressage? Birdie had gotten this estate in part for the horses, who needed acres to graze. They'd moved here from a penthouse on the Upper East Side when Pierre was little. But Birdie still talked like she lived in the city, sometimes New York but more often Paris, especially when she was drinking. Now Pierre was twenty-nine years old and showed no signs of wanting to leave Chateau Blanche. Renee adored Ruby but she would be sad if Ruby hadn't established some independence by twenty-nine. As far as Renee knew, Pierre had never had a job other than that of Birdie's assistant, and he'd lived at home while attending Princeton for college. The whole thing was kind of weird.

Tonight, Pierre greeted the women at the door, as he often did. He was wearing his standard salmon-colored polo shirt over khakis and boat shoes. Valerie and Carmela tended to make fun of Pierre's style. They'd hardly left Shady Pond except to go to Sicily once a decade and they weren't familiar with Pierre's breed of boarding school prep. Renee knew a few guys who dressed like this at NYU, guys who'd gone to New York City private schools and couldn't get into an Ivy. But the guys Renee knew were less effeminate than Pierre, who'd never been explicit about his sexuality, but they all assumed he had to be gay. His frosted blond hair was always styled to precision into a near-pompadour and his khakis were a hair too tight. Also, the dressage. They'd had to watch it once during a filmed episode and Carmela and Valerie couldn't stop laughing. "Look at him riding that thing like a float at the Pride parade!" Carmela had squealed, which had divided viewers—some finding it homophobic (mostly straight women) and others finding it camp at its finest (mostly gay men). Despite her mild homophobia, gay men seemed to love Carmela. When fans approached her, they were always gay men. One fan explained it to Renee, saying that due to internalized shame, gay men are particularly drawn to fabulous women with mild disdain toward them. For example, Brigitte Bardot: gay icon and famous homophobe.

"Hi ladies," Pierre said. He opened the doors to a foyer filled with cameras pointed at them and a massive crystal chandelier overhead. Renee had been to Birdie's house dozens of times, but each time, the grandiosity of the home took her breath away. The forty-foot ceilings, the grand double staircase, the gold-leaf moldings and marble floors. As usual, Birdie's "head of house," Luz, quickly appeared out of nowhere with a tray of champagne glasses. The girls each took one. Renee sipped greedily. Birdie's house always made her want to forget mundane obligations and give way to hedonism.

"Unfortunately, Mother is still sleeping," Pierre said, and Carmela snickered. Pierre glared at her. Classic Birdie to be asleep for her own party, especially one meant to be celebrating her sobriety. Birdie had had a few parties like this, parties held to celebrate some kind of renewal or rebirth. She also loved hosting charity events. Viewers had gone wild for a gala last season for a charity unfortunately called Broke Not Broken, where Carmela had gotten into a fight with last season's new girl for copying her dress, in turn breaking a champagne glass over her head and saying, "I'll show you broken, bitch!" That had become such a ubiquitous meme that even Ruby heard it at school and started repeating it around the house. "I'll show you broken, bitch!" she'd say in a variety of contexts that often made no sense. Renee used to forbid Ruby from watching the show unless Ruby herself was on an episode, but Ruby was reaching that age where these things were harder to police.

"If you don't mind following me into the great room," Pierre said. Renee supposed this was the über-wealthy term for a living room, which Renee could admit would feel inadequate to describe the room to which Pierre escorted them. It had an arched cathedral ceiling, a white grand piano, a marble fireplace, and three-story-high Palladian windows. When it wasn't dark, there were views of meticulously landscaped grounds and an Olympic-size saltwater swimming pool, with horses roaming beyond that. Inside, there was a fully stocked bar and French doors opening to the gardens. Birdie loved anything French, and often spoke as though she had lived in France, although there was no evidence of that. Once Renee had overheard Eden telling another producer that Birdie was the type of delusional that kept Huzzah afloat. Renee tried not to think about that, but sometimes it circled through her brain when she was trying to sleep, nudging her like a sinister mosquito out for blood.

"I'll go tell Mother you're here," Pierre said, and disappeared. "Luz," they heard Pierre call, "can you go tell Mother the ladies are here? The stairs . . ." His voice trailed off and Luz responded in muffled Spanish.

Carmela strutted around the room, her heels clacking on the marble. "I'll go tell *Mother* you're here," she mimicked. "*Mother is sleeping*." She laughed.

"Careful," Valerie said. "I bet they have a nanny cam."

Renee wished she could interject with the obvious, that they were literally being filmed by dozens of cameras for a popular television show. But while reality television had become more amenable to breaking the fourth wall in recent years, Eden was old-school and admonished against it.

"It's not like I'm stealing anything." Carmela picked up a crystal figurine from a table, dragged a finger along it, examined her finger for dust, then put it back.

The doorbell rang.

"Probably Hope," Renee said.

"I *hope* not." Carmela snickered.

EDEN: I love your nails today, Carmela.

CARMELA: I see right through you, Eden.

EDEN: I've never seen tiger-print nails.

CARMELA: You need to get out more.

EDEN: [*Laughs.*]

CAMELA: Okay, chop-chop, Eden, I have to get back to the salon soon.

EDEN: Okay, what do you think of Birdie's New Beginnings party?

CARMELA: I wouldn't call it a party. It's four girls and Leona.

EDEN: Why do you call Leo "Leona"?

CARMELA: [*Laughs.*] It's pretty self-explanatory. He's like a woman. He has long eyelashes and loves attention. He's a diva and a gossip. He's Leona. I tell him she should do drag all the time.

EDEN: What does he say?

CARMELA: I don't think I should repeat that on camera. I don't want to get you people sued.

EDEN: Thank you. What do you think of Leona's wife?

CARMELA: [*Laughs.*]

EDEN: Well? What do you think of Hope?

CARMELA: No disrespect to your family, Eden, but your cousin is a freak.

TEN

Hope couldn't believe this home. It reminded her of *The Great Gatsby*, which had been Eden's favorite book growing up, probably because it was all about someone going somewhere new and reinventing themselves. Hope had watched the movie years later in Yreka, at the closest movie theater to Weed, and she supposed now she was the one going somewhere new and reinventing herself.

"You can't see them, but there are horses over there," Leo said, pointing to the left as they wound up the longest driveway Hope had ever seen. Hope thought the houses in Shady Pond were big, but this was next level. The house resembled a castle, lit up with a billion lights.

Outside, they were greeted by producers and miked. When they rang the doorbell, Hope's heart thudded. This was her first filmed gathering with all the other Goddesses. She'd had a glass of champagne on the drive to calm her nerves, but she felt like she needed ten more.

Birdie's son, Pierre, answered the door. Hope recognized him from her wedding. He was the one who'd saved Birdie after her fall. He was wearing a tight pink shirt and his hair stood tall above his head like a wave about to crash. Behind him were the many cameras Hope had become accustomed to. Hope was not accustomed, however, to ceilings this high and chandeliers this big. She tried not to gape at her opulent surroundings.

"Mother's sleeping," Pierre said. "The women are in the great room."

Hope had no idea what Pierre meant by "the great room" or why the host would be asleep during her own party, but she was thrilled to see a woman carrying a tray of champagne. Leo grabbed two glasses and handed one to Hope, then put his arm around her as he walked her into "the great room." The space was *massive* and filled with plush rugs and oversize white sofas, coffee tables holding up intricate sculptures, and huge impressionist paintings on the walls that seemed plucked from a museum. Hope was staring at another crystal chandelier when Renee came over and kissed her cheek. Hope felt herself blush, which she hoped the cameras couldn't pick up.

"I thought it was girls only tonight," Carmela said, eyeing Leo.

"Me too," said Pierre, seeming irritated.

"Me three," said Valerie, seeming compelled.

"Oh well, it's just Leona," Carmela said. She really did look like that actress on the wall at the Italian restaurant, Jenny Karezi. They had the same striking cat-eye makeup, black eyeliner drawn out past the corners of her eyes and up in a dramatic swoop. Same high cheekbones and dark, wavy hair. Carmela was equally glamorous in a shimmery black dress under a bright blue fur stole. Hope felt wildly underdressed in her cotton dress and the same jean jacket she always wore.

"What are you staring at?" Carmela said to Hope.

Hope reddened again. She sipped more champagne to steady herself. "I love your outfit," Hope said with as much confidence as she could muster.

"Leona," Carmela said, air-kissing Leo, "your wife has taste."

Hope didn't like how Carmela kept calling him Leona, which Hope had heard her do once before at a Fontana family gathering. Hope supposed the implication was that Leo was dramatic and feminine, a diva, and he was these things, which Hope liked about him.

Carmela air-kissed Hope next, followed by Valerie, whose air kiss was accompanied by a hug. "Sorry, I'm a hugger," she whispered in Hope's ear. Leo's sister had always been polite to Hope, even though she spent most Fontana family events whispering with Carmela on the other side of the room.

"You look like that actress," Hope continued to Carmela. "Jenny Karezi."

Carmela raised a single arched eyebrow. "Jenny Ka-who?"

"She's a Greek actress from the sixties," said Hope. She looked at Eden, who gave an approving nod. "There's a photo of her on the wall at Amore."

Carmela shuddered. "Greek?"

"Yes," Hope said, straightening her back to appear more confident than she felt. "She's really pretty."

"She is," Pierre interjected. "My boarding school boyfr—err, best friend went crazy for *The Red Lanterns*. That's her big film. It was nominated for an Oscar in the sixties, for best foreign film. Anyway he'd screen it over and over and *over* again."

Everyone turned toward Pierre. Hope was relieved he was backing her up. But then Pierre started laughing, and it was not a friendly laugh. He was laughing at her.

"It's about a bunch of prostitutes," Pierre continued, whistling at the end of the word. "In a brothel." He grinned.

Hope choked on her champagne. Her face burned.

"Come on," Leo interjected. "She was trying to give Carmela a compliment."

"Leona," said Carmela. "Please tell your wife not to compare me to a Greek whore if she wants to compliment me."

"I—I'm so sorry," Hope stammered.

"So," Pierre said, "why don't you whores make yourselves comfortable?" He chuckled. Hope wanted to disappear. "*Whores* d'oeuvres will be served soon."

"Speaking of whores"—Carmela narrowed her eyes at Pierre—"where's your *mother*?"

Pierre's eyebrows shot up, his face burning with indignation. "Like I said," he hissed, "I'm afraid she isn't feeling well." Offense seemed to fade as Pierre became briefly preoccupied with his own reflection in the mirror over the fireplace. "But she does have gifts for you all," he continued. "Which I'll go retrieve now." Pierre walked off. "Luz!" they heard him shout. "The gifts!"

"Heck yes," Valerie said once Pierre disappeared. "Birdie gets the best gifts," she whispered in Hope's ear.

"Poor Luz," said Renee. "I wonder if she needs help."

"Leona," Carmela said, ignoring Renee, "you couldn't miss out on ladies' night."

"You're the one swinging your dick around like an insecure teen-ager," Leo said to Carmela. Hope was shocked by Leo's vulgarity. He was always so respectful with Hope. But he always bickered with Carmela, which Hope didn't totally understand. She wished Leo wouldn't stoop to Carmela's level.

"Easy, Leona," Carmela said. "I can see your tampon string."

"Do you even remember what a tampon is?" Leo quipped. Carmela was around forty-seven or forty-eight, Hope thought, which meant she likely hadn't hit menopause yet. But either way, Leo was very rude to be making fun of a woman for her age. Hope jabbed his rib cage.

"I asked him to come," Hope said. "I apologize."

"You afraid of us?" Carmela asked. "We don't bite." Then she clicked her teeth together in a way that made Hope shiver. Also, the great room was freezing. The room was so big there was a persistent draft.

Pierre returned with several gold-wrapped boxes. Behind him, Luz carried a few more. Pierre handed the first to Carmela, the second to Valerie. Luz, who seemed out of breath, handed Hope the biggest box, so big she could hardly hold it. Then she handed a smaller box to Renee. Pierre handed a bottle of wine to Leo, whispering, "Sorry, we weren't expecting you."

They all sat down on the couch to open their gifts. Carmela ripped into hers the quickest. Inside was a pink snakeskin handbag. Hope recognized the little *C*'s on the fastener. She'd never owned Chanel, but the logo was famous. It must have been insanely expensive.

"Too bad I don't wear pink," Carmela said. She handed the purse to Valerie, who said, "Lucky me!"

Hope couldn't believe Carmela's audacity, insulting such a gracious gift like this right in front of Pierre.

Valerie ripped hers open next. Hope couldn't tell what it was at first. It looked like a plastic foot with a sandal. Then Hope remembered Valerie's prosthetic foot. Hope had first noticed it at a Fontana pool party this summer. Leo said Valerie had lost it in a childhood accident and she didn't like to talk about it. Birdie's gift appeared to be a prosthetic foot cover with pink toenails and pink Prada sandals. Hope held her breath, wondering if the gift was offensive. The room seemed to go quiet. She heard Renee swallow.

"How adorable," Valerie said, and everyone, including Pierre, seemed to exhale in relief. "I love it!" She held the plastic foot up in the air, watching it change colors under the shifting lights of the chandelier above her.

Renee opened her gift next, a collection of what appeared to be high-quality gemstones—turquoise and emeralds and opals and gems Hope didn't recognize. Renee was a jewelry designer, so Hope figured Renee could use these to make necklaces and bracelets. Renee seemed to love it.

Everyone then peered at Hope, who hadn't opened her gift. The box was so big it made Hope uncomfortable. She began carefully undoing the gold wrapping paper with suspended breath.

"Hurry up, Cali," said Carmela. "This isn't origami class. Just rip into it."

Carmela had developed a habit of calling Hope nicknames that referenced Southern California, things like "Miss Hollywood" or "Malibu Barbie." Hope wanted to tell Carmela that she'd never even been to Southern California, that her hometown was an eleven-hour drive from Los Angeles. But Hope didn't really want to get into where she was from, not with these girls, not with anyone. She wanted to forget about it. Start anew.

Hope did as told, ripping a huge swath of paper after another in quick succession. Behind the paper was a big box, which Hope opened swiftly to appease Carmela, then gasped. Inside was a Fender Jaguar, the same guitar that Sharon Van Etten had played on her more recent albums. It was also baby blue, Hope's favorite color. This was the exact guitar that Hope had been planning to ask Leo to buy her for Christmas. She was absolutely stunned.

"I can't accept this," Hope said to Pierre. "It's too generous. I've had dreams about this guitar." This was true.

"Well, I can take it off your hands if you'd like," Pierre said, approaching Hope.

"No, no," Leo interjected. "She's just being polite. She loves it. This is so nice of Birdie."

"*Too* nice, some might say," Pierre said very quietly, so quietly Hope almost didn't hear it, and Hope was confused. It seemed like Pierre didn't want her to have the guitar. She wasn't sure what to do.

"I hope Birdie wakes up soon so I can thank her," Hope said.

"That reminds me," Pierre said, "I should go check on her."

"I can't believe I got *another* pink regifted purse." Carmela sighed when Pierre was gone. "It's like she gives me every purse she buys and doesn't like. And they're all pink! Why not give Valerie the pink purses? She loves pink."

Hope was embarrassed by Carmela's outburst.

"I love your sloppy seconds," Valerie said, holding the purse up under the light. "Fabulosity!"

Carmela walked over to Hope, who held her breath. "Nice guitar," Carmela said. *"Too nice, some might say."* She mimicked Pierre, perfectly echoing his nasal voice. It was rude, but Carmela had a knack for mimicry. She prayed Carmela would never mimic her. Not knowing what to say, Hope glanced at Leo for backup.

"Don't be bitter, Carmela," Leo said. "Just because Birdie clearly likes you the least."

"Easy, brother," Valerie said.

A voice coming from outside the great room interrupted them. It sounded like Birdie. The cameras rushed to follow it, and the women (and Leo) came trailing after.

In the foyer, Birdie stood at the top of the grand staircase, like a queen looking down on her loyal subjects. "Good evening, my dear ladies," Birdie called, and her voice echoed. She was speaking with what sounded like a British accent, and Hope wondered if she had somehow missed until just now that Birdie was actually British. "I'm so sorry to be late for my own party, but I'm so utterly thrilled you all are here." The accent was starting to sound less British and more French. Hope was disoriented. Birdie held up a glass of what appeared to be champagne. Wasn't this party supposed to be celebrating her sobriety? Maybe she was drinking club soda.

"To new beginnings," Birdie said, then began descending the staircase. Everyone stood in silence, watching her. She was wearing a long red gown, and Hope felt ashamed by her jean jacket again. On the third step, Birdie's heel snagged on the bottom of the gown. Her champagne glass flew out of her hand and Birdie followed, tumbling down the stairs. They all stood, mouths agape, watching her fall. Pierre rushed over, but it was too late.

Birdie hit the marble floor with a thud.

CONFESSIONAL TRANSCRIPT – *GARDEN STATE GODDESSES*
(SEASON 3)
PIERRE ST. CLAIR

PIERRE: Can we get some AC in here? I'm sweating like a cat on a hot tin roof.

EDEN: Really? I'm freezing.

PIERRE: You know the gays run hot.

EDEN: I didn't know that at all. [*Footsteps.*] Okay, better?

PIERRE: It's fine. Let's just get this over with. I have a riding lesson at four.

EDEN: We'll be quick. Okay, first question: Why is your mom asleep when her guests arrive at her New Beginnings party?

PIERRE: You'll have to ask her that.

EDEN: My voice will be edited out, so can you include the question in the answer?

PIERRE: As to why my mother is asleep when her guests arrive, you'll have to ask her that.

EDEN: Are you expecting Leo there?

PIERRE: No, my surprise is genuine.

EDEN: [*Clears throat.*]

PIERRE: I am surprised when Leo arrives. It's supposed to be ladies' night. But then again, I've come to expect not a shred of politesse from this crowd. I'm always saying that forced sterilization wouldn't be a bad idea in many parts of New Jersey. Nearly every day I tell Mother we should have moved to Connecticut.

EDEN: Why do you think your mom chose Jersey?

PIERRE: She didn't. My idiot father did.

EDEN: Why?

PIERRE: My father didn't really confide in me, nor did we converse much. But I'm guessing his decision to move us to America's armpit had something to do with taxes. Billionaires are the cheapest people on the planet, I'm telling you.

EDEN: You could still move to Connecticut, right?

PIERRE: I don't understand how any of this is relevant, but Dorothy and Frances are comfortable here and they don't do well with change.

EDEN: Dorothy and Frances?

PIERRE: My horses, honey. How many times do I have to tell you people this? Does working in reality television make you as brain-dead as watching it does? And I know you don't care, but for the record, Frances is named for the late Princess of Wales. Not many people know that Frances was her middle name. "Dorothy" is obviously a reference to Judy Garland's most iconic role.

EDEN: Noted. Okay, back to more relevant matters. I know you have your lesson. Frances is waiting on us.

PIERRE: Frances is waiting on *me*. And I'm riding Dorothy today, but go on.

EDEN: What do you think when Carmela calls Leo "Leona."

PIERRE: I think it's apt that Carmela calls Leo "Leona." He's *super* femme. Those lashes? Those cheekbones? He gives Natalie Portman a run for her money! Actually, scratch that, I don't want the Fontanas to kill me. I think Leo is hot. Actually, scratch that, too. I don't want the viewers to think I'm . . . a "friend of Dorothy," if you will. [*Chuckles.*]

EDEN: [*Clears throat.*] Right, of course not.

PIERRE: I think it's funny when Carmela calls Leo "Leona." Carmela is clever.

EDEN: What do you think of Hope?

PIERRE: She's pretty but has no idea how to dress herself. I would kill to make her over.

EDEN: What would you do?

PIERRE: Two words: blow-dryer. Is that one word or two? Whatever, the point is: this is prime-time television, not *Hannah and Her Sisters*. I still think the worst thing Woody Allen did to Mia Farrow was to put her on the silver screen with that frizzy hair and in those awful paisley dresses. Hope is married to a Fontana, not a Jewish intellectual—she needs to blow that frizz out, you hear me? Another word: mascara. She needs an eyelash curler. Her skin is clear but she looks tired. I'd give her a little Botox between the brows or at least a laser facial. If I were her, I'd wear black. Dark colors go well with blond. And I'd wear something tight. I have no idea what her body looks like or if she even has one. Everything she wears recalls a potato sack, or Hannah's frumpy sisters. And she's not exactly Mia Farrow, if you get what I'm saying.

EDEN: What about her personality?

PIERRE: Are you implying that I'm shallow? [*Cackles.*] Because I am.

EDEN: You seem upset when Hope opens her gift.

PIERRE: Yeah, I am upset when Hope opens her gift.

EDEN: Why?

Pierre: Because it's my guitar.

ELEVEN

Hope was playing her Fender Jaguar for the cameras when Birdie called. Hope had known Birdie was going to call, as it had been planned, but the guitar-playing had been a spontaneous idea of Eden's. "Play the guitar when she calls, then thank her for the gift," she'd said. This request was easy to fulfill because Hope played the Jaguar all the time. She was addicted to it. Leo had bought her some pedals and she was writing a new song, something sad and yearning, like most songs she wrote, but she wasn't playing that now. She was playing Joni Mitchell's "California," because Eden had told her to play it.

Hope was sheltered but she wasn't dumb. She knew her role on this TV show. The outsider. The naive one. The weird Californian. With several cameras in her face, Hope felt slightly energized to be playing guitar for an audience. She felt like a pop star. She'd had some wine, as had become her pre-filming ritual. Leo had a whole cellar of it, all types. In contrast to the Fontanas, Hope preferred white wine, sometimes prosecco or champagne. Carmela and Leo preferred red. They got all into it, debating vintages and varietals. Sometimes Carmela and Leo acted more like siblings—always bickering and ribbing—than did Leo and his actual sister, Valerie. Hope often forgot those two were even related.

When Hope's phone rang, she put her guitar down and took a

quick sip from her coffee mug. It was currently filled with Nino Franco's 2015 Primo Franco, a dry sparkling wine with notes of ripe green apples and wisteria. Like most of the wines Hope preferred, this one was vinted in Northern Italy, which was somewhat controversial among the Fontanas, who primarily drank Sicilian wine, mostly red and some rosé.

"My darling girl," Birdie said, her face sharpening into view on the tiny screen. Birdie appeared to be in a bathtub, bubbles obscuring the bottom of her face. Hope was embarrassed, even though she couldn't see anything other than the top of Birdie's face, her eyes accentuated by dark liner and surgically lifted to precision. "You look absolutely beautiful as always," Birdie continued, her accent verging on British. "Not to toot my own horn, but I was nearly identical to you at your age."

Hope squinted at Birdie's face on the screen. Hope couldn't even tell what Birdie actually looked like. She mostly resembled a plastic surgeon's creation, stretched and taut, shiny and poreless. Hope couldn't tell how old she was. Eden said Birdie's paperwork indicated she was forty-two, which Eden had relayed with a harsh laugh, guessing Birdie's age was closer to mid-fifties to early sixties. But no one knew for sure, she'd said. Today Birdie's eyes were a little bloodshot, eyeliner slightly smudged, as always. Her hair was an icy, unnatural shade of blond.

"Now I know what my daughter would look like," Birdie said, and laughed. Hope laughed too, but felt uncomfortable, both with the compliment and with the idea of Birdie's naked body under those bubbles. She took another sip from her mug. Eden peered at Hope, who remembered she had been instructed to bring up the guitar.

"I was just playing the Jaguar," Hope said to Birdie, who suddenly had a flute of champagne in her hand. At least Hope wasn't drinking alone.

"Oh, how wonderful, Hope, I absolutely *adore* cats." She grinned. "The bigger the better."

Hope laughed, then held up the guitar. "I mean the Fender," she said, and smiled.

"Oh, I'm so happy, dear," Birdie said. "Truth be told, I originally snatched it up for Pierre but he never played it. This was when I dreamed of him being the next Mick Jagger." Her accent turned slightly cockney. "Well, I've given up on that dream! And I hated the idea of the guitar going to waste."

"Well, it's certainly not going to waste here," Hope said. "I'm addicted to her." Hope cringed at her own use of a female pronoun to refer to the genderless guitar. Eden raised an eyebrow.

"Anyway, darling, we could gab all day about the golden age of rock 'n' roll," Birdie continued, the accent turning French, "but I have a tête-à-tête scheduled with a young man who is a dead ringer for Alain Delon, so let's get to why I'm calling."

Hope had no idea what Birdie was saying. She made a mental note to look up Alain Delon.

"I wanted to invite you to my home in Rhode Island for the weekend," Birdie went on. "I've invited all the girls. I have a little place on the sea."

Hope silently chuckled at Birdie's use of the word *little*, as Eden had shown Hope photos of the house and it was not, by any definition, small.

"That sounds wonderful," Hope said. "I've never been to Rhode Island." Truth be told, Hope was nervous about the trip—mostly about being trapped with the girls and the cameras and no escape.

"Oh, how dreadful," Birdie said. "Well, you're going to absolutely love it. And let me tell you what: Rhode Island is going to love you right back!"

Hope smiled. Birdie's flattery was a tad unnerving, but preferable to Carmela's hostility.

"Thanks, Birdie," Hope said. "I can't wait."

The women hung up.

The room fell silent.

Hope felt many lenses staring at her.

CONFESSIONAL TRANSCRIPT - *GARDEN STATE GODDESSES*
(SEASON 3)
BIRDIE ST. CLAIR

EDEN: All set, Birdie? Do you need some coffee in addition
     to your smoothie? You seem a little tired.

BIRDIE: I'll perk up once the cameras start rolling, don't
       worry.

EDEN: The cameras *are* rolling.

BIRDIE: Okay, I'm up! Fire 'em at me.

EDEN: Why do you FaceTime Hope from the bathtub?

BIRDIE: Why wouldn't I?

EDEN: Remember, put the question in the answer because my
     voice will be edited out. And present tense. Narrate the
     action for the viewer.

BIRDIE: Oh, right. You silly people and your silly rules.
       Okay, I am taking a bath when I remember I need to
       FaceTime Hope to invite her to Newport. My phone is
       right there. I'm relaxed. *C'est la vie, ma chérie.*

EDEN: You say you wanted Pierre to be Mick Jagger. Can you
     tell me more about that?

BIRDIE: I was big into the Stones, you know, especially
       when I lived in London. Everyone was into the Stones.
       I wanted a girl, but when I knew I was going to have a
       boy, I was like well, at least my Pierre can be a rock
       star like Mick Jagger.

EDEN: Did Pierre ever play guitar?

BIRDIE: Oh, no. He had no interest in being a rock star. All
       he liked were dolls and horses.

EDEN: You say you have a date with a young man who looks
     like Alain Delon. *Purple Noon*, right?

BIRDIE: *Plein Soleil*, yes. Very good, Eden. And that's right,
       we had a tête-à-tête.

EDEN: What do you mean by "tête-à-tête"?

BIRDIE: It's French.

EDEN: Right. The literal translation is "head-to-head," right?

BIRDIE: Correct. Except we go more bottom-to-bottom. [*Laughs.*]

EDEN: [*Laughs.*] You say Hope reminds you of a daughter.

BIRDIE: Yes, she looks just like me when I was her age. If you can believe it, I was pretty innocent back then. An ingénue.

EDEN: With all due respect, weren't you married to a billionaire when you were her age?

BIRDIE: *Oh, mon Dieu.* It's impolite to discuss finances. [*Laughs.*] How old is Hope? Twenty-one? I got married at nineteen if you can believe it. That was my first marriage, though. I married Pierre's father later, I can't remember exactly when. I miss him terribly.

EDEN: Hope is thirty-three. And I'm sorry about your husband.

BIRDIE: I'm sorry too. He was a great man, died too young. It didn't make sense to me. He was in such good shape, such a healthy eater—I swore he would live forever. I don't admit this to many, but he was younger than me. Just by a few years, but I was confident he'd outlive me.

EDEN: I'm so sorry. Can I ask how he died?

BIRDIE: Yes, but I don't have an answer. One second we were having cocktails—we'd have martinis every evening at five p.m. on the dot, very Gilded Age—the next he was dead on my antique Aubusson rug. I wanted to get an autopsy, but Pierre convinced me it was too macabre, and what's the point of knowing? Nothing will bring him back.

EDEN: I'm so sorry, Birdie. How long ago was this?

BIRDIE: Who knows. I'm not a mathematician. Time is elusive. In the grand scheme of things, we're all a speck of—

EDEN: A speck of what?

EDEN: Birdie? Birdie? Are you awake?

BIRDIE: [*Snoring.*]

TWELVE

Just before Eden left that afternoon, she told Hope to post something on Instagram.

"You only have that one photo," Eden teased. "When the show comes out, you're going to have tens of thousands of followers overnight. They'll want to know who you are."

Hope swallowed. Tens of thousands of people sounded like a lot. And what did Eden mean they wanted to know who she was? She hardly knew who she even was anymore. Just a year ago, she'd thought of herself as a modest Protestant woman and a Californian. Now, she lived in New Jersey, in a $3 million house, and was married to a flashy Catholic. She'd completely started over. She had no idea who this version of her was. Hope was going to ask Eden what exactly she should post, but Eden was already closing the door, following the cameramen to a big truck. The house was very quiet again. Hope walked back to her studio and sat on the faded leather couch Leo had bought to give it an "authentic rock 'n' roll feel." He was very sweet.

Hope's phone was still sitting on the coffee table, its cover glinting yellow in the overhead lights. She picked it up and went to the home screen. It was Hope's first smartphone and it still amazed her, having a little computer in her palm. Before this, she'd had a flip phone, a phone she'd left in Weed along with everything else. Her old phone could make calls and texts, but there were no apps. She could play Snake. Absentmindedly wondering if she could play Snake on this fancy computer phone, she opened Instagram to try to figure out what to post. A red heart indicated a notification. A new person wanted to follow her. Hope only had twenty-two followers, mostly members of Leo's family and the Goddesses. The follow request was probably from someone associated with the show, like Caleb the audio guy or Johnny the DP. Hope clicked the notification. Her breath caught in her throat.

The profile photo featured a woman in a forest Hope immediately recognized. Tall trees with reddish-brown bark. Redwoods. Caramel-colored hair fell past the woman's breasts. She had her arm around another woman. The other woman was Hope.

The profile was Cheyenne's. Hope's throat tightened, like it was being strangled by an invisible hand. How had Cheyenne found her? Hope had a new last name now, and Cheyenne had always claimed to despise social media. She also didn't watch television, which was why Hope felt safe doing the show. But she should have known better than to feel safe. If the past was any indication, Hope was never safe.

Hope clicked Cheyenne's profile. She only had one photo posted, the same as her profile photo, the photo of Hope and Cheyenne in the woods behind Hope's parents' house, one early evening last summer before dinner. An intense, unwelcome feeling jolted through Hope. Part of her wanted to close the app, throw the phone across the room, watch it smash against the wall, never look at it again. But the other part of her was staring at the app, at the little red dot in the corner indicating she had a message. It was from Cheyenne. Hope clicked the message, which contained a photo and the words *Miss you, my Delilah*.

Why was she calling Hope *Delilah*? Was it a reference to the Book of Judges? Delilah who seduced Samson only to betray him to the Philistines?

With shaky hands, Hope clicked on the photo. It was close-up shot of a book in a poorly lit room. The book was a Bible, with charred edges. Squinting, Hope could see the initials etched into the top corner of the leather.

SDB.

It was her father's initials.

It was Hope's father's Bible.

Hope shut the phone off.

Part Two

I'd rather eat glass than talk about this.

—BETHENNY FRANKEL, *THE REAL HOUSEWIVES OF NEW YORK*

ONE

Renee shifted her gaze periodically from Hope to Carmela and back again. Her stomach was in knots, as it typically was at the beginning of a cast trip. The production company had rented them an SUV limo filled with all the snacks and champagne they could possibly want, and Renee was taking advantage of the bubbly to calm her nerves. Before *Goddesses*, she hadn't been much of a drinker. The occasional glass of wine at dinner. But filming was just so much easier with liquid courage. And cast trips required the most courage of all.

"Do I have something in my teeth?" Carmela asked Renee. "Why are you staring at me?"

Renee diverted her gaze and inadvertently met the eye of a camera lens, which was strictly off-limits. But occasionally, Renee would become unnerved and slip up. She shifted her focus back to Carmela.

"Sorry," Renee said. "I'm just on edge." That was another mistake. She was nervous about the cast trip, which she couldn't say on camera because they weren't supposed to break the fourth wall.

"Yeah, me too," Carmela said, thankfully taking the attention from Renee. "Silverstone Manor gives me the creeps." All of Birdie's houses had names. Last season, they'd gone to her Aspen house, Chalet Bleu, as well as Silverstone Manor. Renee much preferred

Rhode Island, with its rocky cliffs and sea breezes, to skiing, which they all sort of hated. Italians weren't skiers. They were warm-weather people.

"Totally haunted," Valerie chirped, as if on command. Renee sometimes wished Valerie were smart enough to know that she should have the upper hand in her friendship with Carmela. After all, Valerie was the one with the powerful Sicilian family who owned the best vintage car dealership in New Jersey. Carmela was just the ambitious girl next door who'd happened to marry into the family due to sheer persistence. Well, Renee supposed, Carmela was also sexy. She wasn't Renee's type—Renee tended to go for a softer look—but she had an objectively great body and beautiful eyes, and could be very charming when she wanted to be. She seemed to have the Fontanas under some kind of spell. Leo was the only one who didn't seem to buy what Carmela was selling, which made him an enemy, and Hope an enemy by association.

"I'm excited," Hope said, speaking for maybe the first time on this drive. Her champagne glass was empty, so perhaps she was feeling more extroverted. "I've never seen the Atlantic Ocean."

"Huh?" Carmela said. "You've never seen the ocean?"

"I've seen the Pacific," Hope said. "Just not the Atlantic."

"The Atlantic is the one at the Jersey Shore, right?" Valerie asked. The Fontanas had a house there where they'd hosted a few cast parties. Renee couldn't believe Valerie didn't know which ocean it was on.

Carmela tapped Valerie's temple with a navy blue nail. "Is there anything inside there?"

Valerie seemed to shudder at Carmela's touch. Renee wondered what Carmela had on Valerie that made Valerie so afraid of her, so obedient. Valerie took a sip of champagne and appeared to compose herself.

"Just diamonds and dreams!" Valerie chirped. "Oh my God, that would be an amazing tagline." Eden, who was sitting in the front, glared back through the divider. Valerie had broken the fourth wall. "For my future hat business," Valerie said in a vain attempt to recover.

So far they weren't creating compelling content on this ride. Eden clearly wanted more. And Renee wanted to move closer to the city, which meant pleasing Eden.

"Hey, Hope," Renee said, briefly eying Eden. "Ruby really appreciates all you've done for her."

Hope was staring out the window. She turned her head back inside the car, gazed over at Renee, blinked a few times. Hope was a bit of a space cadet. And not in the highly medicated way that Birdie was. Hope seemed to have an active inner life. Reality television mostly called for an active outer life. But Renee could see why Eden had cast Hope. She had that doe-eyed innocence viewers would automatically want to protect. And the more sadistic fans would love watching Carmela torture Hope, like a cat playing with a mouse before slaughtering it.

"Oh," Hope said. "It's so easy with Ruby. She's such a natural."

"You bet she's a natural," Carmela said. "She could win *American Idol.*"

"Ruby has a better voice than Adele," Valerie added.

"She's fantastic," Hope agreed.

Renee smiled, feeling proud of her kid and enjoying the quiet before the storm. She knew she had to deliver.

"Ruby said you have a great voice, too, Hope," Renee said. This was almost the truth. Ruby had said Renee had a "sweet" voice. Ruby had compared her to Taylor Swift, whom Ruby didn't particularly like, but lots of people did like her—the woman was a billionaire.

"I've never heard you sing, Hope," Carmela said, lifting a perfectly arched eyebrow. "I'd love to hear it."

Hope reddened and Renee felt bad for her. She was torn between delivering content for Eden and protecting Hope. Perhaps she could do both.

"Don't put the girl on the spot," Renee jumped in.

"Why not?" Carmela asked, refilling her champagne glass. "Ruby can sing on command. All great singers can."

"Hope's voice sounds better with a guitar," Renee added. "She's an incredible songwriter. Why don't we put on her music?" Renee called up front, mostly to Eden. "There's a way to connect our music, right?"

Hope protested, but Renee felt like this was the best option. Hope obviously didn't want to sing a cappella in front of Carmela, but her music was nothing to be ashamed of. Her voice was moving, and soothing. Renee even listened to it sometimes when she was winding down at night. Carmela would undoubtedly hate it, and Valerie would surely echo her, but the viewers might like it, in which case Renee would be doing Hope a favor.

Renee pulled up Hope's SoundCloud on her phone, then handed the phone up to Eden, who gave Renee a sinister grin when she did. Hope protested again, but it was too late. Eden had hooked up the music and it was playing for the whole SUV to hear. Carmela made a face like she smelled something rotten.

"Does it ever pick up?" Carmela asked after an awkward thirty seconds or so. "This is gonna put me to sleep."

"It's peaceful," Valerie said. "I should play this for my boys to get them to chill out before bed."

Carmela tapped Valerie's temple again, and again, Valerie shuddered for a brief moment. The response caused Renee to wonder if the rumors about Carmela being responsible for Valerie's foot were true. She'd seen a meme on Shady Di just this morning about Leo chopping off Valerie's foot with a massive Italian butcher knife. That account was just so dark; Renee didn't even know why she looked. She silently vowed to stop.

Everyone turned their attention back to the music. Sweat appeared to form on Hope's upper lip.

"Are you okay, Hope?" Carmela asked. "This shit is pretty depressing. Is Leo not pleasing you? Are you homesick for Hollywood?"

Hope's face turned from red to white. Renee felt horrible. She needed to stick up for her.

"This song is moving," Renee said. "I love it. I think I might ask the girls to play it in the store."

"Your customers will slit their wrists," Carmela said without skipping a beat.

Valerie snickered.

"There's a lot of power in vulnerability," Renee said. "Some would say it's much more impressive than being intimidating."

Hope shot Renee a grateful smile. She seemed so sweet. Renee felt a motherly urge to protect her, likely in the same way Eden imagined the viewers would.

"I have no idea what the fuck you're talking about," Carmela said. "But I think we've heard enough."

"It's fine," Hope said. "We can play something more upbeat."

"*Grazie a Dio,*" Carmela said, then crossed herself. "Put on Madonna."

The driver did as told.

"Like a Prayer" played loudly and Valerie refilled everyone's champagne glass.

LEO: Eden, are you smoking again? You smell like Carmela.

EDEN: This isn't about me. But yes.

LEO: You put our shit on blast all season and I can't ask a
simple question?

EDEN: On camera, no, you can't. How do you feel about your
wife going on her first cast trip?

LEO: I'm nervous as hell about Hope going on this cast trip.
I'm tossing and turning all night.

EDEN: What are you nervous about?

LEO: Come on, E. You know what these girls are like.

EDEN: Can you not address me? Remember, I'll be edited out.

LEO: Right, right, sorry. I'm nervous about Hope because
these girls are vicious, like piranhas.

EDEN: Is your sister, Valerie, vicious?

LEO: Valerie? No, she's a sweetheart. But around Carmela?
That's a different story. She's easily influenced,
Valerie. Always has been. She's like a chameleon. It
always made her popular in school, but the problem is,
you never know which Valerie you're gonna get.

EDEN: You and Carmela argue a lot.

LEO: I don't like how she walks all over everyone, the way
she bosses my sister around and intimidates my wife. She
needs to be put in her place. And I'm the only one who
isn't scared of her.

EDEN: She's your sister-in-law.

LEO: More reason to set her straight. She can't be acting up
around family.

EDEN: How is Hope fitting in with the Fontanas?

LEO: She fits like a glove. Everyone loves her. She's such a
sweetheart. An angel, really.

EDEN: Carmela doesn't like that Hope isn't Italian.

LEO: [*Laughs.*] Well, Carmela has no ground to stand on.

EDEN: What do you mean?

LEO: I mean she has no ground to stand on. Did I stutter?

EDEN: I sensed an implication.

LEO: I'm a very literal person, Eden.

EDEN: Got it. Do *you* mind that Hope isn't Italian?

LEO: No, because she has respect for our culture. She
    loves Italian wine. She loves *My Cousin Vinny* and Frank
    Sinatra. She's even learning Italian on Duolingo! She's
    a natural. She'll be wearing leopard print in no time.
    [*Laughs.*]

EDEN: Do you think Hope is becoming friends with any of the
    women?

LEO: I think she'll be friends with Renee. Renee is good
    people. And Valerie, of course, as long as Carmela
    isn't there. But definitely Renee. Renee will be her new
    Cheyenne.

EDEN: Cheyenne?

LEO: Oh, Cheyenne was Hope's best friend in California.

TWO

Hope had never seen such a rich navy blue. She pressed her face to the window as the car crossed a suspension bridge, apparently the longest in New England, according to Renee, surrounded by gorgeous blue water on both sides. The geography was so pretty that Hope briefly forgot about the humiliation she'd suffered thus far on the drive. The driver had said they were just fifteen minutes away from Birdie's and the house couldn't come fast enough. Hope kept her eyes glued to the glass to avoid Carmela's hostile energy.

As the car came off the bridge, Hope could see downtown Newport with its marinas, sailboats, shops, and historic homes. This town seemed so much older than anything Hope had seen in Weed.

"God, the way people dress here is so stupid," Carmela said, looking out the window herself. "Ill-fitting floral smocks." She made a gagging sound. "They're like creepy adult baby dolls."

Hope wished Carmela would shut up for five seconds. She thought the pedestrians seemed put-together and attractive. Hope much preferred the preppy styles here to the acrylic nails and leopard prints of Shady Pond. As they glided out of town, the houses got bigger and older looking. The trees were tall and the leaves were turning orange.

And then, *boom*: the ocean view hit her like a glass of Leo's most expensive wine. The Atlantic in all its glory, stretching out to the horizon and shimmering silver under the late afternoon sun. Hope didn't realize she'd made a sound until Renee said, "Gorgeous, right?" Hope was really grateful for Renee, the only Goddess who was remotely pleasant to her. Hope had been annoyed at first when Renee put on her music, but she knew Renee was only trying to be supportive. Her heart was in the right place.

"I've never seen anything like it," Hope said.

"Just wait until you see the house," Renee said.

"Yeah," Carmela interjected. "It's straight out of your worst nightmares."

"Haunted AF," said Valerie.

"You all are so crazy," Renee said. "It's a famous historic home. We're lucky to be staying there."

"Historic just means old," Carmela said.

"Yeah," Valerie said. "I like new houses. Manny built ours from scratch."

"Dino too," said Carmela. "I don't like sleeping where other people have slept." She shuddered theatrically. "Disgusting."

"Completely sick," Valerie echoed.

A buzzing sound came from Hope's purse. She reached over to grab her phone. When she glanced at her screen, the phone began to quiver slightly in her grasp. She had seven missed calls, all from Cheyenne. She was still haunted by that photo Cheyenne had sent her, the photo of her father's Bible. Hope had not only deleted the message, but she'd also (with Google's help) blocked Cheyenne's account. Why couldn't Cheyenne take a hint and leave her alone? Hope slipped the phone back into her purse and lifted her eyes to Carmela.

"You okay, Valley Girl?" Carmela asked. "You look a little pale."

It took a second for Hope to realize Carmela was talking to her. "All good," Hope said. "Just someone from home." She regretted the words as soon as they left her mouth. Eden was staring at her through the divider. Eden held up her phone at Carmela. The phone had words on it in all caps, but Hope couldn't read them.

"Don't you miss Hollywood?" Carmela asked Hope.

Hope's heart thrashed around her chest cavity. She couldn't decide whether to tell Carmela the truth, that she'd never been to Hollywood, or to just let the women think she was from a more glamorous place than she was. She landed on remaining honest but vague, "I miss the mountains."

"That's it?" Carmela asked. "Don't you miss your family? Friends? Didn't you have friends?"

Hope thought of the seven missed calls from Cheyenne. Saying goodbye to the choir. Her last conversation with her parents. Leaving Weed in the middle of the night, the highways filled with wildfire smoke. The photo of the charred Bible. *Miss you, my Delilah.* She felt dizzy and sipped her champagne to find there was nothing left in the glass.

"Of course," Hope said, remaining vague. She turned to Renee for rescue, but she was preoccupied with her phone. "Of course I miss them."

"Here we are!" Valerie shouted, saving Hope as the car pulled up to an imposing set of wrought iron gates. The wheels rumbled over the gravel bordered by manicured lawns and mature trees turning orange, which gave way to pristine gardens and artificial ponds with bubbling waterfalls. Soon the house came into view—a castle even bigger than Chateau Blanche. Beyond the house were miles of blue ocean on all sides. Hope felt the breath leave her lungs.

"It's from the Gilded Age," Renee said. "Built in the nineteen thirties, I believe."

"Ew," Valerie said.

"Almost a hundred years old," Carmela added. "Imagine how many vile things have happened in this house."

"I just like to think of the parties they had," Renee said.

Hope closed her eyes and imagined *The Great Gatsby*. Jazz music and sparkly dresses, long cigarettes and moonlight gleaming off the water. The car rolled to a stop and Hope opened her eyes. Outside the car, Hope sipped up the ocean air. Crisp, cool, salty, exhilarating.

"You okay, Hollywood?" Carmela asked.

"The air," Hope said. "It's so fresh."

Carmela squinted at Hope. "Are you high?" Carmela asked. "I know what goes down out in California." She lit a cigarette.

Hope shook her head, irritated that Carmela was corrupting the fresh air. Hope had never smoked weed or anything else, just like she'd never been to Los Angeles. But she did feel high. In the movies they always talked about autumn, but she'd never understood it until now. The sun felt like magic on her skin.

"Isn't it incredible?" Renee said. "Wait until you see the views."

"The ocean gives me the heebie-jeebies," Carmela said. "The water here is so choppy and dark. You can't see what's happening under the surface."

"Sea monsters, probably," said Valerie.

"Or worse," said Carmela. She exhaled smoke all over Hope.

Renee grabbed Hope's hand and pulled her up to the entrance.

EDEN: Okay, there's a lot to cover on this trip, but I want
to first ask you about the trip up. How are you feeling
on the drive?

HOPE: On the drive to Rhode Island, I feel nervous but
also excited. I'm excited to see a new part of the
country. And I've heard Birdie's house is incredible.
But I'm nervous about being in such close quarters with
Carmela, who seems to hate me.

EDEN: Why do you think Carmela takes issue with you?

HOPE: I think Carmela doesn't like that I'm not Italian.
That I'm blond. I'm from California. She seems to really
hate California.

EDEN: What are you thinking when Renee puts on your music?

HOPE: Mixed feelings, again. Sorry. When Renee puts on
my music, I have mixed feelings. I'm happy she's
standing up for me, but I know Carmela is going to
make fun of me.

EDEN: How do you feel when Carmela says people will "slit
their wrists" to your music?

HOPE: God, do I have to repeat that?

EDEN: You can paraphrase.

HOPE: When Carmela says my music will make people sad or
upset, I have mixed feelings again. I know she's trying
to insult me, but I like sad music. All my favorite
music is about heartbreak and loneliness.

EDEN: Are you lonely?

HOPE: [*Sighs.*] Sometimes? Sorry, I'm lonely sometimes.

EDEN: Toward the end of the trip, you get a call. Who is it?

HOPE: A friend from home calls me toward the end of the
trip. I'm not sure why anyone cares. My hometown is
boring. My past is boring.

EDEN: Carmela asks if you miss your hometown.

HOPE: Yeah. Sorry, it's just weird talking to you about my
    hometown as if it isn't your hometown too, Eden.

EDEN: I know, it's weird for me too. We can come back to
    it. What do you think when Carmela and Valerie say the
    house is haunted?

HOPE: I think Carmela and Valerie are kind of spoiled. They
    don't seem to appreciate history.

EDEN: What do you think when Carmela asks if you're high?

HOPE: When Carmela asks if I'm high, I'm annoyed. She thinks
    that just because I'm from California, I'm high all the
    time. But I've never smoked weed in my life. I'm just in
    awe of the view. People have always said I have my head
    in the clouds.

EDEN: Do you? Have your head in the clouds, I mean.

HOPE: [*Silence.*]

EDEN: Hope?

HOPE: Sorry, what was the question?

THREE

Pierre greeted them as he had last time. Opening the door, he was surrounded by camera and sound guys, to which Hope had become accustomed. She recognized Johnny, who held a camera, and Caleb, who held a boom mic. Pierre wore a tailored jacket over snug-fitting white pants and tall black leather boots.

"Hi *ladies*," he said, then air-kissed Hope and Renee. "Pardon the getup—I've been training." It took Hope a second to realize he'd been riding horses. Hope had grown up riding horses, but she'd never worn anything like this. Her childhood friend from Brother God had a farm and they'd ride bareback in jeans, no saddles. Everything was different on the East Coast. Hope had never seen a house this big or this old in California. Silverstone Manor was like Chateau Blanche, but even grander, even more opulent, if that were possible. Cream-colored marble floors. Mahogany staircases spiraling upward. Crystal chandeliers sending shimmers of refracted light onto paintings of the glimmering sea. Scents of salt water and old wood lingered in the air.

Carmela nearly pushed Hope out of the way. She greeted Pierre and then kept walking, toward the stairs. Pierre grabbed her arm. Carmela shrugged him off. "Easy," she said, puffing up like an angry cat.

"Mother is sleeping," Pierre said. "But she picked the rooms and told me to show them to you."

Carmela frowned. "Why is Mother always sleeping?" she asked. "You drugging her or something?"

Hope was taken aback by the accusation.

Pierre laughed. "Mother doesn't need me to drug her," he quipped.

Eden, who was crouched in a corner, stifled a laugh. Hope experienced a weird sinking feeling in her stomach.

"She's been having trouble getting out of bed since my father died," Pierre said, looking wistfully out the window. Hope wanted to feel bad for him, but the performance felt so clearly calculated for the cameras. Hope also remembered Leo saying that Pierre's father had died over a decade ago, which was a long time to be in bed. Hope also recalled Leo whispering something about "foul play." Birdie seemed too spacy to orchestrate anything criminal. Pierre wiped at a nonexistent tear, then turned toward the staircase. He charged in front of Carmela.

"Come," he said. "I'll show you to your rooms."

The stairs seemed to go on forever. Carmela made ghost noises whenever the wood creaked. She was so obnoxious. Hope just wanted to soak up the incredible interiors, the paintings on the wall, the majestic light patterns, and the sense of history. There was a camera waiting at the top of the stairs. Johnny and Caleb trailed behind.

Pierre took them into the first room at the top of the floor. The walls were sea blue. The bed had tall posts and a chandelier hung over it, casting the room in a golden glow. Blue velvet curtains framed the windows, beyond which the Atlantic shone even bluer.

"For Valerie," he said.

"I thought I got the pink room!" Valerie squealed. "I always get the pink room."

Pierre shook his head, seeming delighted to disappoint her.

Luz appeared out of nowhere to drop Valerie's bags on the blue Persian rug. Valerie let out a whine.

Pierre exited the room and the rest of them followed him next door. This, Hope could see, was the pink room. It had white-and-blush striped wallpaper and a rose-patterned bedspread. On the walls were framed paintings of pink flowers. Peach velvet curtains framed the windows.

"Carmela," Pierre announced.

"You're kidding," said Carmela.

"Not in the slightest," Pierre said.

Valerie peeked her head in. "We'll switch!"

Carmela nodded, and Pierre shook his head. "No, no," he said. "Mother wouldn't like that at all."

"Please," said Carmela. "She won't notice. Will she even be awake while we're here?"

Pierre didn't respond. The maid dropped Carmela's bags. Hope, Renee, and the cameras followed Pierre up the stairs to the third floor. At the top, he took them to an emerald green room with dark wood furnishings.

"Renee," said Pierre.

"Perfect," Renee said, smiling. She was really the only polite one. The maid followed with her bags.

Hope was the only one without a room. She figured she probably had the smallest, which was just fine with her. She couldn't believe she was going to be sleeping here at all. She hadn't known houses this big existed outside of television.

Hope and the cameras followed Pierre to a final room down the hall from Renee's. To Hope's surprise, this one was bigger and more opulent than the others. The walls had a regal purple-and-gold wallpaper and the massive bed was canopied with sheer gold curtains. The room had a huge dresser, a writing desk, and a seating area with purple velvet chairs. There were large paintings of horses on the walls. Huge windows offered a panoramic view of the rocky coastline.

"This must be Birdie's room," Hope said, unsure.

"Nope," Pierre said, "it's all yours." Hope sensed a hint of irritation in his voice, but she wasn't sure. Pierre was hard to read. She'd never met anyone like him. She'd really never met anyone like the people she'd met since moving to Shady Pond, other than Renee. Hope ran over to the windows and stared at the navy expanse of water, becoming transfixed by the way it crashed up against the rocks in a rhythmic manner. When she finally tore her gaze from the window, she realized she was alone. The room was empty except for Hope and her denim duffel. A draft rushed over her and she shivered. Hope grabbed her phone from her bag and hopped on the bed.

She opened Cheyenne's contact and clicked BLOCK.

RENEE: Eden, you look fantastic. Have you been working out?

EDEN: Not in like seven years. Are you buttering me up so
I'll go easy on you?

RENEE: Maybe.

EDEN: Let's see if it works. So, what do you think of the
room assignments?

RENEE: I wonder if Pierre and/or Birdie is fucking—sorry,
messing with Valerie. We all know Valerie loves pink;
Carmela hates it. Why give Carmela the pink room?

EDEN: Can you think of any reason Pierre or Birdie would
want Carmela to suffer?

RENEE: To suffer? Is this a true crime documentary all of a
sudden?

EDEN: Sorry, I worded that weirdly. Do you think Pierre or
Birdie has something against Carmela?

RENEE: I don't think Birdie has anything against Carmela.
I think she hardly knows who Carmela is. She thought
Carmela and I were the same person for the entire first
season. And Pierre, I don't know if he has anything
against Carmela. She's kind of snarky with him. I mean,
she's snarky with everyone, but maybe he takes it
personally. But I don't think Pierre picked the rooms.
It seemed like he was following orders.

EDEN: Why's that?

RENEE: Because he gave Hope the biggest room. The room with
all the horses. It seemed like a room he'd want for
himself.

EDEN: So you think Birdie picked the rooms?

RENEE: I guess. I don't know. I don't really care. All the
hoopla about the rooms is so boring to me. This is a
seventeen-million-dollar home. All the rooms are lavish.
We're all lucky to be staying here.

EDEN: The girls are hard on Hope on the drive up.

RENEE: You think?

EDEN: Do you think it's strange that Hope is kind of secretive about her past?

RENEE: I don't think it's strange, no. A lot of people have pain in their pasts.

EDEN: Do you?

RENEE: Of course. I mean, I'm divorced. My husband was cheating on me. With his secretary. It's not exactly a pleasant memory.

EDEN: Right, so sorry about that. Who do you think called Hope in the car?

RENEE: I have no idea who called her, and it's really none of my business.

EDEN: She signed up for a reality TV show.

RENEE: It's her first season. Let's cut the girl some slack. Isn't she your cousin? Don't you care about her well-being?

EDEN: Of course I care. [Swallows.] What do you think of Pierre's outfit?

RENEE: [Laughs.]

FOUR

Birdie was already slurring her words by the time they got to the restaurant. Renee couldn't tell if Birdie was more incoherent this season or if Renee had just forgotten how sloppy she was during the months they weren't filming. Either way, Renee tried to enjoy the scenery and ignore Carmela's and Valerie's snide comments about the way people dressed and acted in Newport. Carmela kept doing this faux snooty accent, saying things like, "Do you like my dusty old dress, dahhlinggg?" Valerie would laugh as though she was seeing Chris Rock live at the Apollo.

"My goodness!" Birdie squealed, nearly tripping on the curb. She'd been grabbing onto Hope for dear life since they'd gotten out of the SUV. "These Parisian streets are always so slick!"

Hope held Birdie upright.

"Parisian?" Carmela asked, lighting a cigarette.

"She has no idea where she is," Valerie whispered to Carmela, as if everyone didn't know that.

Miraculously, Birdie heard this. "I know where I am," she said. "I'm just a little unsteady this evening. I'm on some new supplements. My vitapharmacologist . . ." She trailed off.

Valerie stayed outside with Carmela while Carmela smoked. Renee followed Birdie and Hope into the restaurant. Johnny and Caleb trailed behind. The restaurant was in an old inn, and Renee had read that it was one of the best restaurants in Newport. Like that of the other restaurants they'd been to in the area, the decor was preppy and nautical—brass sconces on white-washed walls featuring paintings of impressionist seascapes. Everyone in the restaurant turned toward them and stared. The Goddesses were by no means famous, especially not in an old money town like this, where people likely did not watch reality television, but the cameras always drew attention. And here, so did the leopard print.

The women were seated at a candlelit table in the corner with a white linen tablecloth. Renee instantly imagined spilled drinks. Going to dinner with the Goddesses often felt like being forced to take your colicky toddler to a Michelin-starred restaurant. In other words, it was humiliating. But whenever Renee felt embarrassed, she'd just think of that house she was going to buy right outside of the city, about the store she was going to open near NYU, about Ruby enrolling in LaGuardia High, and a smile would form on her face.

Hope and Renee ordered wine and Birdie ordered a martini. Renee chased down the waiter and quietly asked him to just bring Birdie water and vermouth in a martini glass, explaining that Birdie wouldn't know the difference. The waiter eyed Birdie, who was clutching her knife and gesticulating wildly, and nodded. This was aristocratic territory, filled with the type of people who had never worked a proper job, had nothing to show up sober for—this waiter probably had to do this several times a night.

When Renee returned to the table, Carmela and Valerie were back, stinking of cigarettes. Carmela always reeked, and when Renee had had a glass or two of wine, she liked the smell. But right now, sober, she found the stench a bit nauseating. She sipped some water as she waited for her wine.

"Shady Di is onto us," Carmela announced to the table, before taking a seat.

"Lady Diana?" Birdie looked around and lowered her voice. "She loves this restaurant. I saw her here just last month."

"Isn't she dead?" Valerie said, sitting beside Carmela.

"For like twenty-five years," Carmela said. "I'm talking about the Instagram troll."

"I know that," Valerie said. "I'm just wondering what Birdie's talking about."

"Who knows what Birdie is ever talking about?" Birdie said, giggling to herself. Maybe she was more self-aware than Renee realized.

"What's up with Shady Di?" Renee asked against her better judgment.

"They know we're in Rhode Island," Carmela said. She turned to Hope. "And they know about *you*."

Hope blinked, seeming plucked from dreamland and into the current moment.

"What do you mean?" Renee asked for Hope.

"They know you're our newest member," Carmela said. A smile broke out on her face and Renee braced herself for something rude. "They called you a 'ragamuffin.'" Valerie stifled a giggle.

Hope shifted in her seat, smoothed her hair with her hands.

"Shady Di is horrible," Renee said, feeling bad for Hope. "A miserable troll."

"Hope," Birdie said, one eye slightly closed, "whoever called you a ragamuffin has eye problems." Carmela snickered, probably because Birdie was squinting and seemed unable to see clearly herself. "You look *gorgeous*," Birdie continued. "Spitting image of myself at your age, I'm telling you."

Hope smiled.

"I used to model, you know," Birdie said. She loved to tell the women about her modeling days, days which none of them were sure existed. It wasn't that Birdie was unattractive, it's just that she was so surgically altered it was hard to know what she looked like at all. Currently, she resembled an uncanny blend of Kathy Hilton and Dolly Parton—classier than Dolly, but trashier than Kathy. Birdie had the money to roll in these circles, but it was obvious she didn't have many friends among them. Her taste was a tad too shiny, too flashy, too, well, Jersey.

Apparently Birdie had grown up in Keansburg, widely recognized as the trashiest town in the entire Garden State, famous for its nearly toxic water and rampant bar fights. Birdie had allegedly dropped out of high school to work as a waitress at a casino down the shore in Atlantic City, where she'd met her first husband, the real estate mogul who'd left her as soon as she entered her mid-twenties and was no longer in his desired age bracket of nineteen to twenty-four. But these were all things Renee had learned from Shady Di. Birdie never referenced her white trash past, instead behaving as though she'd been born in Paris's eighth arrondissement with a silver spoon in her mouth.

"I'd love to see photos," Hope said, likely feeling compelled. The waiter handed Hope and Renee their wine, then Birdie her "martini."

"Delicious," Birdie said, taking a sip. "You all really do mix the *best* martinis. You can't find a martini like this stateside."

The drunker she was, the more Birdie seemed to think she was in Europe. Hopefully the mostly water cocktail would sober her up.

Birdie gazed at Hope.

"I'll have Pierre dredge up my modeling portfolio," Birdie said. "It's probably covered in dust by now! Heavens, where does the time go?"

"It flies by, doesn't it?" said Valerie. "I feel like just yesterday I was pushing out Apollo. Can you believe he's twelve? He's about to be a teenager, *Dio* help me." She crossed herself, then took a sip of rosé.

Everyone made sort of noncommittal sounds of affirmation, forever bored of Valerie's 24/7 mom talk.

"My God," Birdie said. "Pierre is nineteen! Can you believe *that*?" Pierre was twenty-nine. They all knew this.

"He doesn't look a day over eighteen," Renee said to humor her.

Birdie laughed. "He can drink legally now." She winked. Renee hoped there really wasn't any gin in the martini glass. All the winking did not bode well.

The waiter came over and they ordered their entrees. Renee got the wild mushroom ratatouille, as did Hope. Birdie got the Cornish game hen, whatever that was. Valerie got the branzino. And Carmela got the filet mignon. Carmela always got the filet mignon.

"Are you a vegetarian too?" Renee asked Hope when the waiter disappeared. It would be convenient to have another vegetarian in this cast of carnivores.

"Oh," Hope said, seeming surprised. Whenever anyone spoke to Hope, it seemed like they were pulling her out of some kind of day-dream. "I'm not." She smiled. "I just like mushrooms."

"Aren't you just adorable!" Birdie leaned over and grabbed Hope's chin. Hope reddened. It was incredible how someone as shy as Hope had ended up on reality TV. Renee was starting to wonder why Eden hadn't tried to shield her shy, sweet cousin from this chaotic, dog-eat-dog world.

Renee turned her head to Eden, who was holding up her phone at Carmela. Eden often did this—held up her phone with notes in all caps, topics for them to bring up on camera. Renee squinted. This note said: ASK HOPE IF SHE SPOKE TO HER FRIEND FROM HOME. Carmela often ignored Eden's notes, but Carmela also seemed to get off on making Hope uneasy, so she was likely to obey in this case.

"Hey Malibu," Carmela said to Hope, who was staring at the ceil-ing, seemingly unaware that Carmela was speaking to her. "Hope!" Carmela shouted to get her attention.

Hope turned toward Carmela and blinked.

"Did you talk to your friend?" Carmela asked. "From home?"

Hope took a sip of her wine and eyed Carmela blankly.

"Cheyenne?" said Valerie, as if to prompt Hope, then covered her mouth. Carmela elbowed her rib cage.

Hope's cheeks were pink.

"Cheyenne?" Renee asked.

"Hope's friend from home," Valerie whispered, as though she'd said something bad.

Hope squinted at Valerie as if silently asking how Valerie knew the girl's name. Renee wondered herself.

"Cheyenne give you any Hollywood gossip?" Carmela asked.

Hope shook her head no. Renee didn't know exactly where in California Hope was from, but she didn't seem like a Hollywood type. She hardly wore makeup and didn't appear to have Botox or filler, unlike the rest of them. Even Renee got a few units of Dysport in her forehead twice a year.

"Hope, where in California are you from again?" Renee asked.

Hope's eyes widened. As usual, she seemed surprised by the question. But it was a standard question. Polite dinner party chatter. Why did Hope seem so unnerved?

"I'm from a small town," Hope said. Queen Vague. Her cousin wasn't going to like this. "You all have never heard of it."

"Huh?" said Carmela. "I thought you were from Hollywood."

Hope shook her head no.

Carmela glanced at Eden, then shifted her attention to Hope.

"Why won't you just tell us where you're from?" Carmela asked. "Why are you so damn secretive all the time? You're my sister-in-law and I don't even know where you were born." Carmela turned to Valerie. "V, isn't it weird we don't know where our own sister-in-law is from? That we know nothing about her family?"

"Well, we know her cousin," Valerie said, then quite literally bit her own tongue when she realized what she'd said. Valerie's airheadedness often made for fun TV, but she was constantly breaking the fourth wall by mistake.

"Other than that one cousin in Hoboken," Carmela said, covering. "They don't even seem close." Carmela turned to Hope, gazing directly into her eyes. "Who were you on the phone with?"

"A friend from home," Hope said. She pulled a strand of blond hair behind her ear. "It really isn't very interesting. My background isn't interesting."

"What did your parents do when you were growing up?" Carmela asked.

Hope swallowed. "My dad is a preacher."

"Oh wow," Carmela said. "Here I was thinking you were Miss

Hollywood when you're really Little Miss Bible Study." Carmela chuckled. "Little Miss Bible Bitch."

Valerie snickered, then composed herself. "Preacher?" Valerie asked. "Catholic, right?"

"Please, V, Catholicism doesn't have preachers," said Carmela.

"My first husband was *verrrrryyyy* Catholic," Birdie interjected. "My second husband, Episcopalian. They're similar, you know. You're Episcopalian, right, Hope?" Birdie sounded more coherent suddenly, so maybe the water was helping.

Hope said nothing, just nodded and reached for her empty glass, then put it down.

Renee could tell Hope was uncomfortable with the hometown talk, so she decided to change the subject to something equally juicy but hopefully easier for Hope to talk about.

"Hope," Renee said, "Leo told me you all are trying to have a baby."

Hope visibly slackened. She smiled. Eden smiled at Renee. Renee felt proud of herself for pleasing both Hope and Eden, a win-win. She loved pleasing people.

"Yes," Hope said.

"If you have a boy, I can give you all the hand-me-downs," Valerie said. "My boys would love to have a little cousin to play with."

Carmela glared at Valerie.

"Won't you want your kids to know their grandparents?" Carmela asked Hope. "Will you have to take them all the way to California?"

Hope shrugged.

Carmela seemed on edge, more so than usual. After two full seasons, Renee could tell when Carmela was reaching a boil.

"Simple question," said Carmela. "Yes or no?"

"I'm not sure," said Hope.

Carmela snapped her head toward Valerie. "I don't get why this bitch is being so shady," Carmela said. "I'm going to start calling you Shady Hope."

Renee felt torn between wanting to defuse the situation to please Hope and egg Carmela on to please Eden. Ultimately, she thought of her future store by NYU and Ruby becoming the next Lady Gaga at LaGuardia, and went for the second option. She didn't know Hope well enough to protect her over her future plans. Renee needed to do the right thing for Ruby, for her family.

"The Fontanas will love having another grandson," Renee said. Carmela's inability to give birth to a boy was her biggest insecurity, and Renee knew that going there would cause her rage to runneth over.

"But what about your parents, Hope?" Carmela was yelling now. "Why weren't they at your wedding? Why did you not have a single fucking family member at your wedding?" Carmela slammed her hands down on the table so hard that Birdie's martini glass tipped over. Luckily it was empty, so nothing spilled.

"Her cousin was there," Valerie said.

"Other than her one fucking cousin she isn't even close to!" Carmela spat at Valerie. "Why wasn't your little friend at the wedding, Hope? What's her name—"

"Cheyenne!" Valerie interjected.

"Of course, a weird fucking California hippie-dippie name." Carmela's voice was steadily increasing in volume and intensity. "So, Hope, why weren't your parents or your supposed best hippie-dippie friend Cheyenne at your fucking wedding?"

"Let's calm down," said Birdie. "This is a classy joint. I won't be allowed back. What will I do without my perfect martinis?" she laughed.

"Aren't you supposed to be sober?" Carmela asked. "Why aren't we talking about the fact that we all went to your house to celebrate your sobriety and you fell down the fucking stairs like a drunk?"

Renee felt bad for Birdie, but Birdie didn't seem to take offense. She just laughed and said, "What can I say? I'm the straw that stirs the drink!"

"You're a drunk," Carmela said, then turned back to Hope, her original prey. "And you're a shady freak." Carmela blinked and the whites seemed to leave her eyes. "I don't want to share a meal with a shady freak who conned her way into *my* family. Who thinks she's going to give birth to *my* nephew. Mixing her creepy California preacher blood into the *honorable* Fontana line!"

Valerie smiled at the compliment of her family. Carmela was still going, yelling, shaking. Everyone in the restaurant was looking at them. Eden was grinning.

"Your grandkids are gonna be a bunch of creepy stoner FREAKS! FUCKING CALIFORNIAN FREAK OF NATURE! SINGING CREEPY-ASS SUICIDAL SONGS! *CHE CAZZO!* IT'S LIKE THE FUCKING MANSON CULT WITH HER AND I DON'T FUCKING TRUST HER...."

At that point, Carmela's words turned to Italian-accented gibberish. She was in the midst of a full-blown rage blackout. Renee removed herself from the table because she knew things were about to get violent. Almost just as she got up, Carmela slammed her hands on the table so hard that several glasses fell. Then she yanked the tablecloth, so that glasses and plates shattered on the hardwood floors. Finally, she put her hands under the table and hurled it into the air. More crashing dishware. A young child nearby screamed. Renee's heart skipped a beat.

Hope gazed at Carmela, still and unmoving.

"DEAD-EYED FREAK!" Carmela shouted, and lunged at Hope. Renee scanned the room for help, but her efforts appeared to be in vain. Valerie was on Carmela's side. Birdie was too drunk. Eden cared more about making entertaining television than she did about any human being's feelings. The crew was working. Renee knew it was up to her. She grabbed Carmela's arm and Carmela shoved her off with more force than she'd expected. Renee fell to the ground with a thud. Her hip bone throbbed.

Eventually, a waiter stepped in between them and ripped Carmela off Hope.

Renee would never forget the look on Hope's face when he did. Her face was completely blank.

EDEN: So, the table flip.

CARMELA: Wow, okay. No foreplay?

EDEN: Okay, I'll back up. You find out at dinner that Hope isn't from Los Angeles. What do you think?

CARMELA: Listen, I never thought Hope was from Los Angeles. I didn't go to college, but I'm not dumb. I just like getting a rise out of her. I didn't know she's a preacher's daughter, but I'm not surprised.

EDEN: You call her "Little Miss Bible Bitch."

CARMELA: Did I say that? [*Laughs.*] That's pretty good. Little Miss Bible Bitch. Hope should tattoo that on her lower back. Tramp stamp. [*Laughs.*]

EDEN: You call out Birdie for not being sober.

CARMELA: Birdie has never been sober a day in her life. She popped out of her mother's belly with a martini glass.

EDEN: Is that enough foreplay?

CARMELA: There's never enough.

EDEN: What makes you so angry that night?

CARMELA: I think the viewers know by now that I am very protective of my family. The Fontanas are my family. They're not blood, but they're family. I grew up next door to the Medusa Motors lot. I ran around with Valerie every day after school. I had a crush on Dino my whole life until I made him my husband. They're my family. And I do not trust Hope. I think she has bad intentions. I don't know what they are yet, but I know they're bad.

EDEN: Bad how?

CARMELA: I don't know, exactly. But I tend to be right about these things. She's hiding something.

EDEN: Like what?

CARMELA: You know what I think? I don't think she left California for Leo.

EDEN: Why do you think she left California?

CARMELA: I think she left California because she's on the run.

FIVE

Hope laid on her sprawling guest bed with an ice pack on her head. The crew had finally disappeared to their hotel for the night. They'd taken two cars back from the restaurant because Carmela had refused to ride with Hope. Hope had ridden back with Renee and Johnny in Caleb's car. Hope hadn't wanted to be filmed but Johnny had filmed nonetheless, and as far as Hope was concerned, she had no choice. She'd signed a contract. Renee had kept asking Hope how she was feeling, but Hope didn't want to talk about it. She said she was fine. And she was, really, minus her throbbing scalp from where Carmela had pulled her hair. But Hope had suffered worse. Much worse.

Hope was relieved to finally be alone. She could hear the waves crashing against the rocks down below. She cracked the windows open and a briny breeze hit her skin. Her nerves were finally starting to calm from all the action when her phone lit up on the bedside table. She put the ice pack down and sent the call to voicemail. It was an unknown number, probably spam. She put the phone on her belly and took a deep breath of cool, salty air. She was exhaling when her phone vibrated on her stomach. Hope eyed the screen. *My Delilah*, the message read. Another floated in. *Please call me.* Hope opened the contact. She pressed BLOCK. Cheyenne needed to move on, like Hope had. She'd find someone else to harass soon enough.

The room was suddenly very quiet minus the sound of the waves. Hope's breath slowed and synced with the crashing against the rocks. She was starting to drift off when there was a knock on the door. Hope jumped. Irritated, she went to answer it. She was relieved to see Renee standing there. In a black nightgown, holding a leather bag hardly concealing a bottle of champagn. Suddenly shy, Hope gazed at the floor.

"I thought you might need a nightcap," said Renee, holding up the bottle of champagne.

Hope laughed and let her in. The women sat at the velvet sitting area in the corner of the room, under a massive painting of a horse. Moonlight shone so brightly on them they almost didn't need to turn on a lamp. A cool breeze shot through the window beside them.

"Is it too cold?" Hope asked.

"No," Renee said. "It feels nice, refreshing."

She popped open the champagne bottle and they both jumped, then laughed.

"I couldn't find glasses," Renee said, then took a swig from the bottle. "This house is, like, overwhelmingly large."

"It's incredible," said Hope.

Renee handed her the bottle and she sipped. The bubbles burned her tongue.

"So," Renee said. "How are you feeling?"

Hope was having trouble getting used to all these people asking how she was feeling all the time. Before *Garden State Goddesses*, no one ever asked her how she was feeling. Well, Cheyenne used to, but Cheyenne was gone, at least as far as Hope was concerned.

"My head is a little sore," Hope said.

"She really went at you," Renee said.

"What about you?" Hope asked, remembering that Carmela had shoved Renee to the floor.

"Oh, I'm okay," said Renee. "My hip is a little sore, but . . . at least I didn't lose a foot!"

Hope shivered. "Thanks for trying to save me."

Renee smiled. "Anytime."

A pause sat between them. Another gust of wind. Water against the rocks.

"How are you feeling emotionally?" Renee asked.

"I don't know."

"You're probably still in shock."

Hope shrugged. "I'm not used to all these people being so curious about my emotions. Asking all these questions. In my hometown, everyone knew who everyone was and nobody cared about how anyone felt."

"I get it," Renee said. "This reality TV world is strange, constantly being expected to weaponize your emotions. It took me a while to get used to it." She paused. "I'm still not sure I'm used to it actually. I think it's healthy to have boundaries."

Hope smiled, feeling seen for the first time in a while.

"And I can see why you didn't want to give Carmela ammunition. I also try not to let her know too much about me. But it's different, because I'm from Shady Pond and I'm Italian American, so I'm not inherently suspect to her."

"At least I didn't tell Carmela the name of my hometown," Hope said. "Speaking of ammunition."

"What is it?" Renee asked. "Only if you're comfortable."

"Promise not to tell?" Hope said. "I mean, Eden knows it, obviously. She's from there too."

"Wait, you and Eden were raised together?" Renee asked. "I thought she's from New York. I thought you were distant cousins."

Hope felt bad for revealing something about Eden that Renee didn't know. But also, Hope didn't feel particularly protective of Eden. Eden certainly didn't feel protective of her.

"She left early," Hope said. "When she was like seventeen."

"I can see Eden escaping her hometown and never looking back," Renee said, and Hope realized that she had done the same thing. Renee took another swig of champagne. "So what's it called, your hometown?"

"It's at the southern tip of the Cascade Mountains," Hope said. "And it's called Weed."

Renee laughed. First quietly, then harder. Hope laughed too. Soon they were both laughing so hard they were crying, tears streaming down their faces. It was a glorious release they both needed.

"Okay," Renee said, still laughing, but trying to compose herself. "Definitely don't tell Carmela that."

"Can you imagine?" Hope said. "She already thinks I'm a pothead." She swallowed. "And that Instagram account. Shady Di. They think I'm a ragamuffin."

"Don't think for one second about that dumb account," Renee said. "They're horrible. Just the other day, they said I needed liposuction."

"Liposuction?" Hope said. "But your body is perfect." Hope's cheeks reddened after she said this, but it was true: Renee's body was lean and flawless.

"Thank you for lying to me," Renee said. "I know I could stand to lose a few pounds, especially by television standards."

"You'd disappear," Hope said.

"Stop," Renee said, playfully squeezing Hope's forearm. "Anyway, you're beautiful. Everyone thinks so. Why do you think Carmela is so threatened?"

Hope tried to suppress a smile. The compliment felt nice, even if Renee was just trying to make Hope feel better. She really did feel like a ragamuffin in this bunch.

"You know, some people think Carmela is Shady Di," Renee continued. "The account always seems to spare Carmela. It says Leo's responsible for Valerie's missing foot—"

"Leo would never," Hope interrupted, feeling compelled to stick up for her husband. She hoped he wasn't capable of violence. Hope didn't always have the best instincts about these things. She'd once thought Cheyenne was harmless too.

"I don't think so either," Renee said, and relief washed over Hope. "And neither does RadarOnline, or the streets." She smiled strangely, then continued. "But Shady Di somehow always spares Carmela. Who knows? Maybe it's just another rumor."

"There are a lot of rumors in New Jersey," Hope said.

Renee laughed. "You think?" She peered out the window, then back at Hope. "So, back to weed—you don't smoke it?"

Hope shook her head. "Never."

"Too bad," Renee said, pulling what appeared to be a joint from her bag. Hope had seen pot, of course, but she typically associated it with dirty-looking people who weren't affiliated with Brother God. Hope had to keep reminding herself that she was no longer affiliated with the church either. Regardless, Hope did not associate weed with people like Renee, who was pretty and polite.

"I was hoping to have someone to smoke this with," Renee continued.

"You can smoke it," Hope said. "I don't mind."

Renee pulled out a lighter. She cupped her hand around the joint due to the breeze from the window. Hope felt something strange inside her as she watched Renee light it and inhale. It reminded Hope of something. Cheyenne, maybe. They both had dark, reddish brown hair, and Cheyenne smoked cigarettes occasionally. American Spirits in the baby blue box.

"How is your friend?" Renee asked after she exhaled, as if she was reading Hope's mind. The room filled with a skunky aroma. Hope walked over and opened the window a little farther to diffuse the smell.

"She's a little angry with me," Hope said. The words *My Delilah* swirled around her head. "For leaving." She hadn't been planning on telling any of the Goddesses how and why she'd left Weed, and she'd never tell the full story, but she felt safe with Renee. And there were no cameras. The champagne, on top of the adrenaline and what she'd drunk at dinner, was rendering Hope loose. She took another swig.

"Why wasn't she at your wedding?" Renee asked. "Or was she?" Renee exhaled more smoke.

"Oh, Cheyenne doesn't know about Leo. No one from home does." Hope worried she might be talking too much, but it felt good to finally speak her mind after months of holding back.

"Why not?"

"Because they wouldn't understand," Hope said. "My hometown is very insular."

"Kind of like Shady Pond," Renee interjected.

Hope nodded. "You know, I hadn't thought of it like that, because my hometown is so much less glamorous."

Renee laughed. "You think Shady Pond is glamorous? You must really be from the sticks."

Hope shrugged. "My town didn't even have a grocery store," she said. "And I said my dad was a preacher, but I didn't really explain. He founded his own church with his brother, Eden's dad. It's called Brother God. They're really intense about it. He would not approve of me marrying someone who wasn't in the church or moving to New Jersey. I had to escape, like Eden."

"Why did it take you so long?" Renee asked. "Sounds horrible."

Hope liked that Renee seemed genuinely curious about her life, rather than just mining her for information to be used in some weird television chess game.

"I liked it at first. The church. I was dutiful, not like Eden or my sister, who were cool and rebellious. I was a nerd. I liked the Bible, I liked the choir, I liked being the good one."

Renee laughed. "You're an interesting bird, Hope." She took another inhale, then let it out slowly. "I can see why you liked the choir, though. You love singing."

"It was the only way I was allowed to sing," Hope said. "And it made my parents happy. And it's how I met Cheyenne. She had an incredible voice. Not quite as good as Ruby, but close."

"You're sweet." Renee smiled. "Cheyenne. She was your best friend?"

Hope nodded. She was still a little weirded out that Valerie knew Cheyenne's name, but Hope had told Leo briefly about

Cheyenne, so maybe he'd told Valerie. They were siblings, after all. But Hope hadn't told Leo everything about Cheyenne, obviously nothing about the true nature of their relationship. And suddenly, she felt like she was going to burst if she didn't tell the truth right now.

"We were more than friends," Hope said, then regretted it.

Renee shot up in her seat. "Ooh la la! Hope—you really are full of surprises!"

Hope's throat tightened. This couldn't get out. That was her past. She was married now, to a wonderful man who had given her a beautiful life. Also, his family was allegedly tied to the Sicilian Mafia. Cheyenne was best left in the past.

"You have to promise not to tell," Hope said, desperation creeping into her voice.

"I promise," Renee said, then offered her hand. "Pinky swear."

The women hooked their pinkies together and shook their fists. Just as they kissed their fists to seal the promise, there was a loud bang on the door.

Hope and Renee jumped.

"Ladies." The voice belonged to Pierre. "This is a no-smoking household!"

Renee laughed, and Hope laughed too.

"It's not a joke," he continued from the other side of the door. "Put it out. Thank you!"

Pierre's footsteps disappeared down the hall.

Renee took a final drag of her joint, then threw it out the window, where it hopefully landed in the ocean or somewhere it couldn't burn. Growing up in California had made Hope perpetually aware of the proximity of fire.

"I should warn you, though," Renee said, returning to the seating area. "When you're on *Goddesses*," Renee paused, sat down, stared right at Hope. "These things have a way of getting out."

A cool breeze hit Hope in the chest.

CONFESSIONAL TRANSCRIPT – *GARDEN STATE GODDESSES*
(SEASON 3)
RENEE RICCI

EDEN: The table flip.

RENEE: I feel so bad for Hope. I mean, don't you? She's your cousin, Eden. And you brought her into this shit show. Sorry, I know I can't say that.

EDEN: It's fine, and I do feel bad. I think the viewers will too.

RENEE: Oh, totally. Hope will be the hero of the season, no doubt. She's coming for my spot!

EDEN: I don't know, Renee. She doesn't quite have your charm, does she?

RENEE: No one does! But those doe eyes.

EDEN: Why do you think Carmela gets so upset?

RENEE: She's very protective of the Fontanas.

EDEN: What do you do after the table-flip dinner?

RENEE: I'm exhausted. [*Coughs.*] I go to bed.

EDEN: Pierre says he smells marijuana smoke on the floor you and Hope are sleeping on.

RENEE: Oh, does he?

EDEN: It isn't you?

RENEE: I don't smoke and tell.

SIX

Renee awoke feeling groggy, like she wanted to sleep for another eight hours. She turned and saw blond hair. She suddenly remembered she'd fallen asleep in Hope's bed. The previous night felt like a dream. Carmela's meltdown, her flipping the table and lunging at Hope. Then Hope telling Renee she'd left a sapphic romance in California? Had that really happened? Was it Renee's dream? She had drunk a lot of champagne, smoked that joint. Maybe she'd imagined Hope's confession.

"Knock, knock."

Renee recognized Valerie's voice outside the door. Valerie would be surprised to see Renee in Hope's room, but it was too late. Hope started to rustle awake as Valerie charged in.

"Oh!" Valerie said, eyeing Renee.

Ever since Renee had come out as bisexual in season two, Valerie had seemed cagey around her, like she wasn't quite sure how to act. Valerie probably thought that Renee and Hope had slept together, that Renee couldn't share a bed with another woman without pouncing on her like some kind of feral animal. Renee remembered Hope's confession from the previous night and wondered again whether or not it was true.

"We debriefed last night," Renee said. "With champagne."

Valerie hopped onto the bed. "Pierre said someone was smoking weed!" she said, then lowered her voice to a whisper. "Don't tell Carmela, but I'm sad I missed it." She winked.

Hope sat up and her eyes darted around the room. Renee felt an eerie sense of familiarity. She knew the look on Hope's face well. She was scanning for the cameras. Renee did this periodically ever since she'd gotten on *Goddesses*, scanned random rooms for lenses, even during the off-season. Hope's face seemed to relax when she saw no one filming.

"How are you feeling, Hope?" Valerie asked. "Yesterday was intense."

Hope rubbed her eyes. She appeared annoyingly flawless for just having woken up. No bags under her eyes, no wrinkles from the pillow. Her hair fell in soft, silky waves. "I feel much better," Hope said. "Renee cheered me up." Hope smiled at Renee.

"Oh, is that so?" Valerie asked, voice dripping with innuendo.

"Not like that," said Renee, casting a nervous glance at Hope, who seemed puzzled. "Is Carmela up?"

"Nope," Valerie said. "It's just been me and Pierre. For the last three hours." She contorted her face into a desperate grin. Valerie was an early riser. Her boys had been bad sleepers, which had turned Valerie into a worse sleeper. Valerie could be annoying and vapid, but Renee respected that she was a devoted mother. Ruby was enough work for Renee, and she was basically an angel compared to those rambunctious boys.

"So can you all, like, hurry up!" Valerie said, shaking the covers. "If I have to spend another second alone with Pierre, I'm going to throw myself into the sea."

"I should get back to my room," Renee said. "I'll get dressed."

"I guess I will too," said Valerie, looking down at herself. She was wearing pink silk pajamas and fuzzy slippers. "Although I'm not totally sure what to wear to see a psychic."

They were seeing Birdie's medium today for the show. Huzzah

was obsessed with psychics. Clairvoyants always seemed to produce the kind of salacious content that viewers went wild for. Last season, they'd seen a medium who'd told Carmela she was an ancient Spartan warrior in a past life, which tracked.

"I think you can wear whatever you want," Renee said. "Regardless of what you wear, the psychic will see right through you."

"So jeans? With cute underwear?" Valerie asked, then hopped off the bed. "See you ladies in a flash." Valerie skipped out of the room and down the hall.

Hope sipped water from a glass on the bedside table. She was so quiet in group conversations, Renee often forgot she was there. Renee wished there was a way to confirm Hope's confessions from the previous night.

"You ready for another day?" Renee asked Hope with a wink, then regretted the wink.

"Do you think she suspected anything?" Hope asked.

Renee wasn't entirely sure what Hope meant. The previous night was fuzzy. Renee remembered smoking the joint, and Hope telling her that she and a girl named Cheyenne had been "more than friends." That meant romantic, right? And Hope had said she was from a town called Weed. Renee laughed.

"What?" Hope asked.

"Was I just really high or are you actually from a town called Weed?"

Hope appeared nervous. A blade of light from the blinds lit up her left eye, rendering it electric blue. She scratched her nose.

"You promised not to repeat anything I said last night." Hope seemed terrified.

Renee reached over and gave her arm a playful tug. "Relax," Renee said. "Your secrets are safe with me." Renee was now certain she had not dreamed the sapphic confession.

"Thanks," Hope said, her body language relaxing.

"I'm going to go get ready," Renee said. "See you downstairs?"

Hope nodded.

A seagull squawked outside the window.

CONFESSIONAL TRANSCRIPT – *GARDEN STATE GODDESSES*
(SEASON 3)
VALERIE DULCE

EDEN: How is your first morning at Silverstone Manor?

VALERIE: [*Laughs.*] God. It's torture, Eden. You know I'm an
early riser? Well, I wake up and everyone is asleep.
So I go downstairs to find some coffee, and Pierre is
sitting there like it's his house and I'm intruding.
He's making this nasty smoothie and I basically have to
beg him to show me where the coffee maker is. And while
he's showing me, he tells me that he smelled weed the
previous night on the third floor!

EDEN: Who is sleeping on the third floor?

VALERIE: Renee and Hope are on the third floor. I bet it
was Hope. Carmela's instincts tend to be spot-on about
these things.

EDEN: You think Hope was smoking weed in her room?

VALERIE: I do.

EDEN: Repeat the question, remember.

VALERIE: No, thank you. I don't want my boys to think I'm
accusing someone of doing drugs. It sets a bad example.

EDEN: Do your boys watch the show?

VALERIE: [*Laughs.*] They have no interest. But people talk
about it at school.

EDEN: Gotcha. So you make your coffee, then what?

VALERIE: I make coffee and I try to engage Pierre, but
he has no interest in me. He pours the nasty smoothie
in this purple tumbler thingy and just puts it in the
fridge, doesn't even drink it. Maybe it's for his horses,
I don't know.

EDEN: You think he's making a smoothie for his horse?

VALERIE: I don't know, Eden. It doesn't look fit for human
consumption. I'm telling you, it smells like batteries.
Anyway, I'm trying to ask him about his day but he sits
at the kitchen table and just starts reading and shushes
me! I mean, rude much?

EDEN: What's he reading?

VALERIE: I don't know, a book? I doubt this will surprise you, Eden, but I'm not much of a reader!

EDEN: [*Laughs.*]

VALERIE: So anyway, I take the hint that Pierre wants me to leave. So I take my coffee and sit outside and watch the water, which is actually really pretty. But then I get bored of watching the water so I look at Insta. And then when it's finally past nine a.m., I go back upstairs to check on the girls.

EDEN: And?

VALERIE: Carmela is *still asleep*. The woman can really sleep in, I'm telling you. Now that Bianca has her driver's license and can take herself to school, Carmela doesn't get up before nine thirty. Lucky bitch.

EDEN: Bianca seems independent. She doesn't come to many cast events.

VALERIE: Are you kidding? She's always there. She's just really shy, a wallflower. Carmela and I always say Bianca has the gift of invisibility.

EDEN: That's kind of sad.

VALERIE: Is it? I think she's lucky. I'd love an invisibility cloak sometimes. Anyway, back to "this morning." Carmela can sleep in, Carmela is asleep. So I go to the third floor to see if Renee is up, but her room is empty.

EDEN: Where is she?

VALERIE: I'm getting there, Eden. So I hear rustling in Hope's room and I go knock on the door, see what's up. And Renee is in her bed!

EDEN: Is Hope in there too?

VALERIE: [*Laughs.*] Yes, Eden. They shared a bed.

SEVEN

Eden was feeling exceptionally cocky.

After fifteen years of hustling at Huzzah, from hidden-camera prank shows to weird addiction shows to, finally, *Garden State Goddesses*, Eden knew when something iconic had occurred in front of her cameras. Carmela's table flip was sure to go down as one of the most legendary moments on *Goddesses*, maybe on Huzzah as a whole. Eden hadn't slept that well in decades. Instead of counting sheep, she counted dollar signs, then lofts in Tribeca. After this trip, Eden was taking herself to the fanciest restaurant in Hoboken and ordering a steak and three to four martinis. She would certainly be promoted after what had gone down in Newport last night. *Manhattan Muses* was next.

The SUV hit a bump and Valerie shrieked. They were on the way to Birdie's psychic. Often Huzzah would bring in outside psychics and one of the ladies would pretend to have a connection to her. But Birdie actually had multiple psychics and mediums who were willing to be filmed. Eden had met this one during preproduction. She went by Harmony Hawk, and her office was in a dilapidated old Victorian. It was perfect for the show. Eden hoped this psychic session would be the icing on the cake of an incredible trip.

The car pulled into Harmony Hawk's driveway. The woman clearly came from money to afford a historic house like this. It was old and in desperate need of a renovation, sure, but in this town, the property was easily worth millions.

The women got out. Carmela put her arm around Renee and said she was excited. After a blowup, Carmela always acted like she was possessed by an overly friendly ghost. It was like she released all the negative energy and was in a cheery mood for at least a day. This had happened last year on the trip to Aspen, after she'd screamed at the last new girl on the slopes for implying Carmela and Dino had an open marriage. Carmela had had a similar rage blackout, though not as intense as last night, and the next day—jolly as hell. Like today. Carmela had even asked Eden questions about herself this morning, like how she'd slept and if she had Thanksgiving plans. It was bizarre. And frankly, mean Carmela was better for television. Hopefully the psychic would say something to piss her off.

Eden followed Johnny and Caleb into the Victorian. Last night, she'd been so high off the table flip, she'd let Caleb sleep with her. They'd been fucking on and off for years. He was tall and lean and good in bed, but he could get needy, so Eden always cut it off whenever she could tell he was about to invite her to meet his mom. The way he kept looking at her today, all smiley and creepy, Eden vowed to never let him hit it again.

Inside, Eden was overwhelmed by the strong smell of incense, which reminded her of Northern California and elicited a mild trauma response. The house was stuffy and dark. Eden could hardly see as her eyes adjusted. The walls were dark wood and the windows covered by thick purple drapes. She followed the cameras and the women through the living room and into Harmony Hawk's office in the back. Eden couldn't fit in the office, but she could stand just outside the door and watch. She liked it here, on the outside looking in.

The women sat around a round table draped in velvet. In the center was a crystal ball, which almost felt too on the nose. A chandelier hanging above refracted various colors onto the room's surfaces. Harmony took the seat facing the door. She had long red hair, an unnatural fiery crimson. Her eyes were a piercing green. She wore a red kimono that nearly matched her hair and several layers of crystal-beaded necklaces.

"I love your jewelry," said Renee. She pointed to one of the necklaces. "Is that red beryl?"

Harmony nodded. "What keen sight you have, my sharp one," she said.

"Renee's an *incredible* jewelry designer," said Nice Carmela. "Seriously, you should check out her store. It's called—"

"The Ruby," Harmony said. "It is all known to me."

The women *oohed* and *ahhed* as if they weren't all insanely easy to google.

"You have a divine gift," Harmony told Renee, who seemed flattered.

"She really does," said Nice Carmela, beaming. Even her face was different. Softer. Renee really hoped Harmony would trigger her somehow.

"Gratitude be among you all for joining me in the sacred space that is Harmony Hawk's Heavenly Insights," Harmony said.

God, Eden thought. *What a grifter*.

"You all are very brave to come into the presence of my celestial bounty," Harmony continued. "But be forewarned, I am but a conduit for revelations that may rattle the very foundations of your being. . . ."

Eden stopped listening to Harmony's woo-woo bullshit and eyed Hope, whose expression was, as usual, hard to parse. She perpetually carried herself with a strange mix of calm and terror. Still body, upright posture, but nervous eyes. Eden felt a little bad for last night, for what Hope had gone through. Carmela had lunged at Hope like an animal. But Eden knew where Hope had come from. She was tougher than she seemed.

"Who among you shall step forth first to embrace the spirit's revelations?" Harmony asked, and made a sort of cartoonish witchy noise.

Such a con artist, Eden thought.

Carmela volunteered.

"You're a firecracker," Harmony said.

The women laughed.

No shit, Sherlock, Eden thought.

"That's what they tell me," said Carmela, still smiling like a freaky doll.

"A sparkler in the night, your light reveals truths and shadows alike," Harmony continued, and Carmela cocked her head and chuckled, clearly not buying the woo-woo language.

Good, Eden thought. Her mean girl was coming out.

"This is no joke, my dear," Harmony said. "Your heart is pure but it is guarded with a dragon's fervor."

"That's true," said Valerie. "The dragon part."

Carmela narrowed her eyes at Valerie, then at Harmony. "With all due respect, I don't know what the fuck you're talking about."

Her good mood was fading, thank God.

Harmony pointed to Carmela's mouth. "I'm talking about this, my dear."

"Huh?"

"Your serpent's tongue," said Harmony. "The way you pounced at me like a jungle cat."

Carmela laughed. "I did not pounce at you," she said. "When I pounce at you, you'll know."

Now Harmony was laughing. "Your speech cuts swift and true." She assumed a serious expression. "And underneath this ferocious visage you wear like a second skin, there's a world of shadows, a whispered heritage of your bloodline," Harmony continued. "And in those shadows, discreet rendezvous take shape." Eden watched carefully as Harmony continued to direct vague platitudes at Carmela, waiting for Carmela to blow. But Carmela just let out a few shrugs and giggles until Harmony moved on. Oh well, Eden shouldn't push her luck. Last night had been incredible no matter what happened today.

Harmony went down the circle delivering nebulous prophecies. She told Valerie in unnecessarily esoteric language that she was a good mom, but to remember not to neglect her husband, advice she'd probably come up with after googling her. She told Birdie to be careful of someone who was after her fortune. Eden figured when you had Birdie's money, people were always after it. Birdie was always talking to a lawyer or talking about talking to a lawyer. She'd famously said in season one, "Everyone should have at least six lawyers on retainer at all times."

Harmony told Renee that she had a love opportunity arising, someone in her close circle. Eden hoped this was true. The viewers would love it if Renee had a love interest, particularly if she was a woman. They'd loved it when she came out as bisexual. A lesbian romance would work wonders for *Goddesses*. Eden imagined winning a GLAAD award. Eden had slept with women herself, which she enjoyed until they became needy, but she'd keep that to herself at the GLAAD awards.

Finally, Harmony landed on Hope, whose wide eyes recalled those of a frightened deer.

"You have a deceptively gentle presence," Harmony told Hope. "Like the petals of a lotus, tender and soothing to the eye, yet concealing vicious strength within its folds. You're unshakable as a fortress, my dear."

Carmela made a strange noise. Valerie giggled.

"And behind this fortress," Harmony said, peering at Hope, "is a latent force, its true nature as enigmatic as the path of a whispering wind, a riddle waiting to be unraveled by the sands of time, but powerful as fire ravaging a forest."

The mixed metaphors were giving Eden a headache. Carmela stifled a giggle. Harmony shushed Carmela, then whipped her vision to the crystal ball, as though possessed. She suddenly looked up, right at Hope.

"You're entwined in a sacred union?"

Hope cocked her head, confused.

"I think she's asking if you're married," Valerie said.

Harmony nodded, and Valerie seemed proud of herself.

"Yes," Hope said, voice shaky. "I'm married."

Eden craned her neck to listen better. She'd set up Hope and Leo but she admittedly didn't entirely understand their connection. The marriage was advantageous for Eden, as it got the audience-adored Leo more airtime and Hope her outsider on the show. But she really didn't see what the two of them had in common. They were both attractive, but Eden often wondered what they talked about when they were alone. She imagined Leo monologuing enthusiastically about cars and Hope half listening, providing vague sounds of affirmation, which would be enough for Leo, who was not the most perceptive person. Eden zoned back in on Harmony.

"I'm seeing a cascade of luscious umber locks," the psychic said. "An ethereal visage, a magnetic beauty."

"Leona," Carmela said with a laugh.

Hope seemed afraid, or embarrassed. Her cheeks were pink. Her cheeks were always pink.

"A feminine silhouette appears before me," Harmony continued. "A fertile goddess."

Carmela's laughter grew richer. "*Leonahh*," she repeated, the name stretched out and twisted for comedic effect. Valerie laughed as if on cue. Harmony narrowed her eyes at them, which effectively shushed the giggling.

Eden sharpened her focus on Hope, whose jaw appeared clenched. Carmela had implied that Harmony was talking about Leo, and while Leo was certainly beautiful, he was by no definition a fertile goddess. No, Harmony was suggesting another woman. Eden didn't believe in psychics at all, but something about the look on Hope's face made Eden think Harmony had struck a nerve.

Could Leo be having an affair?

CONFESSIONAL TRANSCRIPT - *GARDEN STATE GODDESSES*

(SEASON 3)

HOPE FONTANA

EDEN: Ready?

HOPE: Not really, but [*inaudible*].

EDEN: How do you feel the morning you all go to the
    psychic?

HOPE: I'm a little scared to see Carmela, but she seems to be
    in a good mood. She hugs me! It's bizarre. It's like her
    explosion never happened. I'm like, did I imagine this?

EDEN: Is your head okay?

HOPE: My head is fine. *Did I* imagine it?

EDEN: You didn't.

HOPE: Too bad.

EDEN: What do you think of the psychic?

HOPE: Harmony Hawk has a really cool house. It's an old
    Victorian. There's so much history in Rhode Island, I
    love it. Her house smells like copal and juniper. There
    are all these really unique curtains and rugs. She's
    wearing this cool kimono and has amazing bright red hair.

EDEN: What do you think of her predictions?

HOPE: I'm not sure I believe in that kind of thing.

EDEN: She says people take your kindness for weakness; do
    you think that's true?

HOPE: I don't know.

EDEN: She says you're a fortress hiding a latent force.

HOPE: Whatever that means.

EDEN: She says there's another woman in your marriage.

HOPE: Oh, come on, Eden.

EDEN: Carmela says "the other woman" is just "Leona."

HOPE: I don't know why she calls him that. It's so rude.
    Seriously, Eden, you promised you'd take it easy on me
    if I stayed. This is too much.

EDEN: Do you think it's possible that Leo is having an
    affair?

HOPE: [*Footsteps*.]

EIGHT

Hope was done with the show.

As Carmela would say, *basta*, *finito*, done!

When the SUV dropped her off back at home, she set her bags on the floor and ran upstairs to shower. Leo wasn't home; he was never home. He was probably having an affair, like the psychic said. Hope turned on the shower full blast, stripped, and sat on the granite floor, letting the water fall over her until it burned. The bathroom had a rain shower, which Hope loved. It was the most luxurious shower she'd ever used. But right now, Hope didn't feel so luxurious. She didn't feel calm, like she normally did in here. In fact, she was finding it hard to breathe.

Carmela's good mood had turned by the SUV ride back, and she'd spent most of the drive making snarky comments directed at Hope— about her lack of makeup, about her being a Bible freak, about "Leona" being the other woman—comments that, had the weekend gone differently, would not have affected Hope the way they did but, given the context, had tipped her over the edge. And now, Hope took gasps of air but never seemed to get enough. She inhaled some water and choked. Then she laughed at herself. She was falling apart.

Hope had thought that moving to Shady Pond would bring positive change. That she'd start anew. Make new friends. Have time for her music. But so far, she alternated between intense loneliness and being attacked mercilessly on camera. And then Hope had been an idiot and had drunk champagne and confessed her past with Cheyenne to Renee. Well, not all of it, but she'd told her they'd been more than friends. She still could not believe she'd done that. Before Hope had moved to Shady Pond, she'd made a pact with herself: everything in Weed stayed in Weed. Everything.

Dating Cheyenne had ruined any chance Hope had of having a decent life in Weed. Before Cheyenne, her life was fine, really. She worked at the diner. She went to choir practice. She wrote her music back at home. On the weekends, she'd hike to a waterfall or a lake in Shasta-Trinity National Forest. She'd have dinner with her parents on Sundays. Sure, her parents could be difficult sometimes, but she'd mostly figured out how to manage them. Life was easy, predictable.

But then Cheyenne showed up one day at choir practice. She was new to town, freshly divorced. She'd moved to Weed from Mount Shasta to escape her abusive ex-husband. But more than that, she was beautiful. Long, thick hair that hung down to her waist. Sharp green eyes. She looked a little like Renee, but had a more Northern California style, always wearing turquoise or fringed leather. She had a generous laugh that felt like a hug, before it started to feel more sinister, ominous. But at first, everyone liked Cheyenne. Even Hope's parents before they found out the truth.

Soon, Hope and Cheyenne were hanging out after choir practice, going on walks in the woods or getting milkshakes at the diner. At first, Hope thought she'd just made a new best friend. Hope had always had friends in Weed by virtue of her dad's status in Brother God, but Cheyenne felt different. When they weren't together, Hope thought about her. Throughout her days, everything reminded her of Cheyenne. And then one night on one of their walks in the woods, Cheyenne kissed her. And Hope was terrified.

Because it felt perfect.

Hope had panicked and run. She ignored Cheyenne's calls for weeks. She wanted to pretend it never happened, didn't want to believe the truth about herself, something she'd always really known.

She'd never had a boyfriend, despite the fact that men were always asking her out. She'd always believed her purpose was not to marry but rather to serve God through singing. But Cheyenne showed her an option she'd never previously considered, one that felt both unsettling and thrilling.

Eventually, Hope's desire won out. She ran back into Cheyenne's arms but made her promise that if they were together, it would have to be a secret. If the church got word of their romance, it would be over for Hope. She loved her parents, but they could be very scary people. Homosexuality was strictly banned in Brother God. They could not find out.

But they did find out.

Not at first. Hope and Cheyenne successfully kept their relationship under wraps for months. Staying a secret was surprisingly easy. In Weed, lesbians didn't look like Hope or Cheyenne. They were more butch, more obvious. People just thought Hope and Cheyenne were best friends, like sisters. Cheyenne would even come to Sunday dinners at Hope's parents' mobile home. Cheyenne encouraged Hope's songwriting and would sometimes harmonize with her on tracks. Cheyenne knew a lot about music and got Hope into Mazzy Star and Nico and Björk, encouraging Hope to go for an "edgier" sound. Cheyenne got Hope to open up about the things that had happened to her when she was little, the reasons Faith and Eden had left. Cheyenne encouraged Hope to explore inner-child work in order to make peace with her past. Things were going well. Until someone from Brother God moved into Hope's apartment complex. Soon, rumors began circulating. Hope and her parents shut them down. Hope and Cheyenne were just close friends. Cheyenne got weird after that. Aggressive, insecure, possessive.

"Why are you so ashamed of me?" Cheyenne would ask.

Cheyenne didn't understand. Once the rumors started, Hope's parents were more distant to Cheyenne, stopped inviting her to Sunday dinners. But Cheyenne hadn't seen how scary they really were, how dangerous it would be for her and Hope if the romance got out.

Cheyenne kept saying that she and Hope should run away, change their names, be free.

Hope didn't like that idea. It was too risky. Of course, Hope had ended up doing it on her own. But only because Cheyenne had given her no choice. The image of the charred Bible flashed in Hope's mind.

Hope's skin burned under the water. Her knees were splotchy and red. She turned off the water and toweled off. Then she called for Leo. Her voice echoed through the empty house. She put on a robe and went to find her phone, then sat on the bed. She had several missed calls and messages, again from an unknown number, a different one from before. *My Delilah*, Hope saw. Without reading them, she deleted the messages. Then she blocked the contact. Cheyenne would eventually get bored of trying.

Hope was putting the phone down when she remembered why she'd grabbed it to begin with.

She opened her cousin's contact, and she called Eden.

NINE

Eden hadn't even finished her first martini when Hope called. She was sitting at the bar at her favorite restaurant in Hoboken, celebrating her wildly successful cast trip. Through the window to her left, she could see the New York City skyline shimmering in the distance. Before her phone rang, she was thinking about *Manhattan Muses*, about her future loft in Tribeca. But the irritating buzzing from her purse interrupted her pleasant daydreams. If it was just her cousin, Eden would have declined, but Eden wasn't strong enough to deny a call from a Goddess.

"Hi Hope," Eden said.

"I'm off the show," Hope said.

Eden's scalp buzzed with irritation. She gulped her martini before responding, bracing herself for a not unfamiliar task: convincing a cast member to stay. It happened at least once a season, sometimes twice. Eden had talked down two Goddesses from quitting mid-season as a result of Carmela's rages. They'd both quit *after* the season, which was annoying but acceptable. A mid-season exit was not. Eden would never make it to Manhattan if Hope left. So she was going to convince Hope to stay. And she was going to do this by making Hope think Eden was on her side.

"I hear you," Eden said. "You had a rough weekend."

"You can't convince me, Eden," Hope said. "I respect your ambition, but this world is not for me. I don't fit in."

"Are you kidding?" Eden said. "You're perfect! Birdie is obsessed with you. Renee adores you. You're, like, Ruby's idol. You married into the Fontanas, the most relevant family on this side of the Hudson. You're *Goddess* gold."

"I'm not falling for your flattery, Eden," Hope said. "Carmela is vicious. I'm not cut out for this. You know I'm uneasy on camera. I freeze up. I'm drinking too much to cope and acting stupid."

"I've never once seen you act stupid," Eden jumped in. "Valerie? Often stupid. You? Cool as a cucumber. It's impressive. The other new girls went running from Carmela, but you're a fortress, like the psychic said."

"I'm not tough," Hope said. "I'm traumatized."

Eden laughed. "That was good. I want you to say that in a confessional."

"There isn't going to be another confessional, Eden, because I'm done. Are you not hearing me?"

"I'm hearing you," said Eden. "You're upset."

"My emotional state has never once mattered to you, so I don't know why it would matter now," Hope said, and Eden felt something. She was proud of herself for feeling something, something approaching guilt or sadness. Hope was Eden's family. Eden should care about protecting her, should care about her feelings. Eden wasn't a terrible person.

"Your emotional state does matter to me," Eden said. "I know I can be a workaholic. I can be shortsighted when it comes to the show. You have no idea how long I've worked to get here—it can be blinding. But I care about you, Hope. And I brought you on this show because I knew it would be good for you."

"Please explain that to me," said Hope. "Because I cannot grasp how being humiliated by a bunch of grown women for television audiences would be good for me."

"Well, first off, you're out of Weed," Eden said. "Second, you're financially independent. I know Leo has money, but you're making enough that you would be fine without him."

"What are you implying?" Hope asked.

"I'm just saying, you're free."

Hope was silent for a second. Eden could tell she was turning her. She hadn't convinced her to stay, not yet, but she had the potential to get there. Eden had to go for the thing Hope cared about the most. This is what Aria had taught her: always zone in on what makes them tick. Hope seemed to love Leo fine, but that wasn't it for Hope.

"And your music," Eden said. "I've seen the way these women promote their businesses and artistic careers. They *blow up* once they're on the show. You're so talented, Hope. You always have been. Once millions of viewers see you play your music on the show, I will literally be shocked if you don't end up with a record deal."

Hope was still silent. Eden smiled and finished the last sip of her martini. She was so fucking good at her job. Almost too good.

"Listen, Hope," Eden said. "I wasn't going to tell you this yet. But I've been working on getting you a filmed gig in Manhattan." This was a lie, but Eden could make it happen, it could become true. Manhattan was big and filled with mediocre venues for struggling musicians. "You can play your original music, and it will be blasted not just to that audience, but to nearly a million viewers at home."

Hope finally spoke. "I don't know, Eden." She paused. "It comes at a cost."

"Carmela's more bark than bite," Eden said.

"She yanked my hair," Hope said. "She is after me."

"She'll calm down," Eden said. "Isn't a record deal worth it? Hey, I've had my hair pulled for less." Eden laughed, but Hope didn't. She probably didn't get the innuendo. Eden had made Caleb pull her hair earlier when they'd celebrated the trip with a quickie. He'd tried to stick around for dinner, but Eden had shut that down real fast. She needed to find someone less clingy to pull her hair.

"A gig in Manhattan?" Hope repeated. "On camera?"

"You heard me," Eden said.

"I need you to do a better job of protecting me," Hope said.

Eden was shocked that Hope was standing up for herself. She hadn't seen that coming.

"You're the boss and you have the power to prevent me from being humiliated," Hope continued.

"I have less power than you think," Eden said. "But I'll do my best."

"Okay," Hope said. "I'll think about it."

The women hung up. Eden ordered another martini. Her steak arrived. Manhattan shimmered beyond the windows. Eden squinted and tried to locate Aria's building in the West Village, where she had a yearly Christmas party to which Eden had been invited this past year, which felt auspicious. Aria's apartment was a two-story penthouse, with fourteen-foot ceilings, two patios, and a *solarium*, which Aria had of course converted into a home office. Eden dreamed about reviewing footage in a *solarium* overlooking the Lower Manhattan skyline instead of her current setup—a breakfast table shoved against an exposed brick wall in Hoboken.

Eden bit into her steak and imagined she was at Minetta Tavern, the red-boothed French bistro in Greenwich Village where Aria had once taken her, instead of here, at Dino & Harry's in Hoboken. Eden swallowed down her steak with the dregs of her martini.

Part Three

Have a good life, or die. . . . I don't care.

—DANIELLE STAUB, *THE REAL HOUSEWIVES OF NEW JERSEY*

ONE

Renee wiped sweat from her palms onto her dress. She'd seen Ruby perform a billion times, and it always made her nervous, but this time her nerves were next level—Ruby was performing not just for the audience of this Broke Not Broken gala in the great room of Chateau Blanche, but also for a television audience of nearly a million viewers.

After Hope's concert, Ruby had convinced Eden to let her perform on camera. "I'm much better than her," Ruby had said, being the rude teenager she'd recently morphed into, a young woman Renee hardly recognized. Eden had laughed, egging her on. Renee was starting to wonder if Eden enjoyed torturing her cousin. Renee had felt horrible for Hope during her concert, if you could even call it that. Tiny bar, shitty sound system, audience of roughly seven. Making things worse, Carmela and Valerie had shown up drunk and started heckling Hope. Leo had charged Carmela in an apparent effort to protect Hope's honor. But he had actually created a bigger scene that effectively ruined the concert. If that wasn't bad enough, Birdie had drifted off during the show, waking up at weird moments speaking French. The whole thing had been a disaster.

Later that night, Renee had texted Hope to check in. Hope had asked if she could come over, and Renee had obviously agreed. Hope was distraught, but Renee convinced her she'd done a great job. And Renee wasn't lying. Hope had this really evocative, ethereal voice.

And Renee convinced Hope that the audience would side with her over Carmela. Hope seemed to believe her, and then something very strange happened.

Hope kissed her.

Then they kissed again, and again, and did more than kiss. And suddenly Renee felt like she was fourteen again, sneaking around her parents to go see her upperclassman crush Mikey Manzo. Renee was smitten in an obsessive, teenage way, like Hope had hijacked all of her thoughts and it was impossible to think about anything else. Renee spent many hours each day reading and rereading her text thread with Hope, parsing it for clues as to Hope's true feelings about her. Hope was fairly clipped over text, but occasionally Renee would find something that excited her, an exclamation point or an emoji that made Renee stir. Then of course she'd feel silly. A blushing-face emoji didn't exactly say, *I'm leaving my husband for you.*

Renee felt stupid and guilty. She was coming home late several nights a week, lying to Ruby about being at work when in reality she and Hope were going on covert dates in neighboring towns where no one would recognize them. But also, Ruby didn't seem to have much interest in her these days, finding everything Renee said and did to be "extra" or "cringe." And Hope said Leo suspected nothing, which didn't shock Renee, given that his powers of perception seemed limited. When Renee had told Leo last season that she was bisexual, Leo had said that he should really start learning another language.

And with Leo's blessing—he was apparently thrilled that Hope was making friends in Shady Pond—Renee and his wife had gone for milkshakes at a diner in Ridgewood, for a hike in Ramapo Mountain State Forest, to a wine bar in Brooklyn. Without the cameras around, Hope was completely different. Still shy, but softer, more present. She made eye contact with Renee when she spoke, and gently touched her forearm. Her attention felt like a miracle. But there was still a part of Hope that felt impenetrable. Renee still didn't know much about her upbringing. Hope would talk about the church in vague terms, but never really told details. Renee wasn't sure if Hope still had feelings for Cheyenne, who had recently become a source of preoccupation for Renee. Renee wanted to know what she looked like, if she was prettier than her. She'd tried to find her on Instagram, but Hope didn't follow anyone named Cheyenne. Renee knew it was silly to be concerned. Especially now. Hope had been distant since sending a surprising and cold text roughly a week ago. Something along the lines of *Leo and I are expecting. A boy.*

Yes, Hope was pregnant.

And Renee had been avoiding Hope all night. Hope had been surrounded by the Goddesses, who wanted to touch her belly. And Renee was trying to remain focused on Ruby, who had been counting down to this show with pink marker on the kitten calendar in the kitchen. Her daughter had been practicing at all hours, her voice echoing through the house when she was in the shower, when she picked her outfits and did her makeup, through the car on drives to and from school. Renee had even heard snippets of Ariana Grande while Ruby ran up and down the stairs, apparently testing her lung capacity.

Renee scanned the room, the fifty or so guests plus five to ten cameras, massive floral arches, gold balloons floating to the ceiling. Opulence combined with old-money heavy drinkers. She hoped everyone would behave themselves. She hoped she could stop thinking about Hope.

Eden had encouraged Renee to go on a date (with a woman) (for the show), which was a nice distraction, but not enough to quell the anxiety about her uncertain status with Hope. From out of the corner of her eye, Renee saw Leo squeeze Hope around the waist. They seemed happy. Renee felt sad for a second; then the lights lowered and a spotlight shone on the microphone. Renee's sadness morphed back into anxiety as Ruby walked out. Renee still couldn't believe this was her baby girl. She was so confident, so mature. She strutted like a star. The highlighter she'd placed on her cheekbones sparkled under the lights. She took the mic from its stand and seemed happier than she'd seemed in months. Ruby would be singing a cappella. The room fell eerily silent. Renee worried people could hear her labored breathing. Ruby cared about singing more than almost anything else in the world, and Renee therefore wanted everything to be perfect.

Ruby's lips nearly touched the mic as she started to sing her favorite song—Ariana Grande's "Imagine." Her voice filled the room like a bell, clear and commanding, reverberating off the walls and chandeliers to create a delicate cave of sound. Each word swept over the audience like a wave. Her vocal range rose from velvety lows to dazzling highs, every note infused with both soulful emotion and technical precision.

Renee couldn't help but look around the room to watch the guests' stunned faces. Everyone was always shocked to hear a voice this powerful come out of such a small body. And if it was possible, Ruby's voice had gotten even better since the last time Renee had heard her perform, at her middle school talent show a month ago. Renee knew she needed to get Ruby representation soon, and truly hoped this would be her ticket. All pop stars started young these days, as Ruby constantly reminded her. Miley Cyrus had started her music career at thirteen, Ariana Grande at fifteen, Olivia Rodrigo at sixteen. Renee made a mental note to talk to Eden about this in the next few weeks—she might not only have connections but might also want to film Ruby's journey for the show. Eden was playing a game, but Renee could play that game too.

Before long, the last note lingered in the air, and the room broke into furious applause. Those who were sitting stood. People whistled and shouted. Renee recognized Leo's voice cheering the loudest. He really was a decent person. Renee felt bad for sleeping with his wife. Judging from Hope's recent demeanor, the affair was probably over anyway. Renee needed to move on, to forget it all, before Eden and Shady Di and the gossip mill started running wild.

"Thank you so much," Ruby said into the mic as the applause died down. "I'm happy to lend my voice to such a great cause, Broke Not Broken."

Renee's heart swelled. Her daughter was so poised.

"I just have one more song for you all," Ruby said.

Renee tilted her head, wondering if she'd misheard. Ruby hadn't told her she was going to sing another song.

"This is my first original song," Ruby said. "And I'm really excited to share it with you."

Renee's breath quickened. She hadn't even known Ruby was writing her own music. She felt so estranged from her own kid. What if it wasn't good? What if she was disappointed? What if she embarrassed herself? Renee was so nervous, but there was nothing she could do. And then Ruby started singing, and as usual when Ruby started singing in front of an audience, she sounded incredible. Thank God. Renee's body relaxed as she zoned in on the lyrics.

Your sparkling world, so shiny and new
Glimmers with gems, but not a clue
Of the daughter fading, just out of view
Missing the love that she once knew

A cold shiver raced down Renee's spine, her fingers tightening around the edges of her chair.

Remember those nights, just you and me?
Talking of what and who we'd be?
Now you're a star on the TV screen
And I'm all alone, just thirteen

Renee couldn't believe it. Ruby had written a song about missing her. She'd thought Ruby had no interest in Renee. Was it true that Renee had been neglecting her? She fought to keep her composure, to keep from wincing as each lyric unveiled more of Ruby's hurt.

Your new best friend, she sings and shines,
In the light that once was mine
Do you miss me, Mom, like I miss you?
Or am I just a faded view?

Ruby suddenly stopped singing. She was choked up. Renee's breath caught in her chest as Ruby wiped a tear from her eye. Ruby wasn't typically much of a crier; even as a baby, she was more likely to laugh. What was happening? Renee sat frozen, unable to move or speak, as the audience filled with sounds of *aww* and *we love you, Ruby!* Ruby struggled to regain her composure. Leo ran up and put his hand on Ruby's shoulder. Renee felt herself leave her own body.

"You got this, Ruby," Leo said. "You're doing amazing."

Ruby kept singing, with Leo's hand on her shoulder.

I'm here, can't you see me?
In the shadows of your dreams
I'm speaking, can't you hear me?
Or am I just a silent scream?

The song continued in this vein while Renee remained paralyzed, feeling as though she was watching the scene from the ceiling. Part of her wanted to run up and squeeze Ruby and never let go, and the other part of her wanted to disappear forever. Ruby was basically announcing not only to this room but also to nearly a million viewers that Renee was a terrible, neglectful mom. This was Renee's worst nightmare. She cared about Ruby more than anything in the world, and now Renee had epically fucked up by getting lost in her business and the show and her idiotic affair with a married woman. While the song continued, Renee privately vowed to end things with Hope for good—it seemed like that was what Hope wanted anyway—and to cut back her hours in the studio and filming and focus exclusively on Ruby. She could date and focus on herself once Ruby got to college or her own apartment. Until then, Ruby would be her sole focus. She couldn't believe this was happening.

Applause erupted in Renee's ears.

Ruby ran off the stage crying.

Renee ran after her.

CONFESSIONAL TRANSCRIPT – *GARDEN STATE GODDESSES*
(SEASON 3)
RUBY RICCI

EDEN: What do you think of Hope's performance?

RUBY: Well, first off, Hope's show is in a literal trash
venue. Very ratchet. I can't believe my mom takes me
here. I'm like, do you want me to get stabbed, woman?

EDEN: [*Laughs*.]

RUBY: And the performance? It's totally weird. I mean,
she's wearing these corny cowboy boots. Then she starts
singing and it's creepy as hell. Like Taylor Swift's
creepy sister. And my mom is watching Hope like she's
some kind of god, and then she starts crying?

EDEN: Your mom cries?

RUBY: Yes! My mom is crying like she did when I had choir
solos when I was ten. So extra, right? She's like under
Hope's strange spell or something, I swear.

EDEN: What do you mean?

RUBY: My mom is always texting her. I see it. She texts her
and she giggles. It's like she has a crush or something.

EDEN: Do you think your mom might really have a crush on
Hope? She *is* bisexual.

RUBY: Eden, don't make me gag.

EDEN: [*Laughs*.] Sorry, sorry. Okay, so back to Hope's
performance.

RUBY: Yeah, so Hope is on her second or third creepy song
when there's this noise in the back. I turn and see
Carmela and Valerie, stumbling like they're drunk or
something. And I'm like, finally—some action! Carmela
and Valerie start making fun of Hope, and at first I'm
into it, like someone needs to give the girl a reality
check. But then Hope looks so freaked out and I feel
kind of bad for her? I mean, her music is totally weird,
but Carmela and Valerie are just being extra.

EDEN: Then what happens?

RUBY: Carmela and Valerie keep going. Between songs, Carmela is asking if people in the audience want to kill themselves? Pierre joins in and says he's close. It's completely tone-deaf. We had three suicides at my school last year.

EDEN: I'm so sorry.

RUBY: It is what it is. Anyway. They don't stop, then Birdie starts snoring. My mom wakes her up and Birdie starts speaking French? I think? I take Spanish at school. Then Carmela says, "Pick it up, Cali," or something cringe like that. Then Leo *runs* at Carmela. We all turn and watch. Hope stops singing, her mic screeches. And then Carmela scratches Leo across the face with her dang three-inch nails. And he's all bloody. Carmela calls him "Leona"—also tone-deaf, like, gender is a spectrum, duh—and then she stumbles out with Valerie. Birdie wakes up and starts speaking French *again*! It's all so extra! I'm like, *Mom, let's dip*. I think my mom feels bad for bringing me to this shit show because she takes me to Brandy Melville! The one in SoHo is open until ten p.m.

EDEN: That's a fantastic summary, Ruby.

RUBY: Thanks. Do you think you can give me my own show? Because I'm soooo over talking about these boomers.

EDEN: [*Laughs*.] I'll see what I can do.

TWO

Hope stood up and caught her breath.

Renee had told Hope that Ruby was hitting puberty, that she had increasingly less interest in Renee, but her song painted a different story. Was Renee neglecting Ruby? Hope felt especially terrible about the lyrics directed at her, the ones about Renee's "new best friend" who "sings," shining in the light that once was hers. She hoped no one else picked up on the implication. Either way, poor Ruby. She was proud of Leo for going up to comfort her. Leo was a commendable man, and he'd be an exceptional dad. Hope rubbed her belly and went to the bathroom to collect herself.

There, she straightened the red dress Leo had bought her for the party. It was a snug fit, accentuating her baby bump.

Leo had been so happy when he found the First Response box in the trash. And Hope's life had improved so much since that faint line on the test. Leo had been home more, more present. They'd gone on more dates, had more sex, which Hope was almost starting to enjoy. Leo had taken Hope to the ballet in New York City. He'd bought her three new dresses and a new amp for her guitar. Hope hadn't had as much time for Renee, which was ideal. The less time Hope had, the less tempted she'd be.

Sleeping with Renee had been an epic mistake. A mistake Hope had repeated three times, maybe four. She didn't want to think about it. Hope had been vulnerable, not thinking clearly. She wasn't going to mess up her life again like she did last time.

Hope had gone to the gynecologist's office but never left the parking lot. She stayed in the car, watching the sky turn from blue to purple to pink to navy to black. Then she drove home. As the Fiat moved at a glacial pace through traffic, Hope had tried to imagine the results window from the pregnancy test. That second line was there. It was definitely there. A faint line was still a line. A faint line was still pregnant. She'd seen that on Google.

Back at the house, Leo was waiting with flowers and champagne. Frank Sinatra was playing and the house smelled like those fancy candles Leo loved.

"Well?" he said. Leo was so handsome, still in his suit from work, his thick brown hair slightly ruffled from the day.

Hope took a deep breath, smiled, and said: "It's a boy."

Everything was perfect.

Until the next day, when Hope got her period.

She'd had her period twice now since Leo found the First Response box.

So Hope was not pregnant, not at all. But she had yet to advertise this unfortunate truth and ruin her good luck. Everyone was being so nice to her. Even Carmela was sucking up to her, at least in front of the Fontanas.

Hope had been overeating to keep up the charade that she was carrying the next Fontana boy. Two bowls of pasta a night and extra wine or Peronis after Leo went to bed. Her stomach was finally starting to bulge a bit, just enough to be noticeable, big enough that Leo would whisper to the baby every night before bed. Imagining their future perfect family had inspired Hope to be better about ignoring Renee's messages.

Hope hadn't spoken to Renee in nearly eight days, and she only thought about her occasionally. When she did, the feelings were more intense than she liked, but Hope knew it was mind over matter. If she could convince her husband and his family she was pregnant with a baby boy, she could convince herself she did not have feelings for Renee. Hope rubbed her belly and imagined there was a tiny baby inside, not just excess carbs.

The woman in the mirror was very different from the one who left Weed. She'd learned to do her makeup from YouTube and Leo had slowly replaced her shabby wardrobe with all designer clothes. This red dress was Christian Dior and it shaped her fuller body with precision. Hope leaned closer to the mirror and removed a clump of mascara from her lashes. The amethyst around her neck caught the bathroom light, casting a blinding incandescent triangle.

Something about the light brought back a slew of memories. First, a flashlight. The megawatt one Hope's father would shine directly into Hope and Faith's eyes for extended periods whenever they disobeyed, a punishment a step above a bar of soap in the mouth and one below a metal whipping, a punishment that once caused Hope to go blind for several minutes. Then, she saw a camera flash. The one triggered by Hope's neighbor from Brother God, a flash she'd seen from her peripheral vision while kissing Cheyenne. She recalled the expression on his face, one of both intense judgment and supreme delight. He'd caught the pure preacher's daughter in an act Brother God considered a sin worse than murder. Then, a rotating table lamp, one Hope's father positioned directly in her eye when he confronted her with the photo, a photo no lie could explain away, although Hope tried, said it was a camera trick, that Cheyenne was merely whispering something in her ear, but her father didn't buy it. Next, a fire. The one burning at Hope's midnight banishment ceremony, her father's words saying that as far as he and Brother God were concerned, Hope was dead. Then, a second fire, a small home in flames, one she didn't see but could feel—the intense heat on her skin. A Bible sitting beside the flames, the edges of its pages charring. Finally, the headlights of oncoming trucks on I-5 in the middle of the night as Hope sped toward San Francisco.

Feeling mildly possessed, Hope ripped the amethyst necklace

from her neck. She tossed it in the trash with a swift, involuntary motion. Though it would be nearly impossible to hear such a tiny gem land on the bottom of the bin, Hope swore she heard a sound like a bell.

To Hope, it sounded like *yes*, an affirmation from the universe that she was doing the right thing.

"Honey," Leo said, knocking on the door.

Hope opened the door, happy to see her husband.

"Can I talk to you for a second?" he asked.

Leo didn't wait for an answer, just took Hope's hand and led her up to a guest room on the second floor, away from the cameras. He sat on the bed and pulled Hope to sit beside him.

"Ruby's song was something, wasn't it?" Leo said. "It got me really thinking. I think it's time we're straight with each other."

"Could it wait until we get home?" Hope asked. She couldn't wait to get home, away from the temptation that was Renee Ricci in a shimmery black dress.

"It can't wait!" Leo shouted. He grabbed her hands tight and leaned in close. His lips nearly touched her ear. Hope shivered.

"I need to tell you right this second," he whispered, "that I know you're sleeping with Renee."

Hope's heart plummeted into her tailbone. This wasn't good. This was really, really bad. This was terrible. Hope clutched the silk bedspread.

"What?" was all she could manage, but it came out like a whisper.

"That first night at the hotel in San Francisco," Leo said. "I wasn't violating your privacy, I promise. Your phone was right there on the nightstand. And it kept lighting up with these messages from someone named Cheyenne. And I knew Cheyenne was an ex." Leo petted Hope's cheek. "And I knew you had done something very bad."

Fire erupted in Hope's chest. Was she in danger? She couldn't tell. Leo was telling her not to be scared, but she was terrified. His family was in the mafia, or so everyone said.

"And at that moment," Leo said, "I knew you would make a perfect wife."

Hope wanted to run. He wasn't making any sense.

"Because you had your love." Leo twisted a lock of Hope's hair in his fingers and she shivered. "And I had mine."

Wait, what? "What do you mean?" Hope suddenly remembered the psychic, her prediction that there was another woman. Hope had thought it was Cheyenne, then Renee. Was it possible that Leo was seeing someone else?

"Me and Carmela?"

"You and Carmela what?" Hope asked.

Leo lowered his voice to a near whisper. "We're sleeping together, just like you and Renee. We have been. For years." Leo was still smiling. "Ten years, actually."

The air left Hope's lungs. She clutched the bedspread again. Leo and Carmela had been sleeping together for ten years. So this was why they were always bickering like lovers. And this was why Carmela hated her. Was Carmela the other woman the psychic had mentioned? Or was it Renee? And how did Leo know about them? And what was the bad thing he was referring to? She gasped for air.

"I was worried when you first moved here that you were actually in love with me," Leo said, and laughed. "Carmela was worried too."

Hope felt like she was going to pass out.

"But then Valerie told me that you and Renee slept in the same bed in Rhode Island," Leo said, squeezing Hope's sweaty palm softly again. "Oh, Hope. Don't be afraid. Don't you see? This is perfect. You can have your love and I can have mine. We just have to keep it a secret." Leo stopped smiling.

"Because my brother, Dino, he's a very dangerous man."

Hope swallowed, remembering Shady Di's claim that Dino never left the house without a loaded gun.

"Carmela worried he was onto us before I came out to San Francisco with Eden," Leo continued. "At that point, I knew I had to find a wife. I needed to kill any suspicion."

Hope prickled at the phrasing. Her breath shallowed. There wasn't enough air getting into her lungs.

"And then I met you, and you were so perfect. So sweet and so pretty." Leo laughed. "And so incredibly gay."

Hope shuddered. No one had ever called her that word before. She didn't like it. She didn't like it at all. She hated it. She had been duped. She'd wanted a chance at a normal life. She had been so close. And now it was slipping away, evaporating into dust.

"But," Hope started, but she didn't know what to say. She had no leg to stand on.

"Don't you get it?" Leo said. "You can keep sleeping with Renee, and I can keep sleeping with Carmela. We both get what we want." Leo put his hand on Hope's belly. "And we get to have our beautiful baby boy."

Hope felt lightheaded again. This was too much to process.

"I need to get back to the party," Hope said, and left the room.

THREE

Eden was excited.

Ruby's performance had been stellar. Not only did she sound great, but that original song? A devastating surprise. Aria said the audience always turned on Goddesses eventually, even the most loved ones. Would they now turn on Renee? Now that her adorable little daughter had painted a tale of neglect in a seriously moving melody? This season was going to be epic. Epic!

Eden also knew there was much left to be uncovered. First off, a blind item had recently hinted at Carmela not being Italian, which Shady Di was denying, which made Eden suspect that Carmela was behind Shady Di. Eden needed someone to bring it up on camera. Renee was always most likely to do her bidding. Eden could use the fact that the audience was maybe turning on her post–Ruby's song as leverage. Eden was always ten steps ahead. She was thinking like Aria.

Also, Eden suspected there was something going on between Renee and Hope. She kept thinking about Ruby's lyrics. Something about a "new best friend" who "sings"—that was obviously Hope, right? Maybe they were more than friends. Pierre had suggested in one of his confessionals that Hope might be a lesbian given her "atonal voice" and "sensible taste in footwear."

The thought hadn't previously occurred to Eden, but Eden was starting to see it. Hope had never seemed interested in boys grow-ing up the way Eden and Faith were. Eden had just assumed Hope was obedient, trying to please their parents, who strictly forbade romance before marriage. But maybe Hope just had no interest in boys. And then there was the psychic's suggestion that there was another woman. Eden had assumed Leo was having an affair, but what if Hope was the one with the other woman? Was Hope liter-ally sleeping with Renee at this very moment? While pregnant with Leo's baby boy?

This was another exciting turn of events. Carmela was playing nice about it but Renee could see the hostility simmering under-neath, ready to blow. Eden wanted Carmela to break something expensive tonight, maybe swing from a chandelier until it fell onto the grand piano. Eden laughed imagining it. Then abruptly stopped laughing.

Because unfortunately, Hope, Ruby, Renee, Leo had all left the great room shortly after Ruby's big performance. She needed reac-tions, she needed more drama. If she didn't find them and get the shots necessary to round out the scene, Aria was going to kill her. Or fire her. Or, worst of all, make her stay on this dumb show in *New Jersey*. Did these women not understand that this was a job? That they were literally being paid to be in this room and create entertain-ing drama?

Eden never lost the plot. About a week or so ago, Hope had men-tioned offhandedly to Eden that Birdie said she'd put Hope in her will. A less seasoned showrunner might have brushed it off, thought there was no way Birdie was telling the truth, as Birdie never told the truth. Hope herself thought Birdie was either joking or "overserved." The rookie producer would say, *That's a nonstarter*. But Eden's sea-soned producer brain spun with possibilities. If the Goddesses—but mostly Carmela—learned that Birdie was leaving Hope a large sum of money in her will, they would lose their minds, regardless of whether or not it was true.

With Aria's encouragement, Eden had immediately asked Caleb

to mock up a fake addendum to Birdie's will, indicating Birdie was leaving Hope $7 million, an amount Eden had landed on by googling *how much would a billionaire leave a close friend in a will?* Caleb had gotten Birdie to sign it by telling her it was a release form. Then he'd dropped it on the floor of the nail salon as they waited for all hell to break loose.

But so far, no such hell had broken. None of the Goddesses had mentioned it. Maybe someone unrelated to the show had found it, or maybe a Goddess had found it and was waiting to bring it up tonight. Eden grinned, imagining the possibility, one that could potentially end with Carmela rage-hanging from a chandelier, admitting that she wasn't Italian but *was* Shady Di.

"Come," Eden hissed at Johnny, who quickly obeyed. She sensed Johnny was afraid of her, which she liked. Eden snapped her fingers at Caleb, who also came right over. She shouldn't have let him fuck her last night, but she'd been so nervous about the party, about delivering on the climax she needed to sustain the season, that she'd craved a release. Caleb had come over with a pizza they hadn't eaten and a six-pack they'd hardly touched before they did the deed and Eden instructed him to leave. She needed her beauty rest. She could tell by the way he was looking at her that he'd read too much into it. Romance was so fucking corny.

She charged upstairs with Johnny and Caleb following her. There were so many staircases in this house and they all seemed to go on forever. Eden hadn't worked out in years and she was winded. She'd also taken up smoking again due to the pressure, bumming cigarettes from Johnny and even Carmela on set, and she had to pause at the top of the stairs to catch her breath.

"You okay?" Caleb asked. He rested his hand on Eden's waist.

"Footage first," Eden said, shoving Caleb off her. "Feelings never."

EDEN: What do you think of Hope's concert?

RENEE: Hope is incredible. Really. She has a really distinctive, ethereal voice. Kind of like Ani DiFranco or the lead singer from the Cocteau Twins. What's her name . . . Elizabeth Fraser?

EDEN: Yeah, I think so. And that's flattering. What do you think of the lyrics?

RENEE: [*Swallows*.] I like them. They're very evocative, intense. I feel transported to Northern California.

EDEN: Ruby says you cry.

RENEE: I'm moved.

EDEN: What does Ruby think?

RENEE: Ruby's a little moody. She's been sassy lately.

EDEN: She told me Hope sounded like Taylor Swift's creepy sister.

RENEE: Ruby's being very rude. And don't people love Taylor Swift?

EDEN: Taylor Swift is a billionaire.

RENEE: It's sort of a compliment then, right?

EDEN: I guess. What do you do after the concert?

RENEE: What? I go home.

EDEN: Ruby said you took her shopping.

RENEE: Oh, right! We go to Brandy Melville. Thank God it's cheap because Ruby is obsessed. We always leave with half the store. And somehow it's only a hundred dollars? I can't think too hard about it because I'm sure something unethical is happening.

EDEN: And what about after that?

RENEE: After that, we go home.

EDEN: Have you talked to Hope since?

RENEE: Of course.

EDEN: You're becoming close.

RENEE: [*Coughs.*] Yes, you could say that.

EDEN: Am I wrong?

RENEE: No, you're right. We're becoming close.

FOUR

Hope walked through the hall toward the great room.

Around the corner, Birdie's head of house, Luz, appeared. Hope jumped, startled, then laughed. Luz laughed, too, and steadied the glass in her hand. Hope had developed a friendly rapport with Luz after spending more time at Birdie's recently. Like everyone else, Birdie had been extra sweet to Hope since word of her pregnancy got out. Birdie had invited her over to Chateau Blanche for tea several times, both with and without the cameras. And Birdie was really starting to grow on Hope. Hope's own mother wasn't the warmest or most compassionate woman; in fact, she was quite the opposite, so having Birdie's effusive support meant a lot to Hope, even if Birdie was often loopy and incoherent. The other day she'd even said something about putting Hope in her will, which Hope had assumed was a side effect of her medication. Birdie always seemed to be on a new medication for something or other, at least that's what Pierre said. Pierre was always shuffling Hope out early so "Mother could sleep." Luz frequently reprimanded Pierre for his rudeness toward Hope, who appreciated the support.

Luz handed Hope a martini. At least she thought it was a martini. She'd never had one before, but the glass had a slender stem and a conical bowl.

"You need it, *mamacita*," Luz said and winked.

Hope exhaled, relieved. She took a big sip. Wow, it was strong. She didn't want Leo to see her, his allegedly pregnant wife, drinking a martini. So she took a few gulps and then left the rest on a decorative table beside her. She could come back for more if she needed it.

Continuing down the hallway, Hope felt lighter already, Leo's big confession already a distant memory.

But then she turned to the corner to find herself standing face-to-face with Renee. Since the positive pregnancy test, Hope had been trying so hard to trick herself into finding Renee unattractive, into preferring Leo. But right now, as she stared at Renee, Hope's stomach was fluttering like mad. Renee's features were soft, warm, framed by rich brown waves. And those bright green eyes. They put a spell on Hope. All her hard work and discipline flew out the door.

"I need to talk to you," Renee said, grabbing Hope's hand.

Hope felt like she was being dragged around like a sack of potatoes. But suddenly, the martini was hitting her and she was feeling less annoyed and more like she was on a ride at an amusement park. Besides, Renee's skin felt pleasant on hers. She remembered them holding hands at the concert Renee had taken her to, and on late-night drives back from Manhattan. Renee's hand was gentle and comforting. And Hope remembered what Leo had said. Leo knew. Leo condoned her sleeping with Renee. She could continue the affair! Hope felt dizzy, and this time in a pleasant way. That martini was really tasty. She would go back to finish it after this conversation.

Renee pulled Hope through the kitchen to a guest room behind it. How many bedrooms did this house have? Leo said something like fifteen? This room was less fancy than the one she'd been in with Leo, luxurious by Weed standards but plain by Chateau Blanche's, with just a twin bed with white bedding, minimal decor. Hope sat on the bed and it felt like a cloud.

"You have to feel this," Hope said. "This bed. It's incredible."

Hope laid down and spread her arms and legs like she was making a snow angel. Renee stared at Hope like she was crazy. Why was she in here again? Oh yeah, Renee wanted to talk to her. But Hope wanted to share what Leo had said. Hope shot up and looked at Renee, who was now seated next to her on the bed.

"I have excellent news," Hope said.

FIVE

Hope had a crazed look in her eyes. Everyone drank too much at Chateau Blanche, but Hope was pregnant. Maybe it was the hormones. Either way, Renee had to tell Hope the affair was off, once and for all, and leave. Renee needed to focus all of her attention on Ruby.

She'd followed Ruby upstairs after her performance, but Ruby had locked herself in a guest bedroom. She was still in there as far as Renee knew. Renee had to give her some time to calm down. She'd talk to Hope, tell her it was over, and put all of that energy she'd wasted on Hope into being a good mom. She'd be the best mom ever. She'd find Ruby a manager in the city and get them a house closer to Manhattan. Maybe she'd even get them an apartment in the city.

"Leo knows about us," Hope said. She was grinning. But why? This was bad news, wasn't it? The Fontanas were scary people. Hope grabbed Renee's hand. Her skin was cool and clammy.

"It's okay, though," Hope continued. "He doesn't care because he's been sleeping with Carmela." Hope giggled and lay back on the bed, spreading her arms. "This bed is so soft, oh my God." Hope pulled Renee down with her. The bed felt like any other bed. Renee was tempted to join Hope in her intoxicated delusions, but Renee remembered Ruby's song, Ruby locked in the guest bedroom upstairs. She needed to do the right thing for Ruby.

Also, what? Leo with Carmela? Renee's mind raced—half of it trying to connect the dots, the other half telling her to run. But once the words sank in, it oddly made sense. This was why they were always quarreling like an old married couple. And this was why Carmela despised Hope. Was Hope in danger? Was her unborn baby in danger?

Renee sat up.

"Don't you understand?" Hope said. "We can continue the affair!"

She was shouting now and Renee worried people could hear. Renee hoisted Hope to a sitting position. Renee needed to get through to her. But Hope swayed, her eyes glassy and distant, resembling Birdie every day post–3 p.m. Suddenly, Hope's smile vanished. Perhaps she was just mirroring Renee's worried expression. But Hope didn't just appear worried. She seemed afraid. Terrified.

"Leo said I did a bad thing," Hope whispered, eyes wide. "He knows I did a bad thing." Her eyes briefly rolled back in her head; then she refocused her gaze on Renee, eyes bigger than before. "Like Delilah," she said. "A bad thing like Delilah." Her eyes rolled back again.

Hope started to repeat *bad thing* over and over, her words slurring into mush. Her limbs began to shake, her body convulsing. But the refrain continued. *Bad thing. Bad thing. Bad thing.*

Was she having a seizure? Panic surged through Renee. She tried to steady Hope, but her body jerked and thrashed uncontrollably.

Bad thing. Bad thing. Bad thing.

And then, without warning, Hope fell silent. The convulsions ceased. Hope's body fell limp. Her skin was cold as ice.

Renee's scream cut through the air. She bolted for the door, her thoughts a blur of *help*, *help*, *HELP*.

CONFESSIONAL TRANSCRIPT – *GARDEN STATE GODDESSES*
(SEASON 3)
RENEE RICCI

EDEN: How are you feeling going into Birdie's Broken Not
    Broken gala?

RENEE: Nervous. I always get nervous before Ruby performs.

EDEN: She's great. More than great. Just stellar. Like how
    does a voice like that come out of such a tiny body?

RENEE: Yeah, she's incredible. She always is. But she cares
    about singing so much. I just want her to succeed. It
    would kill me if she were disappointed in any way.

EDEN: The song that she writes is very moving.

RENEE: Can we talk about something else, Eden?

EDEN: Listen, I'm just following Aria's orders.

RENEE: Do you think Aria might be a sociopath?

EDEN: I'd be lying if I didn't say the thought hadn't
    crossed my mind. . . . When Ruby's lyrics refer to your
    "new friend" who "sings"—do you think that might be
    Hope?

RENEE: [*Sniffling.*] Sorry, Eden. [*Sobbing.*] I can't do this.

EDEN: Me neither.

SIX

Eden had to be tripping. This couldn't be real. This had to be a dream.

Hope, her cousin, the closest thing she had to a sister, lying lifeless on the floor. Still and pale as marble. A gasp snagged in Eden's throat as she stood in the doorway, eyes fixated on the body. A chill seeped into her bones, pulse thundering in her ears. Renee clutched onto Eden, wailing. Eden opened her mouth to join her, but no sound came out.

Slowly, Eden approached the figure.

Footsteps thundered down the hall. Eden turned toward the sound just as Leo burst through the door. Valerie and Carmela followed, all three of them breathing heavily. Leo started to say something, but his words died in his throat at the sight.

"No," he finally whispered, approaching Hope's body. "No, no." He kneeled, fingers trembling as he checked her pulse. He put his head on her unmoving chest. He looked up, as if seeking confirmation that this wasn't some cruel trick, that Hope wasn't playing some very sick joke on them. Then a guttural wail ripped from somewhere primal inside him. He ran his fingers over Hope's hair, then her belly. "My baby," he choked out, voice cracking. "My baby." His cries joined Renee's. Valerie began crying too.

Birdie suddenly appeared in the doorway, martini in hand, oblivious to the darkness before her. "What's all the commotion?" She quickly drained the glass, apparently unable to see Hope's body. "I can't believe someone left a half-empty martini at Chateau Blanc! No dead soldiers—"

Birdie turned white, then dropped to the floor.

Watching Birdie fall, Renee also fainted.

Eden bolted up, fleeing the room and down the halls.

Sirens wailed in the distance. Thank God, someone called 911. Eden ran to the front door. Maybe Hope could be saved. It was probably just her pregnancy hormones. These Italians were so melodramatic.

Eden flung open the front door. Standing there were two men whose jackets said FBI. They weren't paramedics. There was no ambulance in the driveway. Where the fuck were the EMTs? God, Eden couldn't believe she paid taxes in this dumbass state. New Jersey couldn't get anything right. She was about to scream at them when an agent started talking, an urgent tone in his voice.

"We're here to execute a warrant," he said.

"A warrant? For what?" Eden asked. "We have permits to film." She didn't know why she was saying this. Obviously the FBI wasn't here to enforce SAG-AFTRA guidelines. Eden was dizzy. "We need help," she whimpered to the men.

"So do we," the agent said, holding up the paper in his hand. "It's an arrest warrant."

"Under arrest? Who? For what?" Eden's vision was starting to blur. This had to be a nightmare, right? Her subconscious was always out to get her once the sun went down.

The agent scanned the document. "Arson, aggravated arson, reckless burning, unlawful flight to evade arrest, manslaughter . . ." He paused and swallowed. "And first-degree murder."

"Murder?" Eden held on to a console table for balance. Did someone murder Hope? But they weren't even sure she was dead. She could be alive. She just needed help! Where the fuck were the EMTs?

"We need help," Eden whispered again, unable to form a proper sentence.

"Again, so do we," the agent said. "We need to find Hope Bennett, now known as Hope Fontana."

"Hope?" Eden said, her words feeling unfamiliar on her tongue. "Hope didn't kill anyone. Hope needs help." Eden leaned onto the table.

"Well, according to the United States District Court for the Eastern District of California"—the agent waved the paper in the air— "she's under arrest for the murder of Simon and Ruth Bennett."

The names hit Eden like a physical blow to the chest. Her aunt and uncle. Hope's parents.

"Can you help us find Hope?" the agent asked. "We received confirmation that she was here not long ago, via information from a Ms. Cheyenne Green."

The blood drained from Eden's face.

Eden blinked and fell.

Everything faded to black.

SEVEN

Renee watched the Manhattan skyline disappear in her rearview mirror.

She spotted a sliver of her reflection and noticed tears running down her right cheek. She hadn't realized she'd been crying and didn't even know what she was crying about. It could be a number of things. Was it dropping off Ruby at her dad's apartment indefinitely because Renee had proved in the last week and maybe before that to be a wildly incompetent parent? Or was it her ex-lover dying right before her eyes? Or was it learning that the person who had most excited Renee romantically in the past decade, maybe her entire life, had been accused of murder?

Just minutes before Hope died, Renee had dedicated herself to being a better, more present parent to Ruby. But Hope's death had made being present for Ruby nearly impossible. Ruby was currently at her father's until Renee recovered. Not having Ruby made a difficult situation even harder, but Renee knew it was the right thing to do. She couldn't be there for Ruby right now, couldn't make her lunch or take her to school, couldn't fulfill even the most basic maternal duties, let alone take care of her daughter's delicate teenage emotions. If Renee had been an absent mom before, as Ruby's devastating song had suggested, she was even worse now.

Hope's funeral had been sparsely attended and depressing. She supposed all funerals were depressing, but this one particularly so. Hope didn't have a big network in Weed, and most people didn't seem to want to grieve the death of someone accused of killing her parents. Leo had been there, Renee had been there, and Eden had been there, but beyond that? A sprinkling of bodies Renee didn't recognize. Maybe they'd been hired by the funeral director to give Hope a shred of dignity.

Since the service, Renee had been bedridden, occasionally getting up for a glass of water or a handful of chips, or to text Eden, who seemed to be in a similarly bad place. Eden felt completely responsible for Hope's death, for putting her on this TV show, for setting her up with Leo.

Eden seemed to be directing her grief into figuring out how Hope had died. Leo didn't want an autopsy, which Eden found suspicious. Before the funeral, she'd gone to the police, suggesting that they treat it as a murder. But the police said there was no indication that Hope hadn't died of natural causes. Eden said thirty-three-year-olds didn't just drop dead of natural causes, but Renee knew there were always freak incidents.

At Hope's funeral, Renee had told Eden that before she died, Hope said Leo had confessed to having an affair with Carmela. To Eden, this was proof. Carmela and Leo poisoned Hope so that they could be together. But Renee said Hope wasn't really a barrier to them being together; Dino was more the barrier. Also, Leo wouldn't kill his unborn son. Eden said Carmela would. And were they even sure Hope was pregnant? Eden said there was something off about the baby bump. "Too soft," she'd said. And she'd seen Hope drinking at the party. Hope wouldn't drink pregnant. Renee didn't think Hope would invent a pregnancy, but she also hadn't thought Hope would kill her parents, so Renee had resigned herself to accepting that her intuition was deeply, irrevocably off.

Renee still hadn't told Eden that she and Hope had been sleeping together, that she'd taken Hope into that room with the intention of ending their affair. She knew this would make Renee suspicious to Eden, and Renee just couldn't handle that on top of everything else.

Renee felt shaky at the wheel as she merged onto I-80. She never used to be a nervous driver, and in fact found driving freeing and exhilarating, but right now she felt terrified. Terrified about leaving Ruby alone with her absent father in New York City, terrified by the memory of watching Hope die before her eyes, terrified by the realization she'd been sleeping with someone who had killed her parents, terrified about these cars racing by her on either side of her. Someone behind Renee honked and she got off at the next exit, took the streets all the way home, which added nearly an hour to her drive.

Back at home, Renee heated up a pizza that she knew she wouldn't eat. She had zero appetite. Watching it spin in the microwave, she thought about her first proper date with Hope. After Hope's concert in New York, she'd admitted to Renee that that was her first concert ever. Renee at first had thought Hope meant the first concert she'd played, which was amazing given how compelling Hope was, but Renee soon learned Hope meant the first concert she'd ever even been to outside of a church gathering.

As soon as Hope said she'd never been to a concert, Renee knew she had to take her to one. Renee spent hours scouring the internet for the soonest-upcoming concert that would be exciting for Hope. She wanted to take her to see a female singer-songwriter, someone who made music similar to Hope's. Renee wanted it to be a big enough venue that it would impress Hope, but also something intimate and romantic and hopefully historic, having an old world charm the West Coast lacked. When Renee read that Angel Olsen was playing at White Eagle Hall—a recently restored historic venue in Jersey City—just a week after Hope and Renee first hooked up, it felt like fate.

Renee had picked up Hope at 7 p.m. that Friday. The women Renee had dated in the past tended to be more masculine, so she wasn't used to playing this role with Hope, but she also kind of liked being in charge.

"Oh my God," Renee had said to Hope as she merged onto I-95. "The psychic. She said there was another woman. Is it me?" Renee had felt embarrassed as soon as the words left her mouth. It was presumptuous. Something a man might say. Hope and Renee had only slept together once at that point. That hardly counted as an affair. Renee wanted to take it back until Hope replied.

"I was thinking the same thing," Hope had said. "In the shower earlier."

Renee had blushed the way Hope often did.

The concert had been perfect. The venue had soft red lights and a magnificent stained-glass ceiling, worlds away from the dusty venue where Hope had played in New York. White Eagle Hall had impeccable sound. Renee had grabbed Hope's hand and navigated them up to the front. They were so close they could almost see the pores on Angel Olsen's face. Hope seemed to watch in a state of rapture—mouth open, eyes wide. Afterward, Hope seemed high. She said she didn't want to go home. Renee drove Hope down to the waterfront, where they split a bottle of wine and watched Manhattan glitter in the distance, just like Renee had watched it glimmer in her rearview window tonight. The only difference was that Hope was dead.

After a half-hearted attempt at eating the pizza, Renee tried to sleep. It was only 8 p.m., but she didn't want to be conscious. She tossed and turned in the California king bed she once shared with her husband, before he left her for his twenty-three-year-old assistant. Renee thought her love life had been bad then. But then she'd gone and fallen for a woman with a Mafia-tied husband who'd dropped dead after killing her own family. It sounded like a Netflix true-crime special. But no, it was Renee's life.

Renee reached for the water glass on her bedside table and tipped it toward her mouth, only to find it was empty. Her mouth was dry, but she lacked the energy to fill it back up. She fell back asleep, and, as was the norm lately, she dreamed of Hope. Like most of her dreams of the past week, it began romantically, then morphed into horrific. It ended with Hope's seizure, repeating the phrase *bad thing* over and over until her body stopped moving.

EDEN: What do you think of the Broke Not Broken gala?

PIERRE: I don't understand why we're doing this. This is beyond tacky. Someone *died*, Eden. And frankly, you look close to death yourself. Are you okay?

EDEN: Not really.

PIERRE: Well, I have a riding lesson at four, so let's get on it.

EDEN: Copy. Can we go back in time to before [*indecipherable*] the end of the party. How are you feeling about it?

PIERRE: I'm feeling, to quote a woman from another reality TV show I've seen clips of on Instagram, "not well, bitch!" I never look forward to these things. I find them to be torture akin to the most heinous war crimes.

EDEN: What things?

PIERRE: Filming.

EDEN: [*Clears throat.*]

PIERRE: I know I can't break the fourth wall, but does it really matter now? I mean. Jesus, Eden. This was your cousin. I have friends who love reality TV, call it camp, but I find it trash. If I want camp, I'll watch *Female Trouble* or *Pink Flamingos*. People die, but they're just actors. It's fake. I never signed up to be in a true-crime documentary.

EDEN: Okay, well, we can wrap this up quickly, I know you have your horse thing.

PIERRE: Wonderful, again, I just don't get why I'm here. Also, it's called *dressage* and it's one of the most elegant things a person can do, an art form where precision meets beauty, a dance of poise and finesse that transcends mere sport. It's a harmony, a love affair, between horse and rider, and ethereal spectacle, a ballet of control and dominance, the zenith of human mastery of nature. So please never call it some "horse thing."

EDEN: Copy. Before you go, your mother seemed close with Hope. How is Birdie doing?

PIERRE: She was close with Hope, yes. And she isn't doing well, thank you for asking. There's a reason I'm here and not her. She hasn't left the bed in days, Eden. She's mourning, maybe you should try it. Also, she's ill. She was egregiously overserved at the gala and is still recovering. Now, if you don't mind, I'll be off to my "horse thing," then back to care for Mother. Toodles. [*Footsteps.*]

EIGHT

Eden removed the laptop from her belly and rummaged for her vibrating phone under the twisted duvet. She hadn't left her bedroom since the funeral; the bed was covered in take-out boxes and candy wrappers. She'd been watching footage for days, trying to find a clue, anything to help her figure out who killed Hope. Eden just knew it was a murder. Thirty-three-year-olds didn't just drop dead.

She finally located her phone. Aria's name vibrated across the screen. She'd been ignoring Aria's calls for days, but was now realizing she hadn't spoken to anyone with her voice since the funeral, and nothing really mattered anymore, did it? Nothing except for finding out who'd done this to Hope.

"Eden," Aria said before Eden even said hello.

"Ariaaaa," Eden sang. She didn't care anymore. She was going to sing Aria's name, the way her parents likely wanted it to be sung.

"Are you singing my name?"

"Mmm-hmm," Eden sang.

"My dad used to do that. Before he died," Aria said. "Speaking of death—how are you feeling?"

Did Aria really just ask how she was feeling? She surely didn't mean it, but it felt good to be asked.

"Not great, Aria," Eden began. "I mean, Hope was the closest thing I had to a sister." A strange feeling formed behind her eyelids, in her throat. Was she about to cry? She still hadn't cried yet over Hope. She couldn't remember the last time she'd cried, period. But she craved some sort of physical release. Maybe she could hit up Caleb. But knowing him—she'd end up having to comfort *him*.

"I was the one who brought her on the show," Eden continued. "Her death was all my faul—"

"I'm sorry for your loss, Eden, but I'm going to have to cut you off," Aria interrupted. "I was really just asking to be polite. I'm about to get my hair colored. Also, sorry to bring up the elephant in the room, but the girl burned her parents to death in a fire. She wasn't exactly Miss Congeniality. And if she'd lived, she would have gotten the electric chair, or at least life in prison. Her life was over either way."

Aria's clinical analysis was strangely comforting. She hoped Aria was right, that Hope's life had been over either way, that Eden wasn't responsible. But Eden still refused to believe that Hope had killed her own parents. It just didn't seem like her. Sure, Hope had always been somewhat mysterious to Eden, but Eden's job was all about reading people. She knew Hope was hiding something—her sexuality, it turned out—but her cousin just didn't strike her as a killer.

"Eden, did I lose you?" Aria says. "I just got to the salon."

It was weird to think of people living their normal lives, going to appointments and doing errands. Eden couldn't imagine anything outside of this dark, rancid bedroom.

"I'm here," Eden said, but was she? She felt like she was floating.

"Okay," Aria said. "I almost forgot the reason I called."

"I thought you called to see how I was doing," Eden said, even though she knew it wasn't true.

"No," Aria said. "I wasn't. I was calling to tell you you need to start filming again by Monday. That'll be a week of bereavement. That's all Huzzah allows. I can't stall any further—you need to get back at it, film confessionals, get the girls together to process."

Eden felt dizzy, began to zone out. Was Aria really telling her to keep shooting? Eden hadn't thought about *Goddesses* in the past week other than to watch and rewatch footage for clues. She suspected both Leo and Carmela, especially after Renee revealed the bombshell that they were sleeping together. Eden had known there was something weird about Leo and Hope's relationship. Renee had said Leo wouldn't kill his unborn son, but Eden was starting to wonder whether Hope had actually been pregnant.

"Earth to Eden," Aria said.

"You must be crazy," Eden said.

"According to my psychiatrist, you're partially right." Aria laughed. "But the mood stabilizers seem to be helping."

"I'm serious, Aria. I can't possibly keep shooting. Huzzah will surely scrap the season."

"We don't know that yet," Aria said. "They haven't made a decision."

"This is supposed to be a fun, gossipy lifestyle show, not true crime."

"As blond as you can go without burning my scalp off," Aria said, and Eden was confused until she realized Eden was talking to her hairdresser.

"Look, Eden," Aria said, to her this time. "Sophia's husband, Carter, committed suicide during the second season of *Manhattan Muses*—Huzzah aired that. Lisa's son killed someone in a hit-and-run during season four of *Sunset Sirens*—Huzzah aired that. And we've had too many white-collar crimes to count: embezzlement, fraud, tax evasion, Ponzi schemes—you name it, Huzzah has aired it."

"But this is different," Eden said. "This is murder."

"Not according to anyone but you," Aria said. "More blunt," she snapped at her hairdresser. "A perfectly straight line."

"I promise you," Eden said. "Hope was healthy. She didn't just drop dead."

"Well," Aria said, "use the show. The producers found out Elise was committing insurance fraud on season one of *Scalpels in Stilettos* using confessionals. You could do the same."

Eden knew Aria was manipulating her, but Eden was also getting an idea.

"Okay, they're about to shampoo me, I gotta go," Aria said.

With a click, she was gone.

Eden put her laptop back on her belly and watched the footage from Hope's concert for the billionth time, unsuccessfully willing herself to cry.

CONFESSIONAL TRANSCRIPT – *GARDEN STATE GODDESSES*
(SEASON 3)
LEO FONTANA

EDEN: I'm so sorry for your loss, Leo.

LEO: Thank you. You too, Eden. I know Hope was your cousin.
Family. I'm surprised we're still filming.

EDEN: Boss's orders.

LEO: I get it. You gotta put food on the table. I guess it's
nice to have the distraction.

EDEN: It is. For both of us, I hope. Do you notice anything
off with Hope that night of the Broke Not Broken gala?

LEO: No, that's why I don't think it was natural causes like
they're saying. I mean, healthy thirty-three-year-old
women don't just drop dead.

EDEN: That's what *I* said. So what do you think happened?

LEO: I *know* what happened. Carmela, that jealous cunt,
did it. I'm sorry, I know I can't say that. I'm just so
fucking angry.

EDEN: You think Carmela killed Hope? How?

LEO: Poison. Cowardly way to kill someone. Carmela's all
bark and no bite. At the end of the day, she's a fucking
coward, a baby, a wimp. Couldn't even kill someone with
her own hands like a man. Had to use poison like a
pussy.

EDEN: But you didn't get an autopsy.

LEO: It's against our religion. I couldn't. My parents would
disown me. Also, we don't need one. It's obvious.

EDEN: You think it's obvious that Carmela killed Hope
because she was jealous Hope had taken you from her?

LEO: That's exactly what I'm saying, Eden.

NINE

When Eden called Renee to tell her Huzzah expected them to keep filming, Renee thought she was dreaming, or tripping. But nope, she was unfortunately very awake, and dead sober. And currently, she was on her way to the ten-year anniversary party for Carmela's nail salon. Eden was still convinced Carmela had poisoned Hope. Renee didn't know what to think. She tried not to think at all.

Entering the parking lot, Renee looked at the Ruby out the window. She felt completely disconnected from her store, herself, her body. Approaching Italians Do It Better, part of her was relieved to be returning to the trivial universe of the show. An alternate reality where nothing seemed serious. It was just a party celebrating a nail salon. Maybe Renee could convince herself nothing had ever happened.

A red carpet led up to the nail salon's entrance, which was flanked with green topiary and white floral arrangements. Inside, the salon sparkled even more than usual. Tall vases with red roses and greenery decorated each table. Red, white, and green balloons were clustered in the corners, a likely nod to the Italian flag. Waiters carried trays of champagne and tiny snacks on gold napkins. Caleb came up with a mic pack, which Renee dutifully attached to her shirt.

Renee approached Carmela, who wore a sparkly red dress. Her typical scent of cigarettes and perfume jolted Renee back to an earlier, lighter time. Fake and bubbly as usual, Valerie air-kissed Renee's cheeks. Birdie appeared and held on to Renee's arm, both as a greeting and for balance. Renee felt comforted by the familiarity of it all, until she looked over and spotted Eden.

Eden did not look good. She was never exactly polished, but this was a new level of haggard. Her hair was greasy and unbrushed, nearly matted. She had stains on her T-shirt and dark circles under her eyes, and Renee was pretty sure she could smell her from across the room. If Renee hadn't known better, she'd have thought Eden was unhoused.

Renee averted her eyes, tried to focus on the conversation. Carmela was talking about the party planning. Valerie talking about her boys. Birdie talking about a younger lover. But there was something off. Renee felt like she was floating again. Waiters kept handing them glasses of champagne, which they kept drinking. Cameras circled. Conversation happened, but Renee wasn't aware of any of it. She was floating on the ceiling, changing colors with the sky outside the windows.

Suddenly Renee found herself mid-conversation with Carmela's daughter, Bianca, someone she'd never shared more than a few words with. She learned that Bianca was already a senior—Renee could have sworn she was a sophomore—and was considering whether to go to college or just work full-time at the nail salon like Carmela wanted her to. She also said something about managing a social media platform that had become "unexpectedly lucrative," and that she'd maybe like to get a degree in digital media to help turn it into a career. Renee didn't really understand what she was talking about and was afraid of sounding old, and also still felt like she was in a weird dream, so she mostly just nodded along, feeling herself float right through the ceiling, into the night sky.

Renee blinked and she was outside, sharing a cigarette with Valerie. Renee had never seen Valerie smoke, and she'd never seen her this drunk either. Valerie was holding on to Renee for balance the way Birdie often did. Valerie took Renee's hand and pulled her around the corner, to the side of the building, away from the cameras.

"Take off your mic," Valerie whispered. Renee did as told. Valerie took hers off too.

"How are you feeling?" Valerie whispered. "I know you and Hope . . . were close."

Renee swallowed. Did Valerie know she and Hope had been sleeping together? Did everyone know? Renee supposed Leo knew. He wasn't exactly known for being a good secret keeper. He was rather considered to be a reckless gossip. The thought had crossed Renee's mind that he might be Shady Di. Although the account was pretty tough on Leo, frequently accusing him of violence. Maybe it was a misdirection. But was Leo smart enough for that?

"I'm not doing great," Renee said, and it felt good to be honest.

Valerie put her hand on Renee's. "I'm so sorry, honey," she said. The moon shone bright in the distance. Renee wondered if it was full.

"How do you feel about the news," Valerie whispered, swallowed, "that she killed her parents."

"She's just been accused," Renee said. "It hasn't been proven." Renee didn't know why she was defending Hope. Clearly, Renee hardly knew her. They'd slept together for just a few weeks, had known each other for only a few months. Maybe she *had* killed her parents. Renee didn't know up from down anymore. Currently, she was just trying to stay upright.

"True," Valerie said. "You know, Cheyenne sent Carmela a message," she said, her voice slow. "On Instagram."

"What?" Renee said. Before Hope died, Renee had been frequently consumed by jealousy of Cheyenne, had spent sleepless nights wondering if she was prettier than Renee, wondering how she'd managed to capture Hope's attention in a way she could not. But now the name was associated with the night Hope died, the night the police showed up and announced that Hope was under arrest for the murder of her parents, that they'd been alerted to her whereabouts by Cheyenne Green. A twisted part of Renee wished that Hope was alive to see the famous Cheyenne sell her out to the cops. Renee would never have done that.

"Cheyenne," Valerie repeated. "Hope's mystery friend. I guess she'd seen Hope tagged in a photo with us. And she sent Carmela this *longggg* message when we were getting ready together—in Rhode Island."

"Saying what?"

"She said she needed to reach Hope, that it was urgent, but her calls weren't going through," Valerie said. "And she kept calling her 'Delilah'?"

Renee swallowed. Right before she died, Hope had also called herself Delilah, Renee suddenly remembered. She didn't like to replay that moment in her head, but now it was there in her mind, clear as day. Hope had said she'd done "a bad thing like Delilah." At the time, Renee had figured it was a biblical reference, especially given Hope's background. But Renee's biblical knowledge was lacking.

"I had a feeling that Cheyenne was an ex," Valerie continued, "and that Hope had blocked her number, because I've had to block people too."

Renee swallowed. Where was this going? Why was Valerie telling her all this?

"Before Manny," Valerie continued, "I had the worst taste. One ex used to message Leo and Carmela to get to me after I'd blocked his dumb ass, and I told them to just ignore him. I told Carmela to ignore this one too, from Cheyenne. I'm not sure if she did."

"Why didn't Carmela bring it up?" Renee asked, surprised Carmela wouldn't jump to mention it on camera.

"She was waiting for the right moment," Valerie said. "I guess that moment died." Valerie laughed, then stopped. "Sorry."

Renee swallowed and gripped the side of the building. She kept wanting to wake up from this terrible nightmare.

"But then Cheyenne messaged *me* the night of the Broke Not Broken party," Valerie continued. "I guess someone had posted a photo of Hope and me."

"What did it say?"

Valerie shrugged. "Dunno, didn't read it," she said. "It was so long, and you know I hate reading." She smiled. "I'm dyslexic."

Renee leaned against the building so she wouldn't fall down.

"Normally I would have just deleted it," Valerie continued. "And I did, but that night, I was feeling kind of frisky. So before I deleted it, I wrote: *Hope is busy being fabulous in New Jersey's most expensive estate and was recently impregnated by someone who ISN'T YOU so BUG OFF and GET A LIFE, BITCH!*"

Renee started to slide down the wall a bit. Acting normal was so hard right now. Valerie skipped off around the corner of the building until she disappeared from view. Renee followed.

Eden was smoking a cigarette in front of the nail salon. Valerie pulled a phantom zipper over lips for unclear reasons. The old Eden would have noticed this gesture immediately, alerted the cameras to come outside and catch whatever secret she'd missed. But this version of Eden was in a daze. She smelled terrible, like smoke and sweat.

Valerie pinched her nose. "Pee-ew," she said. "I'm going back inside." Often Valerie acted more immature than Ruby. Renee missed Ruby so much, she couldn't even think about it. Valerie fastened her mic pack and went back inside.

Renee hadn't been face-to-face with Eden since Hope's funeral. Her skin looked translucent up close. She didn't want to tell Eden what Valerie had told her, but she thought it might be irresponsible to keep it to herself. It could be relevant to the pursuit of justice, whatever that meant here. Piecing the puzzle together—if there was in fact a puzzle to be pieced—might bring Eden back to life. She did not look good.

"Can we talk?" Renee said.

"What's up?" Eden asked.

Renee pulled Eden back around to the side of the building.

"Valerie told me a few things that might be of interest to you," Renee said. She paused, looked around.

"Carmela ran over her foot with a vintage car?" Eden asked.

"Not that," Renee said, lowering her voice to a whisper. "Apparently Cheyenne—you know Hope's mysterious friend?"

Eden nodded.

"Cheyenne had been DMing with both Carmela and Valerie," Renee said.

Eden seemed to perk up, blood coming into her cheeks. Renee felt like she was doing the right thing. Helping solve a dark puzzle at best, and if not, at least she was making Eden feel better.

"Saying what?" Eden said.

"When we were in Rhode Island, Cheyenne apparently saw a tagged photo on Instagram with Hope and Carmela, so she messaged Carmela about needing to get in contact with Hope, saying it was urgent and she couldn't reach her. Valerie thought Hope blocked Cheyenne's number, that she was a spurned lover." Renee swallowed. She didn't want to reveal that Renee knew this to be true, that Hope had told her. She wasn't ready to confess to Eden the true nature of her and Hope's relationship, but she knew she'd have to eventually.

"I'd been thinking the same thing," Eden said, surprising Renee. "That Cheyenne was an ex." Maybe it was obvious. Eden paused, then asked, "Was there anything else?"

"Cheyenne messaged Valerie the night of the party, the night the cops came," Renee said. "Valerie responded that Hope was at the most expensive estate in New Jersey, and that she was pregnant."

Eden perked up further. "Wait, so Valerie alerted Cheyenne to where Hope was that night? If you google *most expensive estate in New Jersey*, Birdie's *Architectural Digest* spread comes up. The address isn't hard to find. Do you think Cheyenne told the cops where Hope was? I don't trust that bitch at all. Maybe she was involved with Carmela in making Hope disappear. Cheyenne was a rejected lover; Carmela was the jealous mistress. Together, they conspired—"

"Eden," Renee interrupted, squeezing her forearm. She felt like if she didn't interrupt her, Eden would go on forever. "Who is Delilah? Like in the Bible?"

"She betrayed Samson to the Philistines. Why?" Eden asked.

"Before she died," Renee said, a lump forming in her throat, "Hope said she'd done 'a bad thing, like Delilah.' And then Cheyenne allegedly referred to Hope as Delilah in her messages to Carmela."

Eden squinted at Renee with sallow eyes. Renee could see the gears in her brain turning. At least she looked more alert.

"I think it's the Book of Judges." Eden stomped out her cigarette, then looked back up at Renee. "Samson was known for his strength. And Delilah was approached by the Philistines to find Samson's secret and defeat him. Delilah seduced Samson and found out his strength was in his hair, so she cut his hair while he was sleeping, and the Philistines captured him."

Renee swallowed. "So Cheyenne is saying Hope betrayed her in some way?"

"Seems like the other way around," Eden said.

"What do you mean?"

Eden pulled another cigarette from behind her ear and lit it. "I don't trust the bitch. Why did she keep calling Hope when Hope clearly wanted nothing to do with her? Why did she message Carmela and Valerie? And she alerted the cops to Hope's whereabouts. She seems like a spurned lover wanting to get revenge."

Dread settled in Renee's gut. She couldn't tolerate thinking about Hope anymore. She wanted to go back into the vapid party and listen to Birdie ramble on about her "paramours" who probably didn't exist. Anything to avoid this conversation, the grim realities of her life.

"I'm going back inside," Renee said.

"Wait," Eden said. "Will you go to the police with me? Tomorrow?"

"Sure," Renee said, but she wasn't sure if she meant it.

CONFESSIONAL TRANSCRIPT – *GARDEN STATE GODDESSES*
(SEASON 3)
CARMELA FONTANA

EDEN: How are you feeling?

CARMELA: Death is never a happy time, but we have to keep
  trucking. How are you, Eden? Hope was your family.

EDEN: I hardly know who I am anymore; let's talk about you.
  You didn't really like Hope, did you?

CARMELA: It's against my religion to speak ill of the dead.

EDEN: Well, you wouldn't be speaking ill of Hope,
  necessarily, you'd just be speaking about your feelings.

CARMELA: I'm protective of my family. We've been over this.
  But I never wanted the girl to die, if that's what you're
  implying, Eden.

EDEN: I read that your dad is in prison.

CARMELA: Oh yeah? Where'd you read that? Some meme account?

EDEN: Somewhere online.

CARMELA: Well, I heard your cousin slaughtered her own
  parents, so do you want to go there?

EDEN: She's been accused. It hasn't been proven.

CARMELA: I don't know, Eden, the FBI seems to have a lot of
  evidence.

EDEN: People are falsely accused all the time.

CARMELA: I guess it's in the hands of the justice system
  now.

EDEN: I guess it is. Are you excited for your Italians Do
  It Better ten-year anniversary party? [*Indecipherable
  sounds.*] Sorry, I need a second.

CARMELA: Cigarette?

EDEN: Please.

TEN

Eden returned to the party feeling slightly energized. She and Renee were going to the police tomorrow. Inside, Eden walked over to Valerie, then realized Valerie had a mic on and that Eden was in the shot. She moved behind the cameras and texted Valerie. *Send me Cheyenne's IG.* Valerie looked at her phone, then looked at Eden, then gave her a thumbs-up. Eden smiled. They couldn't bring Hope back, but they could figure out who killed her.

As Eden was checking her Instagram, a body shoved past her. He was stumbling to the bar. It took a second for Eden to recognize the figure as Leo. He looked like shit, probably similar to how Eden herself looked. Except Eden always sort of looked like shit; Leo was normally sharp, meticulously put-together. His hair was always styled with precision, carefully sculpted waves gelled into place. He normally wore tailored, ironed clothes and expensive cologne. But now he was in a tracksuit, his hair greasy and sticking out in various directions. He smelled like stale Coors Light. What was he doing here? Shouldn't he be home grieving his wife? Eden was still suspicious of him. Maybe it was all three of them: Carmela, Cheyenne, Leo. They'd all conspired to kill Hope. Leo and Carmela so they could have each other, Cheyenne to take revenge on her ex-lover for leaving.

Caleb's elbow suddenly nudged Eden's rib cage. Disgusted by

this lame attempt at flirtation, Eden shrugged him off. When he nudged her again, this time more insistently, Eden realized he wasn't flirting—he wanted her to look at something. She followed his gaze.

Leo was staggering through the crowd. He turned out he wasn't on his way to the bar. Rather, he was moving with a clumsy determination toward Carmela, who stood encircled by a cluster of guests. Clutched in Leo's grasp was something metallic and pointed—it looked like a silver nail file, catching the light from the chandelier as he wove through the bodies.

The buzz of the party receded as Leo's footsteps became all Eden could hear. Her eyes narrowed at Leo, who was stomping in a messy zigzag. She'd never seen him so drunk.

A shout sliced through the murmurs, "You did this, didn't you?" Leo flung himself at Carmela. Guests recoiled.

"Jealous bitch," Leo hissed, the nail file now tracing a horizontal line along Carmela's neck.

Carmela stood tall, rigid, and said nothing.

"Leo," Valerie begged, "please stop."

"It's okay, Valerie," Carmela said, her voice oddly calm given the circumstances. "I'm not afraid of *Leona*."

Leo cocked his arm back. "What was that?"

The room held its breath.

Just as Carmela opened her mouth to reply, Leo lunged. The nail file found its mark. A vein burst. Blood gushed out like water from a fire hydrant, a torrent of pent-up pressure.

"*Leona*," Carmela gurgled as a waterfall of crimson spilled from her mouth.

She fell to the floor with a thud.

Valerie's scream pierced the air.

More screams.

Screams layered upon screams.

Eden's heart thudded against her ribs. There was a shrill sound in her ears, and for a moment she couldn't tell if it was coming from her or the crowd. Her mind recoiled, flashing back to Hope's lifeless figure, the memory clawing its way forward. This couldn't be happening, not again.

Dino suddenly appeared from the mass of bodies. He reached his hand into his jacket pocket. When he removed it, he was holding a pistol. Eden blinked, hoping the gun would disappear. But when she opened her eyes, it was still there, the shiny metal object held tightly in his grasp.

"Hey, hey," Eden said, her shaky voice betraying her terror. Her eyes flickered over Carmela's lifeless body, which briefly, in her mind, morphed into Hope's. This had to be a nightmare. She pinched her arm to wake herself up, but unfortunately she was very awake.

Dino was still here, and he was pointing the gun at Leo's head.

"Dino, no!" Valerie said.

But it was too late.

Leo was on the ground before Eden even registered the sound of the gun firing.

Carmela and Leo lay on the floor in two concentric circles of blood.

CONFESSIONAL TRANSCRIPT - *GARDEN STATE GODDESSES*
(SEASON 3)
BIANCA FONTANA

EDEN: I'm so sorry about your mother, Bianca.

BIANCA: Thank you. Carmela was a force of nature. She wasn't always the easiest mom to have, but I loved her.

EDEN: Can you say more on that?

BIANCA: You worked with her for three seasons, right? Would you call her an easy person?

EDEN: [*Laughs.*] Honestly? Seems like a walk in the park compared to my parents.

BIANCA: Never introduce me to them.

EDEN: We haven't spoken in fifteen years, so don't worry. So how have you been coping?

BIANCA: [*Holds up phone.*] Instagram. I have a lot of friends on here. People in similar situations. Dead moms, dads going to prison. You know, I've worried about my dad going to prison my whole life, but I really thought Carmela would live forever.

EDEN: You called her Carmela?

BIANCA: "Mom" never seemed right. She was more like a friend or an older sister. Like a cool older sister who would beat the shit out of anyone who messed with me.

EDEN: That's sweet. Your mom was very protective.

BIANCA: [*Laughs.*] Yeah, you could say that.

EDEN: Were you close with your uncle Leo?

BIANCA: No, definitely not. I knew he was sleeping with my mom and I didn't love that. I never trusted him. The Fontanas always stressed me out. I mean, I guess I'm a Fontana too, but my mom always cared too much what they thought of her. And they didn't treat her so well. And with everything that's happened, it's hard to see them in a positive light. It's hard to see Leo as anything but my mother's murderer. I'm basically an orphan now.

EDEN: I'm so sorry, Bianca.

BIANCA: Thanks, I don't know. I've been worried about my dad killing Leo for years. I just didn't imagine it happening like this.

EDEN: Sounds like a really stressful upbringing.

BIANCA: You think? But seems like yours was stressful too.

EDEN: Don't make me go back there.

BIANCA: Back at you.

EDEN: Okay, so moving forward? What's on the agenda?

BIANCA: Therapy. Community college. Building my brand.

EDEN: Brand?

BIANCA: [*Holds up phone.*] I have an internet brand. It's pretty popular. I can't talk about it right now. Also this whole thing [*gestures to room, to cameras*] feels incredibly weird and low-key traumatic. Can I go?

EDEN: Of course, Bianca. Again, I'm so sorry for your loss.

BIANCA: You too.

ELEVEN

Renee dipped a piece of cheesy bread into marinara sauce. She normally never ate like this, but right now she lacked the energy to control her impulses. It didn't seem to matter if she gained ten pounds. Also, she hadn't been eating much lately. Her mouth salivated as soon as she bit into the gooey bread. She probably needed the calories.

Across from her in a corner booth, Eden wasn't touching the cheesy bread or the mushroom pizza they were sharing. She was on her third gin and tonic and kept disappearing to smoke more. She looked even worse than she had at the Italians Do It Better party— wan, droopy, sallow, especially under the harsh lights of the Olive Garden.

Before this, they'd gone to the police station as planned, although the circumstances had obviously changed from the time of their initial plan—their primary suspects were dead. Nonetheless, Eden had wanted to go, and Renee had wanted a distraction, so they'd met with a surly detective and told him everything they knew: Carmela hated Hope, had been sleeping with her husband, Leo, and had been communicating with Hope's friend Cheyenne, who'd tipped off the FBI to Hope's whereabouts. The detective briefly feigned interest and then said there was nothing he could do. There was still no indication that Hope had died of anything but natural causes. He suggested that she'd maybe overdosed or committed suicide, which upset Eden, who pleaded that her cousin was healthy, didn't do drugs, and would not take her own life. The detective said if there was any suspicion, it pointed to Carmela or possibly Leo, both of whom were deceased. So there was no lead to pursue.

"What about Cheyenne?" Eden had said.

"She was in California," the detective replied. "Nowhere near Hope at the time of her death. I understand the tendency to want someone to pay for the death of your loved one, but I'm afraid there's nothing here."

Eden didn't buy it. She kept saying there *was* something there, she just didn't know it yet.

"I keep thinking about Delilah," Eden said when she came back from her third smoke break. "You know, I reread the Bible passage. I found a digitized version online."

"And?" said Renee, wishing she'd never said anything to Eden about it. She should have known Eden would obsess and read into it things that weren't there.

"You said you thought Cheyenne meant that Hope had betrayed her in some way, which makes sense," Eden said. "But I think Cheyenne used Hope the way the Philistines used Delilah."

Renee nodded but didn't understand. She was also sick of talking about Cheyenne. Eden was checking her phone every ten minutes or so, sometimes every five, to see if Cheyenne had responded to her message. She kept rereading what she'd sent to Cheyenne out loud. *Hi, this is Hope's cousin Eden. I know you were close to Hope. I'm feeling really lost and would love to talk to you about her. Talking to people who knew her helps. I would fly you out to New Jersey if you wanted, or we could just talk on the phone or Zoom. Thanks.*

Eden read it again to Renee, who was frankly sick of hearing the message. She stuffed more cheesy bread down her throat. Eden was bumming her out. Renee missed Ruby. She was still at her dad's, and it made sense, especially with the latest violence. Her dad didn't think Shady Pond was safe right now, and Renee had to agree with him. But she missed Ruby so much. Maybe she should pack her things and drive to New York tonight, get a hotel room for her and Ruby. She could afford it. It wouldn't be as fancy as the places Ruby stayed at on vacation with her dad, but Renee could splurge on a suite in midtown.

"Any reply?" Renee asked. She looked up at a WHEN YOU'RE HERE, YOU'RE FAMILY sign and thought about season one, when Carmela had insulted a former Goddess's Italian cooking by saying, *Haley's as Italian as Olive Garden.* Renee supposed the insult would also apply to herself. She liked the food here and found the kitschy decor soothing. Ruby used to love the garlic knots when she was little. Renee picked up her phone to text her daughter. *Hi honey, how are you?*

Eden shook her head. "No reply," she said, not looking up. "But Shady Di changed its handle to Shady Die." She flipped the phone to show Renee the new spelling.

Renee shivered. "God, that's so creepy." Her own phone buzzed. Ruby had just put a thumbs-up on Renee's text. At least she was alive.

As miserable as Eden was right now, there was something oddly comfortable about her. Renee had known Eden for several years, but this was a new version of Eden—raw, vulnerable. But beyond that, she was a relative of Hope, the person Renee had felt the closest to outside of her own daughter in over a decade. Eden was suddenly the closest Renee could get to Hope. And after several days of spending more time with Eden, Renee was starting to see the similarities between the cousins—their narrow shoulders, delicate features, and laser focus. Hope was focused on her music the way Eden was focused on the show, the way she was now focused on solving the mystery.

"Oh my God," Eden said, staring at her phone.

Renee was sick of asking if Cheyenne had replied, given the answer was always no, but she gave in and asked again.

"No, but it says *seen*," Eden said, again turning the phone to Renee. "She's seen it."

TWELVE

Eden picked up a bottle of red wine from the table and emptied it into her plastic cup until it was nearly overflowing. She hated wine, especially red wine, but apparently Carmela had left detailed instructions as to what was going to be served at her funeral, and the only alcohol was her favorite varietal of red wine. She'd also indicated that the reception was to be held at Italians Do It Better and designed to her specifications. Shadows danced over black tablecloths as gold candelabras flickered, casting an eerie glow. Crimson drapery hung heavily, a morose reminder of the violence that had stained the salon only a few days ago.

Eden had never been to a nail salon funeral. In fact, she'd never been to a funeral period until Hope's. She'd certainly never been to a funeral in the very location where the deceased had been murdered. Eden gulped her wine. She couldn't remember what number glass this was, but she was starting to taste it less. With every sip, the room around her blurred just a little more, the voices becoming a faint hum, which was exactly what she wanted.

"Eden," a voice said, unfortunately not a hum. Eden turned to see Aria in a black suit, her bob shinier than usual. "You look like shit."

"Thanks," Eden said. "At least I kind of have an excuse." She gulped more wine.

"Do you?" said Aria. "When my dad died, I didn't take any time off, didn't cancel a single meeting. And we were close, much closer than you and your estranged cousin."

"Congratulations," Eden said. "You don't have a heart." Another gulp. "I do."

"You do?" Aria asked. "Fooled me."

Eden finished off the wine, ignoring Aria. She didn't want to be here, at a funeral for the woman who'd likely killed her cousin, talking to her heartless boss, who was making her feel worse. She looked around for Renee, her only recent source of comfort. But Eden didn't see Renee. Valerie was surrounded by family, huddled close with Carmela's daughter, Bianca. Their faces looked blank, or maybe Eden was projecting. They were probably all in shock. Birdie was using a handsome young waiter to stand. But no Renee.

"I have some good news for you," Aria said. "The season is scrapped." She gestured around the room. "Apparently all this is too macabre for even Huzzah, the most heartless network, for heartless women like ourselves."

Aria put her arm around Eden. This was the first time Aria had ever touched her. A few weeks ago, the act would have *delighted* Eden, such physical closeness between herself and her hero. But now, Aria's bony arm felt like death. These days, everything felt like death.

Eden wriggled out of Aria's skeletal grip to refill her wine cup. Down the table, she spotted a woman who seemed out of place. Eden didn't recognize a lot of people here, but most of them fit into the same familiar genres: new-money Italian Americans, flashy nail salon employees, Goddesses, jaded Huzzah employees. But this woman didn't fit into any of these categories. She had caramel-colored hair nearly down to her waist and wore faded jeans and a prairie blouse of the variety Hope used to wear. But she had more swagger than Hope. Her body slinked as it moved. Was she wearing cowboy boots? Maybe she was a contestant on Huzzah's *Survivor* knockoff.

"Was she on *Feral*?" Eden asked Aria as the woman walked off to the buffet.

Aria squinted in the woman's direction. "I don't think so," she said. "Why, do you have a crush? She's pretty." Aria craned her neck to follow the woman. "And there's an ass on her, damn. Maybe I should get her on *Feral*."

"She's familiar," Eden said.

"Tinder?" Aria said. She was frisky today. Aria was probably one of those strange people who was so typically joyless and wound up that funerals provided a sense of levity. Had she been like this at Hope's? Had she even attended Hope's funeral? Eden couldn't remember. It was a blur.

The mystery woman turned toward them and Eden nearly choked.

"Your Tinder crush is looking at us," said Aria.

Eden remembered to breathe. She knew exactly who this woman was. She looked back at Aria and whispered, "Cheyenne."

"You think she's Native American?" Aria whispered back. "Or do we say American Indian now? I can never fucking keep track."

"No, no," Eden whispered. "Hope's mystery friend from back home. Her ex, I think."

The woman was now talking to someone Eden didn't recognize, maybe a Fontana cousin, engaged in a conversation as if she belonged.

"Hold up, Hope was a lesbo?" Aria said. "I knew she was hiding something, but I didn't realize she was a murderer *and* a lesbian. She's a regular Aileen Wuornos. God, I really wish they hadn't canned the season. This is TV gold."

"You know Carmela was in contact with Cheyenne," Eden said.

"Like . . . from the dead?" Aria said.

Eden sighed. She had no ability to enjoy Aria's bleak humor, if you could even call it that.

"They were messaging on Instagram while Carmela was alive," Eden explained. "She was messaging Valerie too. Valerie tipped Cheyenne off to Hope's location at Chateau Blanche, and Cheyenne tipped off the cops."

"Hold up," said Aria. "Let me get this straight: Cheyenne is Hope's ex from Buttfuck, California—no offense. And she was messaging Carmela and Valerie, for what purpose? Because Cheyenne knew Hope was a killer and wanted to help the police find her? Jesus, this is good."

"It is not good," Eden said. She was beginning to wonder, was Aria a sociopath? Was Eden? One thing Eden knew: Hope was not a killer. "Hope was not a killer," she repeated to Aria.

"That's not what the FBI says," Aria said.

Aria was pissing her off. Eden said she needed to go to the bathroom, but Aria grabbed her arm before she could get away.

"Wait," Aria said. "Get her in a confessional. The Native American. Or American Indian, whatever."

"You said the season is canceled," Eden said. "And her name is Cheyenne. She is not a member of the Cheyenne tribe."

"You don't know that," said Aria. "Anyway, I think the show is scrapped, yes, but nothing is set in stone."

Eden tried to get away. She didn't want to have this conversation.

Aria gripped Eden's hand harder. "Wait, Eden," Aria said. "You have a gift. I've seen the way you work in confessionals. If I hadn't poached you, the FBI would have. You uncovered that Birdie doesn't have a yacht, that the chick from season one went to Berkeley College in Newark, not UC Berkeley, as she'd previously led people to believe, and you uncovered that the vajazzler was embezzling funds."

"I haven't solved a murder," Eden said. But she wanted to.

"You could," said Aria.

Eden freed herself and went to the bathroom.

But on the way, someone stopped her.

Part Four

Receipts! Proof! Timeline! Screenshots!

—HEATHER GAY, *REAL HOUSEWIVES OF SALT LAKE CITY*

CONFESSIONAL TRANSCRIPT – *GARDEN STATE GODDESSES*
(SEASON 3)
CHEYENNE GREEN

EDEN: Can you state your full name?

CHEYENNE: Cheyenne River Green.

EDEN: Hippie parents?

CHEYENNE: [*Laughs*.] The apple doesn't fall far.

EDEN: Okay, let's cut to the chase. Can you tell me the
nature of your relationship with Hope Fontana?

CHEYENNE: Well, I knew her as Hope Bennett.

EDEN: Right.

CHEYENNE: That's your last name too, right?

EDEN: [*Nods.*]

CHEYENNE: I moved to Weed after my divorce. My ex, well, he
was violent. We don't have to get into it, but I needed
a fresh start. So I drove a few towns over to Weed.

EDEN: What town did you come from?

CHEYENNE: Yreka.

EDEN: I dated a guy from there.

CHEYENNE: Oh yeah? I probably know him. What's his name?

EDEN: God, it was so long ago. Mike? I know that's not
helpful.

CHEYENNE: Did he play baseball?

EDEN: He was in a band. I didn't really mess with jocks.
Anyway, does your ex still live in Yreka?

CHEYENNE: [*Shrugs*.] Who knows. I changed my number. Haven't
seen or heard from him in years.

EDEN: So you arrive in Weed.

CHEYENNE: Yes, I rented a studio apartment in town. I had
some savings, so I wasn't super worried about money.
I didn't need a job right away. I was lonely though. I
found out about Brother God, so I went to a meeting.
I met Hope, who suggested I join the choir. Everything
changed then.

EDEN: Tell me about that.

CHEYENNE: Hope was one of a kind, you know? She had this

angelic vibe, pure and bright. I could tell she'd seen
shit, same as me. It's strange, but I felt this call to
protect her.

EDEN: Is that why you ratted her out to the police?

CHEYENNE: What?

EDEN: According to Valerie Dulce, you'd been communicating
with Valerie and Carmela over direct message.

CHEYENNE: Yes. Hope disappeared without a trace. She was
the love of my life. I was distraught. She wouldn't
answer my calls, and then she blocked my number. I was
about to give up on finding her when my friend, a fan of
the show, messaged me a photo of Hope with Valerie and
Carmela. So I instantly reached out to Carmela.

EDEN: Valerie said you referred to Hope as "your Delilah."

CHEYENNE: [Smiling.] Yes. Delilah was quite the seductress.

EDEN: She was a traitor.

CHEYENNE: Depends on what side you're on.

EDEN: Are you Samson in this metaphor?

CHEYENNE: God, no. I have no special strength. I'm weak.
[Flexes muscle.] I'm probably a Philistine.

EDEN: I figured. So on the night Hope was killed, you were
apparently in contact with Valerie. She told you where
Hope was, and then the FBI showed up, to arrest her for
murder. But she was already dead.

CHEYENNE: I was trying to warn Hope, not rat her out. The
FBI had been looking for Hope since her parents were
killed. She apparently got rid of all her cards, so it
was hard at first. She changed her last name too. But
then she was suddenly affiliated with this popular show
on Instagram. The cops probably found her the same way
I did.

EDEN: The night the FBI showed up, they said they'd been in
contact with you. That you'd tipped them off to Hope's
whereabouts.

CHEYENNE: They were lying. You know cops lie. They probably
breached some ethical rule to get the information and
used me as a coverup.

EDEN: ACAB, et cetera.

CHEYENNE: Right, exactly.

EDEN: I'm going to have a smoke. Hold tight?

CHEYENNE: Can I bum one?

EDEN: Sure.

ONE

Eden knew there was something off with Cheyenne River Green from the minute she walked up to her at Carmela's funeral. Yes, Eden had asked her to come to New Jersey, but she'd expected Cheyenne to at least respond to her message before showing up at a random woman's funeral. Cheyenne had chutzpah. It was probably what Hope had been attracted to. Eden wondered if bad romantic taste was a family trait.

Cheyenne obviously wanted to share a cigarette to get Eden on her side. But Eden wasn't buying it. Outside of the studio, she handed Cheyenne a cigarette, then went off to her car to call Renee. Eden drove around the block while she called, making sure Cheyenne wouldn't hear.

"What do you have so far?" Renee said. Renee had left Carmela's funeral early, feeling overwhelmed with grief and hurt and confusion, so she hadn't seen Cheyenne. But Eden had called her afterward, and Renee had been intrigued, perhaps catching the bug of solving this mystery to avoid her feelings, her lost friends, and daughter at her dad's. Renee said Hope had told her a lot about Cheyenne, so she would be on call to fact-check Cheyenne's statements.

"She said her full name is Cheyenne River Green," Eden began. "She fled an abusive relationship in Yreka for Weed, then met Hope at Brother God."

"Yreka?" Renee said. "Hope said Cheyenne was from Mount Shasta."

"You sure? That's on the other side of Weed."

"Positive," said Renee.

"She said she didn't tip off the police to Hope's whereabouts," Eden said. "But the police told me they'd been directed to Chateau Blanche via a DM from Cheyenne Green."

"Are *you* sure?"

"I wish I could block out that night," Eden said. "But unfortunately, that dialogue is crystalized in my brain."

"Did you call her out?"

"Yes, she said the police are lying," Eden said. "ACAB, etc."

"Shady," said Renee. "Did you ask her about her messages with Carmela and Valerie?"

"She said she was trying to find Hope," Eden said, rounding the corner back toward the parking lot. "And she said the night at Chateau Blanche, she was trying to warn Hope, not tip off the FBI."

"Shady shady," Renee said.

"It's almost like you live in a place called Shady Pond," Eden said.

Renee laughed. She had a nice laugh, like a bell. For a moment it reminded Eden what it was like to think about something other than death. But as soon as she stopped laughing, the thoughts of death returned. As she parked, Eden watched Cheyenne chatting up Caleb outside of the studio. Eden tightened her fingers around the steering wheel.

Time to skewer this creep.

CONFESSIONAL TRANSCRIPT - *GARDEN STATE GODDESSES*

(SEASON 3)

CHEYENNE GREEN

EDEN: Ready to pick it back up?

CHEYENNE: [*Nods.*]

EDEN: You said you're from Yreka?

CHEYENNE: [*Nods.*]

EDEN: Hope said you were from Mount Shasta. That's the opposite direction on I-5.

CHEYENNE: [*Laughs.*] I know. I've lived in Northern California my whole life; I know its freeways better than the veins on my own hand. Hope was a spacy one, wasn't she? Not the best listener.

EDEN: So you think Hope didn't know where you were from?

CHEYENNE: I think it's possible she got confused. She was often confused.

EDEN: Okay, let's go back to your conversations with the police. What was the extent of them?

CHEYENNE: [*Exhales.*] Well, as you know, Hope and I were in a relationship. It was both of our first relationship with a woman, which was strictly forbidden by Brother God. That was less of a big deal to me, as I'd only just joined Brother God, mostly for friends and for the choir. But it was a *huge* deal to Hope. She loved her parents and didn't want to bring shame to the family. But then they found out. And not long after that, their house was burned down, killing them. It didn't look good. The police came to me early, not long after the fire was discovered.

EDEN: Why did it take so long to discover the fire? Couldn't they have been saved?

CHEYENNE: Hope's parents lived deep in the woods. Their closest neighbor was half a mile away.

EDEN: The trailer?

CHEYENNE: What? No, they had a regular house. It was small but cozy. All wood, though.

208   ASTRID DAHL

EDEN: So what did the police ask you?

CHEYENNE: They asked if I knew anything about the fire. I
said no, I found out when they did, probably after. They
asked where Hope was. I said I didn't know. I couldn't
reach her. They asked if she had any animosity toward
her parents, and I told them no, she loved her parents.
I thought it was crazy to think that Hope would hurt
anyone. They asked about Hope's parents being upset
about her relationship with me, which I couldn't deny.
They were upset. They had a fight. But that didn't make
Hope violent. They didn't have anything else to point to
but Hope, I guess.

EDEN: Couldn't the fire have been accidental?

CHEYENNE: The cops said the smoke alarm was disabled. And
I guess they found residue of gasoline. But, you know,
cops lie.

EDEN: Who would have killed them?

CHEYENNE: Brother God had enemies. I mean, I don't have to
tell you this. Sorry for your loss, by the way. I know
Hope's parents were your aunt and uncle.

EDEN: We weren't close. So you don't think it was Hope?

CHEYENNE: I don't know. I meant, her parents did some really
awful things to her. You know this, Eden. No one wants
to believe the love of their life killed their parents.
But if she did: I wouldn't blame her.

EDEN: Sorry, I'm disgusting, but I need another cig.

CHEYENNE: You aren't, no problem. This is heavy.

TWO

Renee hadn't googled the fire until now. She wished she hadn't, but now she had. She'd seen the house burnt to a crisp, imagined Hope's parents burning to death, their cries for help. Hope had said her parents could be scary people, but no one deserved to die that way. The sound of her phone ringing jolted her from her frightening thoughts. She shut her laptop and answered the phone.

"Hey, Eden," Renee said.

"Um, it's Valerie?" said the voice, as if she wasn't sure who she was. Renee had just assumed it was Eden. Valerie never called Renee unless it had to do with filming. Why was she calling?

"Oh, sorry," Renee said. "Eden said she'd call me back, so I thought it was her. How are you, Valerie?" Renee figured Valerie must be distraught with Carmela gone, her younger brother gone, and her older brother being charged with his murder.

"Oh, up and down," Valerie said. "Luckily I'm not the world's deepest person." She laughed. "I don't feel things as strongly as C or Leo did. My dad always says talking to me is like talking to a wall." She sighed. "But Carmela was my best friend. Leo was my brother. And I do miss them. I don't think it's fully sunk in, though. Maybe it never will. I meant it in my season one tagline when I said, 'They say ignorance is bliss, and I love being a ditz.'

I obviously didn't come up with that, I never could have, but I stand by it."

"I'm so sorry, Valerie," Renee said. "I miss them too."

"You think Carmela killed Hope, don't you?" Valerie asked.

The bluntness of the question startled Renee. "No," Renee said. "Eden does, but I don't."

"She didn't," Valerie said. "Trust. *Giuoro su Dio*, she didn't want Hope dead. She just didn't like her. But Carmela loves having an enemy. Honestly, I think she liked having someone to be rude to all the time."

Renee paused, considering this. Valerie wasn't the most trustworthy, especially when it came to Carmela, but Renee agreed that Carmela wasn't a killer. She was more bark than bite. And she loved barking. And Valerie was probably right that she enjoyed being able to berate Hope without consequence.

"She was jealous of Hope, though, right? Because Carmela was in love with Leo?"

Valerie cackled. "Carmela was not in love with my brother, at least not that one. She slept with him, but I don't think she loved him. I mean, you saw them interact. She hated him! And he hated her too." She paused. "I mean, he freaking murdered her, didn't he?" Oddly, Valerie started laughing. "Manny says I have a very strange response to trauma."

Valerie was making more sense than she ever had. If Carmela had wanted Leo, she could have picked him over Dino in the beginning. Clearly, she'd wanted both of them. And she'd wanted to torture Leo. And she'd done it until he killed her.

"Why were you talking to Eden?" Valerie asked. "The show's in the can, isn't it? Don't tell me you're, like, friends with that workaholic freak."

Renee laughed, easing a tightness in her chest. "Eden seems altered by Hope's death somehow. Softer. She feels really guilty," she said, finding a small shard of solace in the shared absurdity of grief.

"Eden has feelings?"

"I think so," Renee said, suddenly doubting herself. After all, she'd fallen for someone who'd maybe burned her parents alive. So maybe she wasn't the best judge of character. "She's talking to Cheyenne right now. Did you see her at Carmela's funeral? I didn't—I skipped the reception—but I can't believe she showed."

"Oh my *God*," Valerie said. "That was so freaking weird. I was like, who is this Earth goddess with the haunted green eyes? She certainly ain't Italian and I know she ain't from Jersey. Carmela wasn't friends with women like that."

"Friends like what?" Renee asked.

"Tall, gorgeous, thin, hair down to her butt—and I don't think those were extensions. I was looking for tracks."

Jealousy swirled inside Renee. She knew it was dumb, but she'd worried and suspected that Cheyenne was some kind of vision. What did it matter now, though? Hope was dead, and likely a killer.

"Let's be honest," Valerie continued. "We all know Carmela kept me around because I wasn't a threat."

Renee said, "Oh, Valerie, of course that's not true," even though it absolutely was true.

"Why is Eden talking to Cheyenne?"

"She's trying to get information," Renee said. "I think her grief is manifesting in an obsession with finding out who killed Hope, with getting clues, with clearing Hope's name on the death of her parents."

"I don't think Hope killed her parents either," Valerie said.

"You don't?"

"Nope," Valerie said. "Carmela didn't either. You know she had really good intuition, like the psychic said."

"But she always said Hope was shady, that she was hiding something," Renee said.

"Yeah, hiding that she was gay as a Pride flag." Valerie laughed.

Renee's cheeks felt suddenly hot. What did Valerie know?

"And fled a cult, et cetera," Valerie continued. "Not that she killed her parents."

Renee's phone buzzed. Another call was coming in.

"Eden's calling," Renee said. "I have to get this."

"Please call me after," Valerie said. "A distraction would be lovely."

"Will do," Renee said, and switched the calls.

"Are you busy?" said Eden.

"No, no," Renee said. "I was just on the phone with Valerie."

"Oh yeah?" Eden asked, her voice perking up. "How's she doing?"

"Oh, you know," Renee said. "Typical Valerie. She's making jokes and pretending she's fine. Although she did tell me that Carmela didn't love Leo."

Eden paused. "Interesting."

"Oh, also," Renee continued, "Valerie doesn't think Hope killed her parents. Carmela didn't either." Renee felt comforted saying these words out loud. She really wanted to believe that Hope hadn't killed anyone.

"Well, that makes three of us," Eden said.

"What's up in Cheyenne land?" Renee asked, not even knowing why she made the silly rhyme. Maybe to minimize Cheyenne's apparently otherworldly beauty.

"She's suggesting Hope killed her parents," Eden said. "I don't trust her. I think she's trying to get the heat off herself."

"You think she did it?" Renee asked. "But why?"

"She said Hope was the love of her life," Eden said.

Renee swallowed. More jealousy. This would be the time to tell Eden. She probably couldn't hide it much longer. But she was worried Eden would put the blame on Renee. The real spurned lover. The uglier, frumpier one.

"Hello?" Eden said.

Renee realized she'd zoned out. "I have to tell you something," she said.

"I'm listening," Eden said.

"Hope and me," Renee said. "We became, well . . . romantic."

"Oh, I suspected that," Eden said.

Renee exhaled.

"I was hoping to make the season about that, actually," Eden said. She laughed. It was nice to hear her laugh.

"Oh God," Renee said. "It all seems so silly now."

"It does," Eden said. "Anyway, I figured that's why you were hurting so much. Because you loved her."

Renee swallowed. She hadn't exactly used that language, certainly not to Hope's face, not even with herself.

But it was absolutely true.

"So I called Cheyenne out on Yreka," Eden continued. "She blamed Hope for mistaking Yreka and Mount Shasta, basically called her dumb."

"What a bitch," Renee said.

"You're jealous, aren't you?" Eden said.

Renee sighed.

"Don't worry," Eden said. "You're much prettier."

This was more comforting to Renee than it should have been.

"Valerie said she's a vision," Renee said.

"She takes up a lot of space," Eden said. "She has freaky energy. Like a butch witch. It's not cute. Also, I'm pretty sure she's a murderer." She laughed.

"Oh, right," Renee said, laughing too. "There's that." It felt so good to be laughing.

"Okay, I'm going back," Eden said. "Wish me luck."

"Break a leg," Renee said.

EDEN: So, you contacted Valerie to warn Hope that the police were after her?

CHEYENNE: Correct.

EDEN: But you suggested that it's possible that Hope killed her parents?

CHEYENNE: Anything is possible. People can be pushed to their limits.

EDEN: You think Hope, the love of your life, could have been a killer?

CHEYENNE: Not under normal circumstances. I think if she did it, there's an argument that it was self-defense. Maybe not legally, but . . . you know what Brother God was like, Eden. I was new and really only involved in the choir, so they were relatively nice to me. But Hope told me what she'd gone through. We'd been doing inner-child work to get her in touch with her trauma. It might have unleashed something.

EDEN: So you think your inner-child work might have stirred up something violent in Hope?

CHEYENNE: It can happen.

EDEN: And you think my aunt and uncle deserved to die?

CHEYENNE: No one deserves to die. But some people are very dangerous. I'm sorry, Eden, but you know they did some really awful things.

EDEN: Did you tell all this to the police?

CHEYENNE: Of course not. I want to protect Hope's name. I want to find out what happened to her. Who killed her. That's why I'm here.

EDEN: Do you have any ideas? About who killed Hope?

CHEYENNE: You're the one who brought her into all this mess.

EDEN: Are you saying I had a hand in my own cousin's death?

CHEYENNE: Anything is possible.

THREE

Valerie was calling again. Renee closed her laptop, where she'd been staring at photos of the burned-down cabin.

"My cousin gave me her Whitepages account," Valerie said. "She stalks all her boyfriends and their exes and really everyone. She's completely nuts, but she's basically a PI, if you need any info. What's Cheyenne's full name again? I can look her up."

"Cheyenne Green, I think. That's what she told Eden anyway," Renee said. "Yreka, California. Or Mount Shasta, California. Or neither, I'm not actually sure. We think she was lying about where she came from. Also try Weed, California. She definitely lived there."

"Okay," Valerie said. Renee heard typing. She opened her laptop and googled *Cheyenne Green*. The first ten search results were about a paint color. It was really ugly, sort of a puke or bile color.

"I'm not finding a Cheyenne Green in Yreka or Mount Shasta," Valerie said, pronouncing it Yreka *Y-reka*. "Not in Weed either. Hope's hometown was really called Weed?" Valerie laughed.

"Yep," Renee said.

"I'm so legitimately sad that Carmela died before learning that." Valerie laughed again, then stopped. More typing. "So I can't find any Cheyenne Green in California. I'm texting my cousin now. She said if there's no record of a Cheyenne Green in California, she's probably using a fake name. I mean, it sounds made up, doesn't it?"

"Yeah," Renee said. "When I googled it, the only thing that came up was a paint color."

"Oh my God, I know, right?" Valerie said. "Vomit color. Nasty. Imagine choosing to paint your walls the color of puke."

Renee laughed.

"My cousin thinks Cheyenne was on the run when she came to Weed," Valerie said. "Why did Cheyenne say she came there?"

"She told Hope and Eden that she fled an abusive husband," Renee said. "Maybe she unofficially changed her name after the divorce, which is why there's no record?"

"Maybe," Valerie said. More typing. "But I don't trust her. My cousin thinks she might have done something to her husband. She has good instincts about these things. She said we should look to see if there's a similar, fire-related death in Northern California, or anywhere in California, at around the time Cheyenne moved to Weed."

"You really think that's possible?" Renee said. "Seems a little crazy." Then Renee remembered Hope's husband was a killer—he'd killed Carmela. Was it so shocking that her ex was also a killer? Maybe Hope was drawn to violent types and that was why it hadn't worked out between them.

"Again, my cousin tends to be right about these things. She majored in forensic science in college," Valerie said, "and now spends like all her time watching true crime instead of watching her kids." She let out a tiny laugh, then paused. "Do you know when Cheyenne got to Weed?"

"I don't," Renee said. "Eden's talking to her now. I'll text her."

CONFESSIONAL TRANSCRIPT – *GARDEN STATE GODDESSES*
(SEASON 3)
CHEYENNE GREEN

EDEN: That's a heavy accusation.

CHEYENNE: I didn't accuse you of anything. I just said anything is possible. It is, isn't it?

EDEN: [*Looks at phone. Pauses.*]

CHEYENNE: Everything okay?

EDEN: Yup. When did you say you moved to Weed?

CHEYENNE: Um, let me think. About four years before I met Hope? In 2018, I think?

EDEN: Got it. [*Pauses, looks at phone.*] So there's no record of a Cheyenne Green in California.

CHEYENNE: Oh, well, that's not my legal name. It's not on my birth certificate or anything.

EDEN: What's your legal name?

CHEYENNE: I changed it for protection. From my husband.

EDEN: You said your hippie parents named you.

CHEYENNE: The Cheyenne and River parts, yes. But Green is my husband's name.

EDEN: If Green was your married name, then there should be a record under that, right?

CHEYENNE: I didn't vote. I didn't want to get jury duty. My parents raised me to not trust the government. We were off the grid.

EDEN: Right. [*Looks at phone.*]

FOUR

Renee, Valerie, and Valerie's rando cousin whom Renee was beginning to suspect didn't exist were all feverishly googling *arson Northern California 2018*.

"Holy fucking shit," said Valerie.

"What?"

Valerie's voice sharpened as she began to read, "In 2018, Randy Cates's residence in Chico, California, was consumed by fire as he slept. Evidence of gasoline at the scene hinted at arson, but no arrests followed. Suspicion circled Cates's ex-wife, Audrey Kincaid, but there was insufficient evidence to sustain an arrest." Valerie paused; said, "Holy fucking shit," again; then continued reading. "Kincaid vanished shortly after the fire was discovered, prompting a search. A public appeal for her whereabouts remains ongoing." She stopped reading and said, "There's a photo at the bottom and a plea for information."

"And? Can you see the photo?"

Valerie unleashed a discordant laugh. "I sure can."

CHEYENNE: Is everything okay? Do you need to take a call? I don't mind if you need to take another break.

EDEN: All good. [*Pauses.*] Does the name Randy Cates ring a bell to you?

CHEYENNE: [*Shakes head.*] Nope. Why?

EDEN: He died similarly to how Hope's parents died. Fire in the middle of the night. Remnants of gasoline.

CHEYENNE: I imagine it's not uncommon.

EDEN: Death by arson?

CHEYENNE: [*Shrugs.*]

EDEN: It happened in Chico, California. Not too far from Weed. And in 2018, around the time you arrived in Weed. Around the time the main suspect in the fire disappeared.

CHEYENNE: Small world.

EDEN: I don't think it's a coincidence.

CHEYENNE: Yeah?

EDEN: I have a picture of the suspect, Audrey Kincaid, and, well . . . it's you.

CHEYENNE: [*Laughs.*] I have a familiar face. I get this all the time.

EDEN: Caleb, come here. [*Footsteps.*] [*Shows Caleb phone.*] This is a photo of the person right in front of you, right?

CALEB: [*Clears throat.*] That's . . . that's her.

CHEYENNE: It's a strange coincidence, nothing more. [*Laughs.*] You're both reaching.

EDEN: Seems like more than a coincidence.

CHEYENNE: Look, even if I was this person in the photo, which I'm not, it doesn't necessarily tie me to any crimes.

EDEN: Like the Philistines used Delilah, you used Hope to get to her parents and kill them?

CHEYENNE: When I called her Delilah, I just meant she's hot.

EDEN: Hot like the fire you started, Cheyenne, or should I say Audrey?

CHEYENNE: You should say Cheyenne because that's who I am. Can we just move on to who killed Hope? That's why I'm here, to find out what happened to her. I loved her.

EDEN: Loved her so much you wanted to kill her evil parents?

CHEYENNE: I wanted to protect her. I didn't want her to suffer anymore. I wanted to give her the freedom to be herself.

[*Distant sirens.*]

CHEYENNE: I came here to help.

EDEN: Just like you helped Hope by killing her parents?

CHEYENNE: I wanted her to be free.

[*Sirens grow louder.*]

FIVE

Snow started to fall in tiny flakes as Renee drove to Birdie's. Birdie had invited Renee over the other day to "process" all that had happened—Hope dying at Chateau Blanche, Carmela and Leo being murdered at Carmela's nail salon, and Hope's ex-lover being charged with the murder of Hope's parents.

Catching Cheyenne had been a thrill. After they'd found the photo of the suspected arsonist on the run who was identical to Cheyenne, it had seemed obvious that Cheyenne—or *Audrey*, rather—had started the fire that killed Hope's parents. Since the Chico police had put a call out for her whereabouts, Valerie immediately called them and alerted them to Audrey Kincaid's location at the studio in Moonachie, New Jersey. The Chico police coordinated with Moonachie police, who sent a squad car to the studios, where Eden had nearly gotten Audrey to confess—on camera! It all felt like a movie.

The FBI was involved because Audrey had crossed state lines to flee numerous felonies, and the FBI, along with the Chico and Weed police stations, were currently deciding whether to consolidate the charges of her ex-husband's murders and Hope's parents' murders and figuring out where to try her. Valerie said that wherever she was tried, they should watch. She said it was possible that they'd be called as witnesses given their involvement. Renee still couldn't believe that Valerie had helped clear Hope's name. Ultimately it made Renee sad, knowing that Hope wasn't alive to see herself redeemed. But Renee was also wildly relieved to learn she hadn't been sleeping with a killer. She hadn't admitted this to anyone out loud, but this was by far the most satisfying part of the Cheyenne revelation to her. Hope had been good, just like Renee knew she was. But in some ways, this fact made Hope's death that much harder, propelling Renee to really grieve, especially now that the thrill of hunting Cheyenne was over. She swallowed down the tears that were always lingering in her throat these days, ready to burst free, as she wound up Birdie's very long driveway.

For maybe the first time in three years, Birdie herself answered the door. "Pierre's out riding," Birdie said. "Tuesday and Thursday afternoons I'm all alone." She laughed. "Well, this is typically when I have my gentleman callers, but today it's just you, my dear," Birdie said. "Although I know you like the ladies." She winked and Renee smiled awkwardly. Birdie led Renee into the kitchen, where Luz was reading a tabloid.

"Smoothie time?" Luz got up and removed a clear tumbler of a purple smoothie from the fridge.

"Can I offer you a smoothie, dear?" Birdie asked. "Pierre is on my ass to get more protein. Or fiber?"

"Protein," said Luz, opening the fridge.

"I can never remember." Birdie took a sip. "They're really delicious though."

Watching snow fall outside the massive kitchen windows, Renee thought it seemed a little cold for a smoothie, but she didn't want to be rude. "Sure," Renee said. "A smoothie sounds great."

Luz handed Renee her smoothie, which was beside several identical tumblers in the fridge, and they went to sit in a room Renee had never been in before. It had wood-paneled walls and a big fireplace in which a fire was currently burning, its flames casting the room in orange light. It was cozy until Renee thought about Hope's parents. These days, Renee couldn't look at a fire without seeing people burning to death. She couldn't look at a nail salon without thinking of someone getting stabbed to death. And being in Birdie's house for the first time since the Broke Not Broken party also made her think of death. She tried to stop thinking of death as she sat across from Birdie in a plush hunter green chair.

"How are you feeling, dear?" Birdie asked. "I know you and Hope were close."

Renee took a sip of her smoothie before answering. The sensation of the cool blended drink combined with the warmth of the fire was a pleasant contrast. And Birdie was right, it was tasty. Blueberry and vanilla. "I'm okay," Renee said. "It felt good to catch Cheyenne—or Audrey, rather—and clear Hope's name." She swallowed. The smoothie had a strange aftertaste. Chemical.

"Good, isn't it?" Birdie said, holding up her tumbler.

Renee nodded, holding up her own, and they clinked tumblers. Renee took another sip. Same thing. Pleasant, then acrid.

"I knew that girl wasn't a killer," Birdie said. "She had a heart of gold."

"I know," Renee said. "Hope was a great girl."

"She really was," Birdie said. "I miss her terribly. We were becoming close ourselves, you know."

"Hope loved you," Renee said, although she wasn't sure if it were true. They'd never really talked about Birdie, or the show in general, when they were together.

Birdie looked behind Renee, as if making sure they were alone. "I spoke with my lawyer shortly before she died," she said. "Well, one of them—I have six." Her voice was lower now, so low that Renee had to lean in to hear. Birdie turned around and scanned her surroundings again. Renee remembered the psychic had said someone was after Birdie's money. Although Renee supposed that when you were as rich as Birdie, there was always someone after your money.

When Birdie continued to speak, no sound came out. Renee tried and failed to read her lips.

"Sorry, Birdie," Renee said. "I can't hear you."

Birdie leaned in close to Renee, so close her lips were almost touching Renee's ear. Her breath was hot and smelled of something rotten. Renee supposed it was the aftertaste of whatever they were drinking.

"I put Hope in my will, dear," Birdie whispered.

Renee blinked in disbelief, certain she'd misheard. She leaned in and asked Birdie to repeat herself. Birdie then said exactly what Renee had heard the first time: that Birdie had put Hope in her will. And she added that she had been planning to leave Hope "quite a lot."

"She was the spitting image of myself at her age," Birdie continued. "I couldn't help but see myself in her. She was like the daughter I always wanted."

Renee smiled, unsure what to say. It seemed odd, especially to say about someone she'd only known a few months, but Birdie was nothing if not odd.

"Ever since Pierre's father died unexpectedly," Birdie continued, "I've been very meticulous about my affairs." She sat up, suddenly businesslike.

"That makes sense," Renee said. "I'm so sorry about your husband," she continued, suddenly remembering all of the rumors on Shady Di—or Shady Die, rather—accusing Birdie of being responsible for his death. Renee really hated that account. She still was trying not to look at it, but sometimes she got an itch she couldn't help but scratch. Last night, Shady Die had accused Leo of sleeping with many more women than just Carmela. Renee thought it was possibly true, but very tasteless of the account to speak poorly of the dead. Leo was such a people-pleaser, he'd hate to be spoken about this way after his death. Although Leo *had* killed someone, Renee remembered—but only to avenge his wife's death. Her head spun with the moral implications of it all. Had she lost her ability to tell right from wrong?

"It was a horrible tragedy I'll never get over," Birdie said. "But that's life, isn't it?"

Renee nodded. She felt loose suddenly, maybe from the coziness of the room or the sugar from the smoothie. "You know," she said, feeling like she just had to get the truth off her chest to someone who wasn't Eden, "Hope and I were together. Before she died."

"Oh, I had a feeling," Birdie said, giggling. "I watched you two. Quite a lot of *yeux doux*, if you get my drift."

Renee felt embarrassed. Was the affair that obvious? That someone as out to lunch as Birdie picked up on it?

"*Yeux doux*?" Renee asked.

"Sweet eyes, my dear," Birdie said. "Puppy love." She sighed. "I just *love* love."

She picked up her smoothie and clinked Renee's tumbler again.

"Dead lovers' club," Birdie said.

And the two of them, oddly, broke out into hysterical laughter.

Then Birdie fell out of her chair.

SIX

Eden was watching footage on her laptop, still trying to place the final piece of the puzzle—*who killed Hope?*—when Aria called. Eden didn't want to answer, but reluctance gave in to loneliness, a desire to talk to someone other than the harrowing voices inside her own head.

"Eden," Aria preempted Eden's greeting, per usual.

"What's up?" Eden said.

"*What's up?*" Aria echoed, accompanied by muffled sounds in the background suggesting she was rummaging through something. "You snag a murder confession and become a skater boy? What about, *How are you, Aria?* I liked when you sang my name. That felt more appropriate. Not professional, exactly, but charming."

Eden sighed. Aria's quips, once amusing, were now just annoying.

"Aren't you going crazy not working? Climbing the walls yet?" Aria asked, her attention clearly split—Eden heard cabinets opening and closing. "I'd be going crazy. I'm surprised you haven't gatecrashed my office yet, wide-eyed and begging for a spot on *Yacht Wars*." Aria giggled in a way that sounded sadistic. She knew that back when Eden was ambitious—just a few weeks ago, but it felt like an eternity—she'd wanted *Manhattan Muses*, not a third-tier show like *Yacht Wars*. But Eden wasn't thinking about any of that right now.

"I'm trying to focus," Eden said.

"Coming up with new show ideas? Something about your amateur sleuthing?" There was a clink of glass, a pour—Aria was mixing a drink. "Pitch me, baby."

"Not show ideas," said Eden. "I'm trying to rewatch footage, trying to solve the murder."

"Ah, got it," Aria said. "I still think Huzzah should air the season. Not my decision to cancel it, for the record. But again, nothing is set in stone. You solve another murder, and I think we're back on the table. Your work with the Native American was absolutely incredible."

"Again, she is not actually a member of an Indian tribe," Eden clarified. "And her name isn't even Cheyenne—it's Audrey Kincaid."

"Audrey Kincaid. That's an incredible name," Aria said. "Star quality. Why would she change that?"

"Because she was wanted for murder," said Eden.

"Oh, right." Aria laughed. "Anyway, I think this sleuthing would make a great show."

"I'm not doing this for television," Eden said. "I want justice for my cousin." Eden still wasn't convinced that Audrey Kincaid hadn't killed Hope, who knew the truth (Audrey had apparently told Hope about the fire she'd set just before Hope bolted), to save herself. Sure, Audrey hadn't been in New Jersey at the time of the Chateau Blanche party, but she could have gotten Carmela to do her bidding, to poison Hope's drink like Leo suspected. After all, Audrey and Carmela had been in contact. And Carmela had hated Hope, who'd allegedly been pregnant with the first male heir to the Fontana line, an obvious source of pain for Carmela. Even if Eden was still suspicious about the baby bump, Hope had been presenting herself as pregnant.

"*Justice for My Cousin*," Aria said. "It's a bit of a mouthful, no? Maybe just *Cousin Justice*. We'll workshop it."

Eden suddenly felt nauseous. Just as she was about to dry-heave into a plastic bag that once contained Chinese food, someone knocked on the door. She wasn't expecting anyone, but she was grateful for an excuse to get off the phone. She said bye to Aria and made her way to the door, joints stiff from lack of use. She hoped it wasn't Caleb. Eden swung open the door to find Renee—hair ruffled, eyes bloodshot, grasping the doorframe for support. How had Renee even found her address? Before Eden could react, Renee lunged at her, sloppily kissing her cheek.

"Eden, you look gorgeous," she said, holding Eden's face in her hands. "Just like your cousin."

"What are you on?" Eden asked, wondering if she had any more to spare. Eden craved an escape from the dark, obsessive corridors of her mind.

"Nothing," Renee said, laughing. "Just a smoothie Birdie gave me." She tumbled onto Eden, who held her up. "I love your place, Eden," Renee slurred. "Very bohemian."

"That's generous," Eden said, guiding Renee to the leather couch she'd found on the street and sitting her down. Her apartment was a dump. Four hundred square feet with just two tiny windows. Dusty, stuffy, cluttered with piles of dirty clothes and hard drives. She didn't have much of an eye for decor. Most of her furniture was inherited from friends or colleagues or found.

Eden went to get Renee a glass of water, maybe sober her up. Renee called something out, but Eden couldn't hear her over the sound of filling up the water glass.

"What is that?" Eden asked as she walked over to hand Renee the glass.

"I got some information for my little detective." Renee leaned over and tapped Eden on her nose. Renee then performatively examined her finger and grimaced. "You might consider washing your face," she said.

"Thanks for the advice," Eden said, sitting in the chair across from Renee for fear that Renee might try to attack her again. Although if Eden was being honest, she didn't entirely mind being attacked by Renee. It was a nice alternative to Caleb, who always smelled of sweat and pizza. Even completely shit-faced, Renee was more poised, softer, and better-scented than any man she'd kissed in the past decade. She smelled like blueberries and cinnamon.

"What did you learn?" Eden asked.

Renee banged her fists on the coffee table as though doing a drumroll.

"Birdie put Hope in her *will*," Renee said, reaching over to tug the sides of Eden's face so that her eyes became large and distorted.

Eden pulled away from Renee, then realized what she was saying.

"Wait, what?" Eden choked out, her throat tightening. But Eden knew what Renee was saying. Eden had forgotten about Birdie's will, had forgotten how Hope had mentioned being added to it, forgotten how she'd had Caleb mock up a fake addendum to plant in Carmela's nail salon. Eden had been so focused on catching Leo and Carmela, who were now both dead, that she'd failed to see the obvious. Someone must have found the fake will, someone who was looking to inherit from Birdie and wanted to off Hope to secure their inheritance. Eden's brain spun.

"Where did you go, *madaaame*?" Renee said, again squeezing Eden's cheeks.

"God, you hang out with Birdie once and you're slurring your words and speaking French," Eden said, trying to conceal the panic rising inside her.

Renee laughed too hard. She then hunched over and took off her boots, put her feet on the coffee table.

"Birdie said it was a lot too," she said. "*Millions.*"

"Jesus," Eden said, feigning surprise. "I need to start hanging out with Birdie."

"Me too." Renee laughed. "I'm trying to get the hell out of Jersey."

Eden perked up. "Me too." She was feeling weirdly attracted to Renee. Maybe Eden was just jealous of whatever Renee was on. Also, she needed to focus.

"Wait," Eden said, remembering a confessional she'd watched just this morning. "Pierre. It has to be Pierre." It was suddenly so obvious to Eden. They'd all joked that Pierre had been drugging Birdie. Pierre had always seemed hostile toward Hope in his confessionals, angry that Birdie had given her his guitar and his room in Rhode Island. She'd been watching a confessional about Rhode Island just this morning. And with Hope getting millions in Birdie's will, Pierre would obviously want her gone. Pierre had never had a job as far as Eden knew. He needed that money. And Pierre's father had mysteriously dropped dead, just as Hope had. Eden was embarrassed she hadn't seen it sooner. She'd been so focused on Carmela and Leo and Cheyenne, she'd forgotten all about Birdie and the will. Had Pierre gone to the nail salon? Eden was having trouble picturing Pierre somewhere so aesthetically Jersey. Maybe someone had found the fake will there and told him about it?

There was a more sinister realization, one that had yet to fully form in Eden's mind as it would be too difficult to bear: in orchestrating the creation of the fake will, had Eden inadvertently set in motion a chain of events that had resulted in her own cousin's murder?

"Did Pierre make that smoothie?" Eden asked, mostly to drown out her thoughts.

"Stop thinking so hard," Renee said, putting her hands on Eden's face again and dragging them down it theatrically as if she were trying to reshape Eden's jawline. "You have a very serious detective face," Renee slurred, squishing Eden's cheeks into a mock scowl.

"Just watch this with me," Eden said, getting her laptop.

EDEN: You miss the table flip.

PIERRE: Thank God I miss the table flip. Although I feel guilty that Mother is there unsupervised. After losing my father . . . [*Sniffles.*] I worry about her.

EDEN: I'm so sorry, Pierre. Your mom said your father's death was unexpected.

PIERRE: I appreciate where you're going with this, but I will not be discussing my father's death on *Garden State Goddesses*.

EDEN: To be fair, you brought it up.

PIERRE: Literally who raised you?

EDEN: You don't want to know. Your mom seems taken with Hope.

PIERRE: [*Long exhale.*] It's a phase, I'm sure. Mother loves her projects.

EDEN: What do you mean?

PIERRE: You know how she loves her charity work? Well, sometimes she mistakes human beings for charities. Who was that girl on season one? The one with the bikini waxing business? Or, like, bikini bedazzling?

EDEN: Vajazzling.

PIERRE: [*Shudders.*] Good Lord. There's a reason I don't remember that. What was her name again?

EDEN: Michelle. Her business was called "Luxe Landing."

PIERRE: Jesus, right, Michelle. Mother pronounced it like the French, like in the Beatles song, *Mi-chelle, my belle*. Such a sad woman. But so familiar. Like the woman Mother met on an airplane, Sandra? The one time she flew commercial, she had to pick up a stray in the line for the bathroom. Then there was the busboy at our favorite French restaurant in the city, Louis. At least he was cute. He lived with us for like three months. Mother always lets them go eventually, once they gain some

footing. Although didn't Luxe Landing go under? I feel
like I read that somewhere.

EDEN: Yeah, I think Michelle is selling real estate now.
Anyway, are you suggesting Hope needs financial help?

PIERRE: It isn't always financial. Mother once had a stray
who was a literal princess. Of Liechtenstein. Helena.
Mother met her at a Broke Not Broken event. She had
emotional problems, like Hope.

EDEN: What makes you think Hope has emotional problems?

PIERRE: Well, I have eyes. Poor girl is hanging on by a
thread.

EDEN: Hope's room in Rhode Island has paintings of horses on
the walls.

PIERRE: Yes, it's my room.

SEVEN

Renee, Eden, and Valerie were nearly at Birdie's, ready to execute a plan mostly concocted by Valerie, who'd finally admitted there was no expert stalker cousin—just Valerie itching to play out her private-eye fantasies.

It was Thursday afternoon, the same time Renee had come over last time, meaning Pierre would be riding. Renee had told Birdie that spending time with her the other day had helped her process, that it was healing, that she'd love to do it again with Eden and Valerie, who were also hurting after the deaths. Birdie had seemed delighted, and had said she'd have Pierre make extra smoothies.

But to their surprise and dismay, Pierre answered the door. This was not the plan. The plan was that Renee and Valerie would occupy Birdie while Eden searched Pierre's room for evidence. But now Pierre was here.

"I thought I was finally done with you all," Pierre said. He was wearing chaps, so hopefully he'd be leaving soon.

"On your way to a lesson?" Eden asked.

"Just got back," Pierre said.

What the hell? This was going to make things difficult. Renee was annoyed, and Eden looked furious. Valerie always had the same facial expression—amused but slightly confused. Maybe she'd come up with something. Too bad Pierre was gay, or one of them could seduce him. Maybe Eden could call Caleb; he was decently handsome.

Birdie appeared in a lilac muumuu. "*Mes amies*," she said, opening her arms and hugging each of them. She led them into the same room they'd been in last time, the one with the dark wood walls and the fireplace, which was on again. Luz arrived with a tray of smoothies for them all.

"I've heard these smoothies are incredible," said Valerie. She took a big sip. Renee had warned both Eden and Valerie that the smoothies were obviously drugged, but that didn't stop either of them from gulping. Renee took a small sip of hers, wanting to maintain some clarity. She supposed Valerie and Eden wanted some escape, and Renee couldn't blame them. Thursday was the first time since Hope's death that her brain—and heart—had had a break.

"Yum," Valerie said. She smiled, then grimaced, Renee assumed due to the aftertaste. "Oh, wait!" Valerie said. "I recognize this taste! Batteries! This is the smoothie Pierre was making in Rhode Island— I could smell it from ten feet away." Valerie stopped talking, seeming to realize that what she said might be considered rude, but luckily Birdie, as usual, didn't seem to be paying attention.

Renee tried to make eyes at Eden. Her expression had lightened somewhat, likely from the smoothie.

"Cheers," Birdie said, holding up her tumbler and clinking glasses with everyone the way she had with Renee the other day. Was it possible that Birdie was onto them? That she was in on this whole thing with Pierre? Renee gripped the sides of her chair, suddenly nervous.

"I'm so happy you all came over," Birdie said. "It's nice to have a break from . . ." She trailed off, but everyone understood.

"Valerie, dear," Birdie said, taking her hand. "You must be distraught."

"Manny convinced me to start seeing a therapist given everything that's happened," Valerie replied. "He said I have incredible powers of denial." She acted as though it was a compliment. Maybe to Valerie it was.

"I'll drink to that," said Birdie with a wink.

Birdie opened her mouth to say something else when yelling broke out down the hall. Renee couldn't make out what was being said, but she heard Pierre's voice and another, that of a woman, maybe the woman who'd brought their smoothies. Renee's heart quickened as she strained to catch snippets of the heated exchange.

Birdie's eyes darted away for a moment. "Oh my," she murmured, a hand fluttering to her neck. "Pierre is . . . well, he's having some issues with Luz," she confessed.

Eden leaned in. "What's going on?" she asked.

Birdie sighed. "Oh, you know," she replied. "Pierre is very particular about his things."

The yelling beyond the door rose in volume. Frustration vibrated down the halls.

Eden straightened. "Why don't I go check on them?" she offered, already standing up and taking a step toward the conflict.

"Oh, that's not necessary—" Birdie objected, but Eden was already out the door.

Once Eden was gone, Valerie lifted her smoothie into the air and looked at Birdie. "Let's chug these," she proposed. "Whoever gets brain freeze first wins."

"Game on," Birdie declared with a wink.

EIGHT

Eden didn't like being back in this house, where everything reminded her of death. She swore she could smell Hope's decaying body, even though it had obviously been removed. Walking down the hallway, she couldn't stop thinking of that night, of looking for Hope with Caleb and Johnny, dragging them up and down the billion staircases, searching the billion rooms. This hallway was too freaking long. Eden trudged forth, feeling slightly off-balance, toward the yelling. She had to stop and hold on to the wall a few times for support. Now she knew what it was like to be Birdie.

Just when Eden was almost in the foyer, the front door slammed. Eden silently prayed it was Pierre who'd walked out the door, even going so far as to cross herself. When she arrived in the foyer, Luz was standing under the chandelier, muttering in Spanish under her breath.

"Luz?" Eden said. "Everything all right?"

"*Maricón*," she said toward the door.

Eden didn't know Italian but she did know a little Spanish; she'd picked it up when she worked in a kitchen when she first moved to New York. She knew this word too. It was a gay slur. This woman was pissed. Now was Eden's chance.

Eden reached out to put her hand on Luz's arm. "Let's go talk," Eden said. "You can tell me everything."

"Who the hell are you?" Luz said, raising an eyebrow. Eden had seen Luz a billion times, but they'd never been formally introduced or talked one-on-one. And Eden was paid the big bucks to fade into the background while they were filming, so she didn't blame Luz for having no idea who she was.

"I worked on the show with Birdie," Eden said, leading Luz into one of the countless sitting rooms. This one was pink and floral, an explosion of flowers at odds with Luz's suspicious expression.

"I hate that show," Luz said. "Pierre ran me like a dog to make everything perfect." Her words began to tremble, and Eden noticed the tightness around Luz's eyes, the clenched jaw slowly giving way to sadness.

"I'm sorry," Eden said. "It's over now, though."

Luz took a deep breath. "I mean, I'm sorry someone died, but . . ." Her voice cracked, and she paused to compose herself. Then she crossed herself, the way Eden had earlier, the way Carmela used to. "That lady was very sweet," Luz continued. "Hope. She was nice, unlike the rest of them."

Eden realized she was still holding Luz's hand. She squeezed it to comfort them both.

"You look like her," Luz said. "But older and more tired."

Eden smiled. "Thanks," she said, not even offended, because an older and more tired version of Hope was still very beautiful. "She was my cousin."

"Your cousin?" Luz said, softening. "I'm so sorry." She crossed herself again. "*Lo siento mucho*," she repeated a few times. As she exhaled, Eden saw the first glimmer of tears. Then, surprising Eden, the tears began to flow freely. Luz's hand, which Eden was still holding, started to shake slightly. Eden squeezed it again.

"It's okay," Eden said. "It's not your fault." She didn't know why she said this. Obviously it wasn't Luz's fault.

Luz locked eyes with Eden, her watery eyes shimmering. Luz leaned in and whispered something, barely audible.

It took Eden a second to register the words as: "It was my fault."

NINE

This smoothie was acting as some sort of weird truth serum on Valerie. Whatever was in it was probably similar to what they gave people for surgery. Either way, Renee couldn't believe what Valerie was saying.

In hushed tones, she had told Birdie and Renee that growing up, she and Carmela used to play together after school every day. Carmela lived next to Medusa Motors and Valerie was always there. Then one day at the lot, when Valerie was ten and Carmela was eleven, they were playing this make-believe game where they pretended to be dragon babies. It was hard to imagine Carmela as a little girl playing make-believe. Renee wiped a tear from her eye imagining it. Grief always washed over her at the strangest times. Valerie explained that Leo had come over and started shooting them with water guns, getting them soaking wet in the cold. Carmela yelled, *Vaffanculo*, which is Italian for "fuck off," and Leo said something along the lines of *What do you know, Grecko!*

And that was the first time Valerie had seen Carmela's rage.

Carmela had picked up a giant crowbar off the ground and started running at Leo.

Leo spotted a vintage Maserati with the keys inside and ran over, jumped inside, turned on the ignition, and started driving it toward Carmela at full speed.

Carmela darted aside and Leo swerved, running over Valerie's foot.

"And that's how I got this puppy," Valerie said, pointing at her prosthetic foot. The artificial appendage caught the warm glow of the fire, casting a soft metallic sheen across its surface. Renee felt a chill that had nothing to do with the temperature. Then she wiped another tear from her eye. After all the rumors, it really had been Leo. Renee felt somewhat vindicated because she'd never thought Carmela was capable of such violence. She'd never thought Leo was either, but obviously that instinct had been, well, dead wrong. Renee looked over at Birdie, who had drifted off in her chair. A wave of isolation washed over Renee, the only witness to Valerie's confession.

"We lied to our parents," Valerie continued. "To protect Leo."

"Did you tell them Carmela did it?" Renee asked. "Is that why everyone thinks that?"

"Oh God, no," Valerie said. "We told them someone forgot to put the parking brake on and it just rolled. We also never told them about Carmela being Greek." Valerie lowered her voice to a whisper. "Her mom is English. Like, from England." Valerie contorted her voice into a British accent. "Like, *time for tea, darling*!"

Surprising Renee, Valerie started to cackle, the sound growing increasingly loud, eventually morphing into a bellow. She tilted her head to the ceiling and howled like a coyote. Then she laughed again.

Valerie grabbed Renee's arm and Renee jumped.

TEN

Luz didn't want to talk in the house. She said there were cameras everywhere. So Eden took her for a drive in her car. When she got in, Luz said it smelled "very bad . . . like garbage." She was really no bullshit, this woman. Eden was beginning to like her. Especially since Luz despised Pierre so intensely.

As Eden drove past $10 million estates, Luz told Eden that on the night of the Broke Not Broken party, Pierre had given her a martini and insisted that he get it to Hope. Luz had followed orders as usual. But when Hope dropped dead that night, she knew there had been something in the drink. She'd been consumed with guilt since. In Eden's car, she started crying again.

"It's not your fault," Eden kept saying to Luz, but she also felt she was saying it to herself. Ever since Eden remembered the fake will, she'd been convinced that Pierre had gotten ahold of it, that he'd killed Hope for that reason, that it was all Eden's fault. But Luz was saying it was her fault. And there was still no proof that Pierre had seen the fake will. Maybe Birdie had told him she was leaving Hope the money herself. Or maybe Pierre was just pissed that Birdie had taken such an interest in Hope. Maybe he just couldn't stand the way Hope dressed, like he'd told Eden. She'd always suspected Pierre was at the very least vaguely sociopathic. Maybe it had been a thrill kill. Either way, it wasn't necessarily Eden's fault.

"You didn't know," Eden said, patting Luz's shoulder with her free hand. Eden didn't know either. She hadn't known Pierre would find the fake will. She still didn't know if he had found the will.

"I should have known," Luz said. "The lady who worked at Chateau Blanche before me, she told me to be careful. She said Pierre is a very bad man. She didn't say anything else, but I had an idea what she meant." She looked out the window.

"What do you mean?" Eden asked, feeling somewhat comforted. Pierre was a sociopath, or a psychopath—she could never remember the difference. Either way, he hadn't needed a fake will to kill Hope. He'd been going to kill Hope regardless, and Eden had had no power to stop it. She certainly hadn't put it in motion. Eden hadn't killed anyone, she kept reminding herself.

"You know Pierre's dad, he died in a similar way," Luz said out the window. "Martini, then dead." She sighed. "Maybe more people, who knows?"

Eden remembered the Pierre confessional she and Renee had watched just before hatching the plan with Valerie, when Pierre talked about Birdie's "projects," the multiple women she'd taken under her wing and then grown tired of. But had Birdie really grown tired of them, or had Pierre offed them, like he had Hope, like he potentially had his own father? Eden recalled an earlier confessional in which Pierre had complained about his father being cheap. Did he kill his dad to get to his money? Did he kill Hope to prevent her from getting money? Maybe it was Eden's fault. Maybe he had seen the fake will. Eden felt vomit rise up in the back of her throat.

"So what are we going to do?" Eden asked Luz.

"We?" said Luz. "I'm out of here as soon as you drop me off. Pierre fired me for giving the women the smoothies. Birdie asked me to do it, but whatever. It's her money, his rules. I can't wait to be out of here. I'm going back to Mexico tomorrow."

"Mexico?" Eden said. "You can come talk to the police with me first, right?"

"Police?" said Luz with the same disgusted face she'd made when she got in Eden's car. "Hell no. I don't talk to the police, no. Are you stupid? I could go to prison." She crossed herself again.

Eden felt herself deflate. She was so close. She knew how the cops were—they weren't going to investigate Pierre without definitive proof. If Eden just recounted what Luz had said, they'd probably think she made it up.

"Well, you have to give me something," Eden said, circling the block once more.

"I don't have to give you nothing," Luz said. "I told you the truth, that's it. Take me home. I can't stand this creepy neighborhood. No kids, no people. Just these big gates." She glanced at the nearest wrought iron threshold, stark and black in the late afternoon sun.

Eden couldn't help but agree; the area did have an unnerving sterility to it. Eden stared at the iron monstrosity towering over them, casting intricate shadows on the pavement. It felt like a heavy-handed metaphor for the barriers between her and getting Pierre locked up, where he belonged.

"Watch the road, lady," Luz said, and Eden realized she was swerving toward the gate she'd been staring at.

"I need proof," Eden said once she'd straightened the car out. "I want to send Pierre to prison."

"A prissy boy like that will never go to prison," Luz said.

Eden refused to believe this.

"Can you take me back now?" Luz said.

Eden turned the car back onto Birdie's street. It would still take a while to get back and up the driveway; maybe she could convince Luz to talk to the cops or at least point her to some proof. "Can you show me his room?" Eden said. "Or at least point me in the direction?"

Luz laughed. "His room is locked. Always."

Eden wanted to cry. She had to get something. She couldn't let Pierre get away with this.

"Where did he go?" Eden said, approaching the driveway. "When he left?"

"Who knows," Luz said. "No job, no girlfriend, no boyfriend, no life. Just horses. And poisoning people."

Eden sighed. They went through the gates, and Eden craned her neck to look for Pierre.

"Do you think he's riding?" Eden asked.

"No idea what that weirdo killer is doing," Luz said. "I'm out of here."

"Okay, okay," Eden said. "I get it."

At the top of the driveway, Luz nearly leaped out of the car. "Sorry about your cousin," she said. "I really am. But there is nothing I can do." She jogged over to her own car and got inside.

Eden sighed and retrieved her phone from her pocket. She had a text from Renee.

Where did you go? it said. *Birdie passed out and Valerie is high as a kite.*

I got proof it was Pierre, Eden typed.

Luz stepped on the gas and sped away toward the gate, flashing a peace sign out the window as she drove.

Eden deleted the text and exhaled.

What the fuck was she going to do?

ELEVEN

Valerie was bouncing up and down on the couch while Birdie snored on the chair across from Renee.

"Dead!" Valerie yelled as she jumped. "Dead! Dead! Dead!" Her voice was getting louder and louder. "Everyone I love is dead!"

Footsteps sounded from down the hall, just barely over the sound of Valerie's screaming. Renee hoped it was Eden. She also hoped Eden was okay. After the events of the past month, Renee had started to worry about everyone. She was texting Ruby several times a day to confirm she was alive, then calling her dad if she didn't respond. Everyone told her to chill, but Renee had no idea how to chill when two friends and one lover had been murdered in the span of just a few weeks. It was hard to know how to do anything, hence the reason Renee partially understood Valerie's strange dance in front of her.

"What the hell is going on in here?" Pierre asked, storming into the room. He stomped over to Valerie and screeched at her to get off the couch, which she did. Renee had seen Pierre be sassy and passive aggressive many times before, but this was different. He was being outright aggressive. He tapped Birdie to wake her, but she was out cold.

"Oh God," Pierre said. "And Luz isn't here to help me carry her upstairs." Pierre squinted at Valerie and Renee. "I don't suppose either of you has a lick of upper-body strength."

Valerie shook her head. "I'm a cardio girl."

"I'm a no-exercise girl," Renee said.

"What about the butch one?" Pierre asked. "Where did she go?"

Renee shrugged.

"You don't know where she is?" Pierre huffed. "I leave for *twenty minutes* and everything goes to *shit*." He grabbed Valerie's arm, then Renee's. "We'll let Mother sleep this off. You all are out of here." He squeezed Renee's arm so hard it stung.

"Ouchiee," Valerie whined.

"Buck up," said Pierre, tightening his grip.

In the foyer, they saw Eden.

"What are you doing to them?" Eden ran over and shoved Pierre off Renee and Valerie. It felt romantic. Renee had been seeing Eden differently since the night she'd showed up at her apartment. Eden had taken care of her, ordered her Thai food, nursed her back to health. Renee had been too tired to drive, so she'd slept in Eden's bed. Eden had said she'd sleep on the couch, but Renee hadn't let her. Feeling Eden's warm body beside hers had been comforting and had reminded Renee of that night in Rhode Island with Hope.

"Get away from me, butch!" Pierre shouted. "The show is *over*. You bitches—and you butch—are out of our lives. Forever."

He tried to grab Eden but Eden shoved him off. She was stronger than she looked. Scrappy.

"I need you to leave," Pierre said. "Now."

"Or what?" Eden said. She was being heroic. Despite herself, Renee was charmed.

"Or I'll call the police," said Pierre.

"And tell them what?" Eden said. "That your mother, who owns the house, invited us over for tea and that your housekeeper served smoothies that you'd made and *drugged*? And then you fired her for it?"

"Are there any more of those special smoothies?" Valerie asked in a strange voice. "I could take another. My nanny's staying the night. I'm free as a *birdddd*." She sang the last part, which morphed into that Nelly Furtado song. Then she stopped singing and asked, "Is Nelly Furtado Italian?" Pierre ignored her.

"What are you talking about?" Pierre said to Eden. He pulled his phone from his pocket and performatively pressed the numbers 911.

"I'm sure the cops have better things going on," Eden said.

"Not in Alpine, New Jersey, they don't," Pierre said. "I've called for less."

Valerie got on the floor and lay down on the rug. She looked up at a chandelier above her. "So sparkly," she cooed.

"Call them," Eden said.

Eden pulled out her own phone. Renee could see the screen. Eden opened her notes app like she used to on *Goddesses*. She wrote: *I'M GOING TO PRESS RECORD AND TRY TO GET HIM TO CONFESS. YOU RECORD TOO IN CASE HE CATCHES ON. BE DISCREET.*

Renee got on the floor next to Valerie. "Oh my gosh, so shiny," Renee said, pretending to be equally drugged. She pulled her phone from her purse and said, "Let's take a picture."

"Good idea!" Valerie said.

Renee opened her voice memo app, pressed RECORD, then opened her camera app.

Pierre appeared to be calling the police. "I'd like to report a case of trespassing," he said into the phone. "There are three women in my house without permission and they refuse to leave." He gave the address as Eden mumbled, "It's your mother's house."

When Pierre hung up, Eden said, "I look forward to seeing the police."

"Oh yeah?" Pierre said. "I could see you in prison, Eden. You have the aesthetic, for sure."

"I'm not the one going to prison," Eden said.

Pierre laughed. "Who's going then? Valerie? For public intoxication?"

"We aren't in public, honey," Valerie said. She rested her head on Renee's stomach. Her head was heavier than it looked. Renee petted her hair the way she used to do with Ruby when she was little. Renee missed Ruby so much it hurt, in addition to all the other hurt.

"No, you," Eden said, looking at Pierre. "For murder. Luz told me everything."

Renee perked up. She wondered if this was true or if Eden was bluffing like she often did in confessionals.

"Told you what?" Pierre said.

"Told me that you gave a martini to her and insisted she get it to Hope," Eden said. "Hope drank it and then she dropped dead."

Renee's mouth hung open.

"So Luz poisoned the martini," Pierre said. "I'll tell the police."

"She's talking to them now," Eden said. "Telling them everything."

Pierre cackled. "Nice bluff," Pierre said. "You reality TV people are so dumb, seriously. You think our illegal immigrant housekeeper is talking to the police? Try using your frontal lobe for once."

"She doesn't care," Eden said. "She's going to Mexico tomorrow. By choice. She has nothing to lose."

Pierre shook his head, laughing. Renee wanted to punch him in his smug little face. The doorbell rang, and Pierre went to answer it. "That was quick," he said. Eden followed him. Renee got up off the floor, but Valerie stayed. She seemed to be drifting off like Birdie had. Renee hoped Valerie and Birdie were okay. She could never be too sure in this house.

"Good afternoon, officers," Pierre said to the two policemen at the door.

"Hi again, Pierre," they said, seeming vaguely irritated. Pierre probably called them for mundane nonsense all the time.

"These women," Pierre said, pointing to Eden and Renee, "and another down the hall are the trespassers."

"We're very dangerous," Eden said facetiously.

"Seems like it," one officer joked.

"Officers, chop-chop," Pierre said. "My tax dollars aren't paying you all to banter. Flash the guns, get them out of here."

"We're friends of Pierre's mom," Eden said. "She invited us here. This is her house. She pays for everything, including Pierre's taxes, I assume."

The officers laughed. "Where is Birdie?"

"Down the hall," Eden said, leading the officers. "I'll show you."

Renee was impressed by how Eden was handling herself, charming the officers the way she often coaxed her cast to open up in confessionals.

"There's no need for that," Pierre said, but they were already on their way. Eden was running the show now. She was a literal showrunner after all.

In the den, Birdie began to stir. "Oh goodness," she said, clocking the officers. She clutched the armchair. "Please tell me no one else has died. My tender heart can't handle it."

"Everyone's fine," Eden said. "Pierre called the cops to kick us out."

"Pierre," Birdie said, "how incredibly rude." Birdie blinked, eyeing the shorter cop, the one with the blue eyes. "Officers, can I offer you something to drink? Pierre, fetch these handsome young men some tea or a smoothie or something?"

Pierre frowned. "Mother, these women are not good influences on you."

"Again, we're very dangerous," Eden said.

The officers laughed again.

Then, suddenly, the front door unlatched with a click that resonated down the long hallway. Pierre's head snapped up. The annoyance etched on his face swiftly morphed into alarm. Confident, methodical footsteps approached down the hallway. Pierre rose quickly, his chair scraping back with an urgent screech, and rushed toward the hallway.

There was a beat of silence, a held breath, as the footsteps drew nearer. Renee could almost feel everyone tensing. The stranger was still out of sight, but each step seemed louder, closer, a steady drumbeat.

Pierre's voice barely carried over the sound of the approaching steps. "Tristan, you're early," he said, his voice extra nasally. "We have company."

But the stranger didn't seem to register the warning in Pierre's tone. "Yeah, I had some time to swing by before the barn." His voice boomed down the hall. "I've got the goods you asked for—seven grams of Special K, one gram of China white."

"Shut the *fuck* up," Pierre hissed, but it was too late.

The stranger's words hung in the air, stark and incriminating. Renee felt a jolt of adrenaline at the implication. The meaning was clear to everyone.

The police officers sprang into action, their earlier lackadaisical attitude replaced by sharp focus. Renee and Eden followed them into the hallway, where a tall man in chaps and riding boots stood holding two bags of powder, right there in the open. There was their evidence, before their eyes, held by a man in freaking chaps. Was this Pierre's horse trainer? Was this why he had ketamine? Did the smoothies contain horse tranquilizers? Renee couldn't help but laugh.

She locked eyes with Eden, who was grinning.

TWELVE

Pierre wiped a bead of sweat from his forehead.

JFK was a fresh hell: hot, stuffy, long lines, howling babies, fluorescent lighting, and some of the worst fashion he'd ever seen in his entire life. Had the general public always been this unattractive? He couldn't remember the last time he'd flown commercial, but Mother had jetted off with the PJ as soon as she paid Pierre's bail. Pierre was furious. They'd set his bail at a million, which for mother was like buying a latte. He couldn't believe she'd just up and left him to fend for himself, in this trashy country with its famously corrupt criminal justice system. The American empire was long since on the decline, and Pierre was eager to leave it behind to die.

The security line inched forward. Pierre's phone buzzed in his pocket. He'd gotten a burner phone so he'd be harder to track. When he got out of that revolting jail cell, he'd had to promise not to flee the country, et cetera. Pierre laughed now to himself, in the security line with a ticket to Charles de Gaulle. His boarding school boyfriend lived in Maisons-Laffitte, an elite Parisian suburb known for its equestrian culture and nicknamed Cité du Cheval, meaning "City of the Horse." There was no more obvious place for him to go. He loved horses, his name was French. It would be easy for him to start over in the City of the Horse. He would surely fit in better there than he did in *New Jersey*. He shuddered at the mere thought of the state.

THE REALLY DEAD WIVES OF NEW JERSEY   251

Pierre looked at the phone screen, knowing it could realistically be just one person. He'd only given his new number to Tristan. He really shouldn't have, given it was Tristan's fault that Pierre was having to flee the country. But Tristan had a narcotic effect on Pierre. Those broad shoulders, that tapered torso, those curved biceps. The way he rode a horse like he was part of the animal itself, a majestic union of man and beast that made Pierre's heart gallop. He also had access to the purest drugs in the tristate area. His ketamine was medical grade, and, well, only the best for Mother! Pierre wasn't a user himself—he liked to be clearheaded. But Pierre had realized a long time ago— after Mother's first facelift—that Birdie was easier to manage when sedated. At first, Pierre would only slip her the ketamine only on certain occasions, like when he wanted to up his allowance or needed a new car, or horse. But then Mother signed up for that godawful television show. That tasteless, tacky show for which she was being paid pennies to embarrass herself.

Pierre had tried many times to convince Mother to quit, had begged her not to join the cast in the first place, but she was attached to the ridiculous show for reasons that eluded him. So he'd upped her ketamine infusions, as he called them, hoping he could subdue her into hardly showing up for filming, let alone causing the drama they required to keep her staffed. The show had finally been canceled, but Pierre had had to pay a price—a rather large price that had landed him in a jail cell.

At least that odd country bumpkin was gone for good. Of all of Mother's projects, Pierre had hated that white trash freak the most. She was so frumpy and, beyond that, so *boring* it was almost criminal. Yet Mother was walking around talking like she was the second coming of Judy Garland. Maybe the ketamine smoothies had clouded her judgment. First, Mother had given Hope his prized guitar. Sure, Pierre didn't play it, but he had an affinity for the instrument, its baby blue paint providing an aesthetically pleasing pop of color in his bedroom, and, better yet, it seemed to impress his suitors, seemed to impress Tristan. And then mother had given Hope *his* room in Rhode

Island, saying it was "fit for a queen," which made Pierre think Mother needed to get her head checked. And the bumpkin had smoked *weed* in there. Disgraceful. But not the worst that would happen, little did Pierre know at the time.

Pierre had just settled onto the couch with a glass of chilled Sancerre one afternoon when he opened his Instagram account to see that fated message. From Shady Di. Pierre had unfortunately been exposed to posts from the sordid account over the years. He'd even been accused several times of running the account. The accusations had not only offended him deeply but also made no logical sense. Why would he be behind an account that made tacky speculations about his sexuality and accused him of having narcissistic personality disorder? It was obviously run by a zoomer, someone obsessed with identity politics and melodramatic diagnoses. Pierre wasn't out, not even to Mother. He found it chic to be closeted, like Cary Grant in the thirties. And he wasn't a narcissist; he was simply confident. The spineless troll behind this account should try it.

Anyway, this message was the first and only one Pierre had received from the troll. And Pierre still wished he could unsee it. It made him sick to even think about. The message from the zoomer, whoever it was, simply contained a photo. Of a document Pierre had to retrieve his glasses to read. It was an addendum to a will. Mother's will. The document said Mother was amending her will to give money to the bumpkin. *Seven million dollars.* He refused to believe it.

Pierre had thrown his phone against the wall so hard that the screen smashed to pieces. It just couldn't be true. He used his backup phone—Pierre had a habit of breaking his phones when activated, and he was often activated—to call the estate attorney, who said that lawyer-client privilege prevented him from revealing the content of their communications. At that point, Pierre broke his backup phone. Because he knew it was true. There was Mother's signature right there at the end of the document. Flowing, cursive letters in ornamental loops, the *B* and *S* larger than the others, to prove she was "no BS," as Mother would sometimes crudely say. The iPhone was smashed to smithereens on the stone mantel.

Seven million dollars. Of course that was only a small fraction of Mother's money, but she was also leaving a substantial percentage to her charities, particularly Broke Not Broken. And Pierre had zero to no earning potential. He needed to be left with enough money to sustain his cushy lifestyle until he died, which, given modern medicine and his vigorous exercise routine, would likely be well into his hundreds. He would need at least $10 million, probably more. And he wasn't going to have his inheritance taken away by this white trash freak.

It wasn't Pierre's first rodeo with the fentanyl martini trick. The first time he used it was on his father. That man was a menace and needed to go. He was taking too much of Mother's time and kept insisting Pierre get a "job." As if. Pierre wasn't a peasant. He was a king. And his dad had nearly $1 billion. Why on earth should Pierre have to work like some kind of regular Joe? Mother had been upset when Father died, but Pierre knew he'd done the right thing for both of them. He'd felt the same when he'd used the fentanyl trick on mother's project Helena, that sad princess. She was too draining of Mother's time, always calling, crying, showing up unannounced, seeking emotional support. Helena was harder to poison because she didn't drink martinis, or any alcohol. Pierre had put the fentanyl in her iced tea, which she'd made a big stink about "tasting funny," but the nice thing about fentanyl was that it didn't take much to do the deed. Mother's life was better without Helena, just as it was better without Father, and without Hope. Hope wasn't doing their family any favors. She was a parasite. A white trash parasite. And now she was a dead white trash parasite.

Bon voyage, mon ami! said the text. God, Pierre had made Tristan promise not to mention that Pierre was traveling over text or anything that could be tracked. What a beautiful idiot. Pierre dropped the phone in the trash can beside the line. Afterward, he noticed a woman staring at him. She was red in the face and wearing an ill-fitting fuchsia dress, more of a smock. The fashion in this airport was so horrific it should be studied.

"Did you just throw away your phone?" the woman asked.

"Did someone pay you to wear that outfit?" Pierre retorted. "If so, I hope for your sake that it was a lot."

He turned away from her, thinking about the text. *Mon ami*. My friend. Pierre wished he and Tristan had become more than friends, at least one time before Pierre jetted. Well, at least he'd always have the image of Tristan riding Dorothy and Frances, which Pierre had seen him do at least one time shirtless. Oh, how Pierre would miss Tristan. And how he'd miss Dorothy and Frances. He was hoping to fly them out as soon as he got settled in the City of the Horse. Maybe he could relocate Tristan too. Or maybe there was an even hotter French version of Tristan with even classier French musc—

"Hey!" Pierre yelled. There was a hand on his arm. He turned to see two armed police officers. The fuchsia smock lady was staring at him. Everyone was staring at him.

"Sir, you need to come with us," the first officer said firmly.

Pierre felt a cold wave of dread wash over him. He couldn't go back to jail. The lighting in there was so unflattering.

"There's been a mistake," he said, but it was obvious there was no mistake. Maybe he could get really fit like celebrities did when they went to prison. The food was shit, so he'd have, like, zero body fat. He could start doing pushups or write a memoir. Maybe prison could be chic.

"We have orders to detain you," the second officer interjected. "Attempting to leave the country while out on bail is a serious offense." They started putting handcuffs on Pierre. He wondered if he could run. The fuchsia smock lady was still staring at him. He glared at her. This was probably her fucking fault. He'd bought the ticket under a fake name, obviously, with a fake ID he'd obtained through Tristan. How had the police tracked him if not for her nosy ass?

"I knew there was something shady going on when he threw away his phone," Fuchsia Smock said to a woman next to her.

"Well, at least I don't look like the 'before' photo in a makeover shoot," Pierre hissed at her.

"Well, at least I'm not going to prison." Fuchsia Smock laughed.

Pierre was escorted off to the sound of the ugly woman's laugher.

THIRTEEN

One year later

"Mom!" Ruby called up the stairs. "Eden! Let's dip."

Hands shaking slightly, as they always did these days, Renee placed her lipstick back on the counter. In the bedroom, Eden tapped away on her phone. She'd become addicted to Candy Crush since the writers' strike. And after four months, all the dings and chimes were getting a bit grating. And Renee was getting scared. When they'd first moved to Los Angeles, Eden had had a job on a high-paying scripted television show, which stopped filming when the strike started, meaning the checks stopped coming. It was nice having more time with Eden, but they weren't sure how much longer they could afford their lifestyle without those checks. The rent on their Laurel Canyon Spanish colonial wasn't exactly cheap.

"Eden"—Renee squeezed Eden's thigh—"let's go."

Eden grabbed the keys from the bedside table. At the foot of the stairs, Ruby was tapping a Converse sneaker on the terra-cotta tiles. She was wearing a feathered minidress that Renee had bought her this week at Nordstrom's teen section for the competition. Ruby was trying out for *Echo Star*, a new show in the vein of *American Idol* and *The Voice*, where contestants were tasked with mimicking famous musicians. Ruby would obviously be singing Ariana Grande.

As the engine hummed to life and the car backed out of the driveway, Renee's mind shifted from the rearview image of their home to the dread of an uncertain future. Renee worried about Ruby ending up back on reality TV after the epic disaster that had been last year. Eden had convinced Renee that competition shows were nothing like *Goddesses*, didn't rely on secrets and drama, Eden reassured Renee, just talent. Besides, with Eden out of work, they needed the money.

But at what emotional cost? Ruby would be singing the same song she'd sung that fated night at Chateau Blanche, the night the woman Renee loved was killed. But it was Ruby's favorite song, the one she'd practiced the most and the one she thought she could sing the best. Renee had been discussing the upcoming performance all week in therapy, as well as the frightening possibility that Ruby—and by extension Renee—might end up back on television.

Renee had put herself and Ruby into trauma therapy as soon as they moved to LA. Eden was going too. Eden was actually in the most therapy—she went five times a week, whereas Renee and Ruby went twice weekly. After a year, Eden was unrecognizable from the person Renee had known on *Goddesses*. Renee hardly saw them as the same person. After solving the mysteries of who killed Hope and Hope's parents, Eden had space for the grief to set in. She had started showing up at Renee's every night, frantic and bawling. Renee would let her in and remind her that none of it was actually her fault, that Pierre's sociopathic behavior had set in motion an unstoppable chain of tragic events. And comforting Eden was actually helpful to Renee's grieving process. It meant Renee had less time alone to dwell on her own scary thoughts, less time to miss Hope. And Eden was Hope's relative. After a few weeks of Eden coming over every day to cry, Renee couldn't stop thinking about the similarities between them. And when Eden kissed her one night, Renee knew it was a bad idea, but she also couldn't help it, just like she couldn't help but kiss Hope.

But kissing Eden hadn't turned out to be the bad idea Renee thought it would be. Nor was she repeating her relationship with Hope, as she'd feared. Unlike Hope, Eden wasn't closeted, or married, or suspected of killing her parents. And she'd launched into "hero mode," as Ruby later put it, after the murders. Eden was comfortable with her bisexuality. She even kissed Renee in public. And she was vehemently committed to changing her ways, committed to becoming a better person, to putting love and goodness over career. And Ruby was already comfortable with Eden from *Goddesses*. It was sort of amazing how quickly and easily they became a family.

Not long after the cops showed up at just the right time to Chateau Blanche, Pierre was taken in for interrogation. And Renee went to New York to see Ruby, where her daughter admitted—to Renee's absolute thrill—that she was bored of living with her absent father. Renee took her home that night. And soon, Eden was spending most of her nights with them, grilling veggie burgers for her and Ruby and watching movies with them on the couch after. And when Eden got the call about showrunning a scripted show in LA, Renee decided they should go with her. Actually, the move had been Ruby's idea. LA, Ruby said, would be even better than New York in terms of following her pop star dreams.

In LA, they moved into their Laurel Canyon rental and Ruby was signed by a young and hip manager at Maverick, which famously managed Madonna and Miley Cyrus. It was that manager—her name was Piper—who'd suggested that Ruby try out for *Echo Star*. Kelly Clarkson and Carrie Underwood, she'd emphasized, had both been contestants on *American Idol*. And Olivia Rodrigo, Miley Cyrus, and Ariana Grande had all been on television before they were pop stars. Piper said *Echo Star* could help Ruby break through. Ruby had been singing at smaller venues along the Sunset Strip and had been posting videos of herself singing to TikTok regularly, but Piper said Ruby needed more exposure. And Ruby's performance that night at Chateau Blanche had never aired because the season had never aired due to the tragedies, which was fortunate in every way except that Ruby never got her big TV performance.

As the car emerged from the leafy calm of the canyon and onto the chaos of Hollywood Boulevard, Renee's palms began to sweat as they now did whenever she left her neighborhood. Her therapist said it was a trauma response. Renee was over it. She'd like to leave her neighborhood more easily, go to the beach, take Ruby shopping without having to take a pill or have a glass of wine first to calm her nerves. But the therapist said it was only natural for there to be an adjustment period. *Healing isn't linear*, she'd say. *Your body's response is a testament to what you've survived. Allow yourself grace.* Renee wanted her old life back.

In the meantime, she mostly focused on making jewelry in their rental's ADU, which Eden had helped her convert into a studio, and selling through her online store. Huzzah had given Renee and Eden sizable chunks of cash to not sue, but that money would not last forever. Los Angeles was far more expensive than New Jersey, and Ruby's journey to fame wasn't turning out to be cheap either. Each performance required a new outfit. Her vocal coach was stellar but insanely expensive. And every show and meeting required spending gas money or a fortune on an Uber. Piper promised that the payoff would be worth it, but Renee had yet to see a dime. And she hated to see her own daughter as a means to make rent.

The sound of a phone blaring through the Bluetooth speakers on their leased Honda CRV caused Renee's heart to slam against her rib cage. She was so over feeling on edge all the time, jolted into full-blown panic mode based on the mere sound of a phone ringing.

"Hi, Valerie," Eden said. "You're on speaker. We're driving Ruby to an audition."

"Oh my gosh, hi fam!" Valerie squealed. Eden and Renee had been in semi-regular contact with Valerie since the three of them had trauma-bonded over the deaths and then low-key solved two murders together. Renee always had mixed feelings whenever she talked to Valerie these days. She was inspired by Valerie's positivity, her ability to see the bright side of things even after all the tragedy she'd suffered—losing a foot at the hands of her best friend, then losing her best friend at the hands of her brother, then her younger brother at the hands of her older brother, then that brother to prison. Dino had taken a plea deal for manslaughter, with the charge reduced due to duress. "I don't like saying 'break a leg,' for obvious reasons," Valerie continued. "But kill it, Ruby—I know you will!"

"Thanks, Valerie," Ruby said. Then she started singing a few lines of Amy Winehouse's "Valerie." She'd been on a Winehouse kick since the three of them watched the documentary recently, which Renee later worried was inappropriate for Ruby given its depiction of alcoholism and drug abuse. But Eden said it was important for Ruby's "artistic growth," which Ruby was now repeating constantly with a North London accent, mimicking Amy. Everything, now, was *impawtont for my ahtistic growth*.

"Wow, Ruby, I thought I heard Amy's ghost for a second—that was you?"

Ruby laughed, then stopped, scrunching her nose. "Should I do Amy instead? For *Echo Star*?" she asked Renee and Eden.

"Valerie," Eden explained, "Ruby is trying out for a singing competition where—"

"Oh, I know *Echo Star*!" Valerie chimed in. "I love that show! My boys hate it because I sing along and, well, I don't have Ruby's voice. Ruby, you do a great Amy. But an even better Ariana, right?"

"Yeah," Ruby said. "I was planning to do 'Imagine.'"

"Perfect. You *killed it* at the Broke Not Broken party," Valerie said. Renee wished Valerie would stop using the word *kill*.

"It was magical, seriously," Valerie continued. "Italians really do it better, don't we? Amy was Italian, too, right?"

"Probably," Eden said, although she and Renee both knew that Amy was an Eastern European Jew. Eden was becoming more agreeable by the day. Renee mostly liked the new and improved Eden, but she suddenly wondered if there was anything Eden was keeping from her.

"Anyway, I can't keep it a secret anymore—guess where I am?" Valerie asked. Before any of them could say anything, Valerie shouted, "California!"

"No way," Eden said. "Are you in LA? You have to come over for dinner."

Renee's stomach tightened. Her social life had been nonexistent since they'd moved to LA. She used to love seeing friends, but she didn't really have any in LA, and making new ones felt dangerous. The only people she really saw were Eden, Ruby, and their therapist. That was all she could manage. If Valerie was in town, would Renee remember how to socialize? And would seeing Valerie bring back an onslaught of torturous memories?

"Not LA," Valerie said, and Renee exhaled with relief. "I'm in Butte County? This place is a shithole! Eden, I can't believe you grew up here. Is all of California this terrible? I don't ever want to find out! It's so dry, I feel like I've aged twenty years. I'm currently standing over a pot of boiling water."

"The place I grew up is way worse," Eden said. "Why on earth are you in Northern California?"

"Audrey Kincaid's trial, *helloooo!*" Valerie said. "Aren't you watching the news?" At their therapists' suggestion, Renee and Eden had stopped reading the news. They were trying to move on, to live normal lives. Birdie apparently felt the same way—she'd fled the country not long after Pierre was charged, causing many to wonder if she'd had knowledge of his crimes. Renee liked to think she hadn't, that she just didn't want to stay and watch her son go to prison. Last Renee heard, Birdie was living on a young suitor's yacht off the South of France. Renee was comforted by the facts that not only was Pierre being prosecuted, but Birdie was living her dream.

"We aren't allowed to watch—or read—the news," Eden said. "We're trying to heal et cetera."

"Well, there's nothing more healing than justice, baby," Valerie said. "First day of trial starts tomorrow, and my Airbnb is definitely a lot shittier than it looked in the pictures, but there's an extra bedroom if you all wanna come up. There's a pullout couch for Ruby."

"I don't think that will be good for us," Renee said before Eden could be diplomatic. "Also, we have Ruby's audition."

"Yeah, no way that *Goddess* bullshit is derailing me once again," Ruby said. Her tongue was getting spicier with each passing year. "Also, I don't sleep on couches."

"Me neither, Ruby. It's good to have high standards," Valerie said. "Well, it's just good to hear your voices. I'm bored out of my mind up here. And I've only been here three hours. Is there literally anything to do? No mall, no nail salon, no wine bars. Just like, grass? And trees? Maybe I should catch up on *Echo Star* now that Ruby might be on it."

"You could go on a hike?" Eden said. Renee was still curious about the place Eden and Hope had grown up—it looked so beautiful in pictures, with tall trees and snowcapped mountains—but Eden maintained that she didn't want to go anywhere near Northern California. Southern California was fine because it felt like a different state, she said, but if she so much as got near a redwood, she'd have PTSD. Renee felt similarly about the tristate area. So LA it was, for the foreseeable future.

"Ew," Valerie said. "You know I don't like nature. Don't they have snakes here? And, like, bears? I'm not trying to lose another append-age, okay. Don't you think I've been through enough?"

"Fair," Eden said. "Well, you could go for a drive? And after the trial, you should come down to LA. Stay with us for a few days. I'll sleep on the couch, not Ruby."

"Thank youuu," Ruby sang.

Renee's stomach tightened again. The idea of having a house-guest, especially someone who was linked to all the deaths they were trying to recover from, felt impossible. She could up her therapy to prepare. Or maybe she could get a hotel for herself and Ruby. No, that would be crazy and would defeat the whole point of Valerie stay-ing with them.

"Sorry, but no," said Valerie, and Renee relaxed again. "As soon as that psycho is convicted, I'm out of this creepy-ass state. I hate it here, no offense. And my boys are going crazy without me."

"Probably best for you to get back to your family," Renee said.

"So are you all ever coming back to New Jersey, or does someone have to die for that to happen?" Valerie asked.

Renee swallowed. She didn't want to ever think about death again. She never used to. The hard fact that she and everyone she knew was going to die had hardly ever crossed her mind before. But now it consumed her at all hours. Ways to die, to get murdered. An earthquake could hit, the big one, and their roof could collapse, crushing them, or the house could slide down from the hill, into traffic. They could get shot during a burglary. Ruby could get kidnapped. Eden could have a heart attack, a stroke, an aneurysm. Renee could slip and hit her head on the terra-cotta tiles. She could eat yogurt poisoned by a disgruntled Fage employee. . . . How did other people avoid thinking about all these fatal possibilities? How had she before?

"We're just trying to focus on healing right now," Renee said.

"Ugh, I'm so freaking sick of that word," Ruby whined. "*Healing* this, *healing* that. It's all anyone ever talks about in my house."

"I'm sick of it too, Ruby," Valerie said. "Everyone says I need to grieve. But that sounds so . . . depressing."

"Preach," Ruby said.

Guilt washed over Renee. When she wasn't thinking of death, she was feeling guilty for what she'd put Ruby through. Her poor daughter, living in this house with two women marred by trauma. She'd probably be better off with a ditzy, dissociated mom like Valerie, who'd take her shopping and shower her with endless praise and refuse to acknowledge a single negative feeling.

"Well, I'll let you all go," Valerie continued. "I'm not going to lie and say I have something else to do, because I have literally nothing, but you all don't seem to be buying what I'm selling. It's times like this I miss Carmela. She would totally drop everything to watch a murder trial with me. You know I started smoking? I miss her smell. I guess that's my form of grieving. Maybe I'll go smoke a cigarette now. Then ten more."

"Smoking kills," said Ruby, which relieved Renee. Ruby was sassy as hell, but at least she wasn't rebelling with drugs and alcohol. At least not yet.

"Yes, it's very bad to smoke, Ruby," Valerie said. "Sorry, I forgot Ruby was here. But also, she's a teenager now. And Carmela smoked over a pack a day and died at the hands of a silver nail file. So life is random, may as well enjoy it."

Ruby said nothing. She was typing away on her phone, probably texting her friends about her mom's cringe friend. Renee often wanted to take the phone away, but Eden said it would negatively impact Ruby's socialization, which was crucial for her, especially now. Eden was typically right about these things, and despite everything, Renee had to admit it was nice to have a partner who actually gave a shit about parenting Ruby, unlike her ex-husband.

"Okay, so I know you all are going to say no," Valerie continued. "But I still think you all should fly out to the lovely Garden State for Pierre's trial! You all might be *healed* by then."

"Crossing my fingers and toes," Ruby said without looking up from her phone.

Before Renee stopped reading the news, she'd learned that Pierre was locked up awaiting trial—the court had declared him a flight risk after he tried to board a plane to Paris shortly after his indictment. She'd also read that Hope's murder had not been a double homicide, because a later autopsy had revealed Hope had not actually been pregnant . . . as Eden suspected. Renee was still grappling with this revelation—why and how had Hope faked her pregnancy? Eden surmised that Hope was afraid people were catching on to her affair and wanted to please the Fontanas by doing the thing that would please them the most: carrying a male Fontana heir. Renee thought this was pretty crazy, but she supposed Hope had been very traumatized, both by her upbringing and by shacking up with a sociopathic murderer, so it had likely distorted her thinking rather significantly. In the past year, Renee had learned the hard way how trauma impacted a person's brain—the flashbacks, the nightmares, the paralyzing panic attacks, the persistently shaky hands, difficulty concentrating, lack of energy, survivor's guilt—the list went on forever. But Renee prayed her symptoms wouldn't.

Renee had also read that Pierre was additionally being charged with the murder of his father and the Princess of Liechtenstein based on newly uncovered evidence. The prosecutor was consolidating the charges so that he was being charged with triple murder. If convicted, he'd likely die in jail.

"I've been talking to the prosecutor," Valerie continued. "He says he's aiming to secure a trial date by spring. Think about it! It's been over a year since we trapped his arrogant ass. You can't be healing forever, right?"

"Amen, sister," Ruby said.

"At least me and Ruby are on the same page," said Valerie. "Toodles!"

Eden and Renee said bye, and then—poof—Valerie was gone.

Eden turned on Fairfax and Renee's heart continued to race at the sight of all the activity. Cars honking and skateboards zooming, teens laughing, the metallic clangs of construction. Every person Renee now saw was potentially dangerous. After watching two friends and one lover killed before her eyes, Renee was on the lookout for danger everywhere. She hated being like this. She used to be trusting, to see the best in everyone. But now she trusted no one after realizing her gut had been completely off. She'd once seen Hope as trustworthy, then found out she'd been faking a pregnancy. She'd seen Leo as incapable of hurting anyone, and then she'd seen him stab Carmela in the jugular with a nail file. She'd seen Dino as kind, then saw him shoot his own brother in the head. And she'd seen Eden as a coldhearted workaholic, but now Eden was the most important person in Renee's life, the person she trusted the most.

Renee squeezed Eden's knee while Ruby did vocal warm-ups in the back seat. The sound of her voice soothed Renee a bit. The therapist said Ruby was adjusting remarkably well given what she'd been through. But she said it also made sense, because Ruby was at a resilient age and hadn't actually seen anyone killed the way Renee had.

Renee had been right there. Hope had died in her arms. And two other people had died within ten feet of her. She had no idea how long it would take to feel normal again, or if that was even possible.

The audition was at Television City, a production studio owned by the same company that owned Huzzah. Renee felt dizzy as Eden drove through the gates. Ruby was shaking with excitement. Renee was trying to be here for Ruby, to be present. But all she could really think about was the audition being over, the three of them being back at home eating mac and cheese on the couch and watching *Succession*. Renee used to like *Kardashians* and *Selling Sunset*, but she hadn't been able to watch reality TV since last year, and neither had Eden.

Piper greeted them in the parking lot. She had a great reputation and Ruby loved her, but her energy made Renee nervous. So flattering and energetic. Renee didn't trust it somehow. Piper told Ruby she looked gorgeous, which was true, and took her off for a pep talk. Eden grabbed Renee's hand and squeezed.

"It's going to be okay," Eden told Renee.

"You promise?" Renee asked, unsure.

"I promise," Eden said.

Eden pulled Renee close. Renee sniffed Eden's neck, its scent indescribable but comforting, salty and sweet and just a little bit sour. Eden's embrace always calmed Renee down. She was taking a second whiff when someone called Eden's name. Eden turned. Renee froze, her breath stopping.

She saw a woman attached to a blond bob that wasn't moving.

FOURTEEN

Eden spoke to Aria in private, away from Renee's shaky nerves. They stood under a young oak tree that felt out of place on the sterile production lot.

"How are you doing, Eden?" Aria asked. Her head moved but her hair did not.

Eden searched the practiced concern in Aria's eyes for a glimmer of sincerity and found none. Aria didn't give a shit how she was doing.

"Fine," Eden lied. No one wanted to hear how she was really doing, about the night terrors, the PTSD symptoms, her newfound trust issues, her irrational fear of slipping back into the violent hell that had been last year, of history repeating itself, her rational anxiety about being jobless with a new family to support.

"Great to hear that, Eden," Aria said flatly.

Eden felt like she was looking at someone other than the person she used to idolize. But more likely, Aria was the same, and Eden was different. Now, Eden wanted nothing to do with Aria. Huzzah had arguably been nice to give Eden and Renee those lump sums, and Aria had helped land Eden a new job in Los Angeles, which had been going smoothly until the writers' strike. But now, things were looking a little precarious. Ruby's burgeoning career was expensive, and Eden cared about Ruby as though she were her own daughter. Renee's business was also expensive, more expensive than Renee seemed to realize.

With the closing of the brick-and-mortar store and *Goddesses'* new, macabre associations, sales had plummeted, and Renee was buying more jewels than she was selling. Eden felt a responsibility to her new family, to the women who'd saved her from the darkest period of her very dark life.

"I heard Ruby's trying out for *Echo Star*," Aria said. She had a look in her eyes that Eden recognized but couldn't precisely identify. She'd been away from Huzzah too long to parse the subtext.

"But I have a better idea," Aria continued.

Oh. Eden understood. Aria wanted something from her.

"You know Bianca's in talks with Huzzah about having a spin-off?" Aria said.

"Bianca?" It took Eden a second to place the name. "Carmela's daughter?" In three years of filming, Eden had only done one confessional with Bianca, and only after her mom had been murdered and Aria had demanded it. Eden felt terrible for the girl, but Bianca didn't exactly have star quality. She was shy, insecure, always glued to the corners of rooms. Being bad for reality TV wasn't necessarily a negative quality. In fact, Eden used to see it as a green flag, until she started sleeping with one of Huzzah's most beloved stars of all time, and it had ended up being the best relationship of her life—by far. Renee, and Ruby, had made Eden a better woman. Despite all the troubling events that had gotten her here, Eden much preferred this kinder, family-oriented version of herself than the icy workaholic, the Aria derivative, that had preceded it.

"Yes, you didn't hear?" Aria said. "Bianca recently came out as Shady Di."

Eden's heart skipped a beat. She and Renee had deleted Instagram upon moving to LA, and Eden hadn't thought about that account in a very long time. She'd always sort of assumed it was Pierre. But now that she thought about it, it sort of made sense that it had been Bianca, given how much the account knew about the Fontanas—it had to be someone on the inside. Eden suddenly remembered that Bianca had said something to her about her "internet brand" in that one confessional. If Eden hadn't been in a death haze, one she'd frankly yet to come out of, she would have clocked that immediately as a giveaway.

"That makes sense," Eden said nonchalantly, not wanting to give Aria the pleasure of a big reaction.

"Bianca really went through hell in that house," Aria said. "She's like a new woman since Carmela died. It's like she's free for the first time. It's giving Gypsy Rose."

Eden felt nauseous again, the way she had the last time she'd spoken to Aria, and the time before that.

"Have you seen her recently? She's on Ozempic. Bianca, obviously, not Gypsy Rose, although Gypsy Rose might be on Ozempic too. Anyway, Bianca looks incredible. She has this fresh air of confidence. We're thinking of calling her show something along the lines of *Shady Di: The Makings of a Troll*."

"That title will be great for her newfound self-esteem," Eden said. Aria cackled. "Anyway, I digress." She stopped laughing and looked Eden dead in the eyes, her gaze stiff and cool. Her irises were very narrow slits of icy blue.

"You want me to showrun," Eden said, suddenly realizing what Aria wanted from her. "That's a hard no. I told you, I'm done with reality TV."

"But Ruby's trying out for *Echo Star*," Aria said. "Last I heard, that's reality TV. But I think she can do better. I don't want you to showrun Bianca's show—that's below you, frankly."

Eden was nervous. Aria was flattering her.

"Ruby should have her own show," Aria continued. "Focused on your . . ." Aria paused, ran a finger along the edge of her bob. "Unconventional family."

"Because Renee and I are women?" Eden asked. "It's 2024, Aria, come on."

Aria laughed. "I don't mean you being gay," Aria said. "I mean raising a pop star." Aria pulled a pack of Trident gum from her purse, pierced a square, and popped it in her mouth, then put the pack back without offering a piece to Eden. "The show will mostly focus on Ruby," Aria continued. "The pay will be substantial," she said.

Eden said nothing. She looked at Renee, pacing in circles around the car, taking labored breaths. Then at Ruby, practicing with Piper, belting her heart out and looking happier and more excited than she ever looked at home, a testament to what was at stake. Eden wanted to do the best thing for her family.

"Or!" Aria said, as though a lightbulb was going off in her head. Eden braced herself. "You and Renee could be on the next season of *Sunset Sirens*! The cast is great, you'll—"

"You must be joking," Eden said, her words trembling on her tongue. "Why in God's name would we go back on that franchise?"

"To heal!" Aria said. Eden was glad Ruby wasn't near enough to roll her eyes. "I mean, what happened on *Goddesses* was horrific, obviously. But it was a fluke. Nothing to do with Huzzah or the franchise. More to do with your cousin, right? And the chain of events she put in motion?"

Eden bit the inside of her cheek.

"Or was it really you?" Aria continued. "Who hired her? Who fabricated the will that gave Pierre the motive to kill Hope?"

"Aria," Eden said, swallowing blood. This was Eden's biggest fear, the one that kept her up at night, the one she talked about three times a week in therapy. The fear that Eden's intentional actions had led to the deaths of three people. "How do . . . you . . . know about that?" She could hardly get the words out.

"The fake will?" Aria said. "It was my idea!" Her shrill laugh chilled Eden's bones. "That's not fair," Aria continued. "We came up with it together."

Eden's memory had been less sharp since the deaths, which her therapist said was a common side effect of trauma. But that afternoon over a year ago was starting to take shape in Eden's mind. Eden had called Aria while driving back to Hoboken, as she often did. She'd told Aria about Hope mentioning being in Birdie's will, and they'd both laughed about how Birdie had also recently said that Elon Musk was scouting her to go to Mars after seeing her quick reflexes on the dance floor at a recent charity function. And while they were laughing, Eden had started to think about how Carmela would *flip* if she found out Birdie was leaving Hope a massive sum of money. And then she'd suggested . . .

"Fine, it was your idea," Aria said, and Eden knew she was right. "I signed off on it, and you put it in motion. Obviously, we could not have anticipated that Bianca would take a picture of it and send it to Pierre as Shady Di."

Eden choked on the metallic-tasting blood in the back of her throat.

"Sorry, that was out of line," Aria said, and Eden exhaled, head spinning. "But just think about it. You can come on the show and we can focus on how tragedy brought you and Renee together—it's honestly *so* beautiful—and the show will be part of your healing journey. It will also help you financially, help you get back on your feet! A powerful story of two queers beating the odds and coming out on top, which is everything Huzzah is looking for right now."

Eden couldn't locate words. The leaves on the tree above her started to blur.

"Think about it," Aria said. "And let me know by the end of the week?"

Eden stood still—nauseous, frozen.

"Great," Aria chirped, as though Eden had said something, which she hadn't. "More soon!" Aria air-kissed Eden, then walked off along the manicured studio path.

As Eden watched Aria's body shrink in size as she moved farther away, the offer echoed in her mind—each repetition more distorted, like a bad cover of a classic played on loop at a grocery store—until Aria disappeared from view.

CONFESSIONAL TRANSCRIPT - *SHADY DI: THE MAKINGS OF A TROLL*
(SEASON 1)
BIANCA FONTANA

CALEB: You remember the drill from *Goddesses*?

BIANCA: I only did one confessional, and it was after my mom died, but I think so?

CALEB: I'm so sorry about your mom.

BIANCA: Thanks. We had a complicated relationship, but I loved her. And I miss her every day.

CALEB: I miss her too. So let's cut to the chase. You came out roughly a year ago as Shady Di, the Huzzah gossip account with now nearly a million followers. Can you talk about when and why you started the account?

BIANCA: Well, I was always a Huzzah fan. I was super psyched when Carmela was cast on *Goddesses*. My mom was protective and guarded with people outside the family but extremely trusting with family. None of her devices were password protected or anything. She told me everything. She took me everywhere like a little dog. And I knew a lot. I was a big fan of Deux Moi and gossip sites of the like, ones with a sense of humor. I'm very shy in person, or was. Carmela took up a lot of space, and I enjoyed giving it to her. Online, I felt more able to take more space for myself. So starting a gossip account regarding a Huzzah show I had inside access to felt like a no-brainer.

CALEB: And how old were you when you started it?

BIANCA: I was fourteen.

CALEB: There was heavy stuff on there for a fourteen-year-old.

BIANCA: [*Laughs.*] I was exposed to much heavier much younger.

CALEB: Like?

BIANCA: [*Laughs.*] I could tell you but I'd have to kill you.

CALEB: Okay, let's not do that. How did the account gain so much traction?

BIANCA: It happened kind of organically. I had all this information no one else had. I DMed a few things to Valerie, suspecting she'd repost them as she's the pettiest, and it worked, she did. She had a lot of followers from the show, so it just picked up from there.

CALEB: Were you worried about being exposed?

BIANCA: When Carmela was alive, yes. Although I partly think she would have been proud of me. But also I don't think she ever suspected me.

CALEB: Why not?

BIANCA: She had certain ideas about who I was, am. She thought I was soft and harmless. She would *never* think I was capable of something like that.

CALEB: That must have been frustrating.

BIANCA: Carmela loved me in the way she knew how. I was always proud to be her daughter.

CALEB: So can you tell me about what happened once the account started gaining more traction?

BIANCA: I have a skill. Or had a skill. I could go to parties and no one really noticed me. And I worked at the nail salon, where people came and gossiped and never thought to lower their voices around me like they did around Carmela. I picked up a lot at the nail salon. That's where I found out that Birdie was leaving Hope seven million dollars.

CALEB: Pardon?

BIANCA: Don't you read the news? That was Pierre's alleged motive for killing Hope. I am wracked with guilt about it even though I didn't actually do anything, as my therapist keeps reassuring me. But I told Pierre, as Shady Di, that Birdie was leaving Hope that money. I worry every day that if I'd never said anything, Carmela would still be alive.

CALEB: And your dad wouldn't be in prison.

BIANCA: Yeah, I guess. Although he probably would have found his way in one way or another.

CALEB: How's that?

BIANCA: Once I became Shady Di, people started DMing me stuff. That's how I learned that Leo and my mom were sleeping together, and that my dad wasn't actually in the Mafia like everyone thought, but he lost a lot of money acting like he was. He's a con man. Didn't treat my mom very well either.

CALEB: I'm sorry.

BIANCA: I told you I was exposed to a lot as a kid. The Fontanas were kind of assholes to my mom. I don't know why she worshipped them so much. My dad cheated. Leo was always bitching at her. My grandparents would call my mom "Grecko" behind her back. They always ignored me because I'm a girl and part "Grecko," I suppose.

CALEB: That's too bad. I'm sorry. It makes sense that you channeled some of that hurt onto Shady Di. Wait, so how did you know for sure that Birdie put Hope in the will?

BIANCA: Birdie told me herself! She came into the nail salon about once a month. Always the same French manicure and pedicure. She was drinking this smoothie that I now know was drugged. And she kept calling me over and talking to me in hushed tones. It almost seemed like she was talking to herself. Anyway, she told me about the will that day. But I figured she was lying.

CALEB: Why?

BIANCA: [*Laughs.*] Before she left, she told me she was going into the city to meet Jay Z to "talk real estate." Birdie lies constantly. And seven million dollars is a lot of money.

CALEB: Fair.

BIANCA: But then I found this piece of paper on the floor of the salon the next day. It was an addendum to a will. It looked legit. Birdie had signed it and everything. I took a photo of it and then put in my purse.

CALEB: [*Coughs.*] Sorry, something in my throat. [*Coughs.*] So you found the will addendum, took a picture, and then sent the photo to Pierre?

BIANCA: [*Exhales sharply.*] I wasn't going to at first. But then we had Sunday dinner at my grandparents' house. And Hope had just announced she was pregnant, as we all now know with a *fake baby*. What a creep. And my grandparents were just being so over-the-top nice to Hope, showering her with all this attention and all these gifts for a baby that didn't even exist. And my mom was so depressed. I felt so bad for her. I was just really angry on her behalf. I wondered if I could maybe do something as Shady Di to make her feel better.

CALEB: What were you expecting when you sent the photo to Pierre?

BIANCA: [*Clears throat.*] I'm not sure. I thought he might bitch out Hope or something. I definitely didn't think he'd do anything violent.

CALEB: Okay.

BIANCA: Yeah, I didn't think he'd do anything violent. Can I get some water?

CALEB: Of course, Bianca.

BIANCA: I didn't mean for anything [*inaudible*].

FIFTEEN

Eden was lying on a rusty green lounge chair that had come with the yard and playing Candy Crush when Aria's name appeared on her phone. Goose bumps rose on her forearms despite the fact that she was in direct sunlight. Aria was saying hello before Eden made a conscious decision to answer the call.

"Eden," Aria said, and Eden felt catapulted back to over a year ago, before the deaths, before LA and the writers' strike, back when Eden loved hearing Aria bark her name, back when it excited Eden rather than formed an intense pit in her stomach.

"I told you we're not interested in reality TV," Eden said. It had been over a week since Aria had appeared at Television City. Ruby had nailed the audition, had gotten a callback. Renee had been even more on edge since then. Eden hadn't even told Renee about Aria's offer, mostly because she didn't think Renee could handle it. The slightest shift in barometric pressure could tip Renee into panic these days. Eden could see Renee right now in the kitchen through the window, rubbing an ice cube on her temple. The AC was being finicky. Eden had come outside hoping to get a breeze. She'd encouraged Renee to do the same, but Renee's phobias had intensified since Ruby had gotten the callback. Leaving the confines of the house proved challenging, even if it was just to the yard.

"Well, I need your help," Aria said.

"Obviously," said Eden.

Aria laughed. A breeze bristled Eden's arm hairs as an extremely clear and incredibly disturbing revelation made its way to the surface of Eden's brain: She missed Aria. She'd been secretly hoping Aria would call. Her life of Candy Crush, driving Ruby to and from school, and cooking dinner was no longer stimulating her. It had been nice at first, the free time, the break from the grind. But Eden liked the hustle of television. She liked the action. The deaths had altered her, no doubt, but trauma couldn't permanently erase her personality. Sometimes Eden thought Ruby was right, that Renee's obsession with healing was counterproductive. Specifically, Eden worried it was keeping Renee trapped in the dark corners of her mind and making her worse.

"I'm not talking about showrunning," Aria said, a hint of urgency creeping into her voice. "Although that's still on the table if you're interested."

Through the window, Eden watched Renee pace in circles while tapping her third eye. Maybe Aria was right. Maybe it would be good to get Renee back on television and out of her head.

"Eden, are you listening to me?" Aria said.

"I'm listening," Eden said. It was true now, even if it hadn't been just five seconds earlier.

"We need your detective skills, Eden," Aria said. "There's been an incident with one of the Sirens."

Eden swallowed. Getting back into a high-intensity work situation seemed partially attractive to Eden during this moment of tedium and pressing bills. But her detective era felt over. Had there been another murder? Eden didn't want to know, but her mind couldn't help but wonder. A rigged stiletto had snapped during a swimwear fashion show, causing a Siren to fall to her death or be seriously disfigured? Or a mysteriously tampered-with Pilates reformer had led to a similarly tragic outcome? Or was it a financial crime, like tax evasion, or theft? Maybe it was a missing diamond, or a pair of $25,000 sunglasses?

"Pass," Eden said, adopting Ruby's surly teenage lingo. She didn't want to think about what had happened on *Sirens*. Curiosity killed the cat.

"Don't you think you owe it to us?" said Aria. "To your cousin?"

Eden bit her lip. Renee cracked open the door, stretching her fingers into the sun. She started to hyperventilate, then slammed the door shut. Sound echoed off the stones of the small yard.

"I cleared her name," Eden said, anger gurgling up inside her abdomen. "I exposed Audrey Kincaid and cleared the horrible accusations she made against Hope." Eden found herself sounding more heated than she would have liked. "And I solved Hope's murder. Pierre is in jail thanks to me." Eden clutched the chair's armrests, but they were hot from the sun and burned her.

"But Pierre killed her because he was sent a photo of that fake will you planted at the nail salon," Aria said.

"You said the fake will was your idea," Eden said, feeling like a producer again, turning the accusation on Aria at the drop of a hat.

"Well, there's no record of that," Aria said, her voice flat and cool. "We only have footage of you instructing Caleb to plant the fake will at the nail salon."

Was this true? Was there footage of Eden ordering an action that had gotten her own cousin killed? Or was Aria manipulating her, the way she did everyone? If it was a manipulation, Eden realized too late that it was working, because she heard herself say, as a tiny black bird landed on the foot of her chair:

"Fine, I'll do it."

ACKNOWLEDGMENTS

Massive thank-you to my agent and friend, Sarah Phair. And another massive thank-you to my editor and friend, Olivia Taylor Smith. Thank you to Math Monahan for the gorgeous cover. Thank you to Martha Langford, Danielle Prielipp, Brittany Adames, and the whole Simon & Schuster team. Thank you to my girlfriend, Vanessa Roveto, for your Italian-American expertise. And of course, thank you to my parasocial friends Teresa Giudice, Danielle Staub, Nene Leakes, Phaedra Parks, Kenya Moore, Bethenny Frankel, Sonja Morgan, Luann de Lesseps, Lisa Rinna, Kim Zolciak, Dorit Kemsley, Lisa Barlow, Aviva Drescher, Meredith Marks, and Dorinda Medley for your endless inspiration.

ABOUT THE AUTHOR

ASTRID DAHL is an author, fangirl, and law school dropout. She lives in Los Angeles, where she plans to die.